LEIGH GREENWOOD

JUST WHAT THE DOCTOR ORDERED

SPECIAL EDITION®

Published by Silhouette Books

America's Publisher of Contemporary Romance

To my father,
who didn't live to see that first book.
Boy, would he be surprised at what's happened since then.

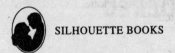

SILHOUETTE BOOKS

ISBN 0-373-24223-9

JUST WHAT THE DOCTOR ORDERED

"Whatever happened in your past has nearly destroyed the man inside the doctor's coat.

"I say *nearly*," Liz continued. "Little bits and pieces have survived. Enough for everybody in Iron Springs to like you. Enough for my two children to think you're the best thing that's happened to them."

Liz turned and hurried inside. She knew she shouldn't have gotten so personal with Matt. But it irked her to see him intentionally cutting himself off from every human emotion.

Besides, he did care. It showed in the way he treated his patients. He might call it good medicine. She called it caring.

And much to her dismay, she'd started to care about Matt. She hardly knew the man, yet somehow she knew he was most like his real self when he was with her kids—and that Matt had enough heart and soul for any woman.

Dear Reader,

Special Edition welcomes you to a brand-new year of romance! As always, we are committed to providing you with captivating love stories that will take your breath away.

This January, Lisa Jackson wraps up her engrossing FOREVER FAMILY miniseries with *A Family Kind of Wedding*. THAT SPECIAL WOMAN! Katie Kinkaid has her hands full being an ace reporter—and a full-time mom. But when a sexy, mysterious Texas rancher crosses her path, her life changes forever!

In these next three stories, love conquers all. First, a twist of fate brings an adorably insecure heroine face-to-face with the reclusive millionaire of her dreams in bestselling author Susan Mallery's emotional love story, *The Millionaire Bachelor*. Next, Ginna Gray continues her popular series, THE BLAINES AND THE McCALLS OF CROCKETT, TEXAS, with *Meant for Each Other*. In this poignant story, Dr. Mike McCall heroically saves a life and wins the heart of an alluring colleague in the process. And onetime teenage sweethearts march down the wedding aisle in *I Take This Man—Again!* by Carole Halston.

Also this month, acclaimed historical author Leigh Greenwood debuts in Special Edition with *Just What the Doctor Ordered*— a heartwarming tale about a brooding doctor finding his heart in a remote mountain community. Finally, in *Prenuptial Agreement* by Doris Rangel, a rugged rancher marries for his son's sake, but he's about to fall in love for real....

I hope you enjoy January's selections. We wish you all the best for a happy new year!

Sincerely,
Karen Taylor Richman
Senior Editor

Please address questions and book requests to:
Silhouette Reader Service
U.S.: 3010 Walden Ave., P.O. Box 1325, Buffalo, NY 14269
Canadian: P.O. Box 609, Fort Erie, Ont. L2A 5X3

Books by Leigh Greenwood

Silhouette Special Edition

Just What the Doctor Ordered #1223

LEIGH GREENWOOD

has authored twenty historical romances and debuts in Silhouette Special Edition with *Just What the Doctor Ordered*. The proud parent of three children ranging in age from seventeen to twenty-four, Leigh lives in Charlotte, North Carolina. You can write to Leigh Greenwood at P.O. Box 470761, Charlotte, NC 28226. A SASE would be appreciated.

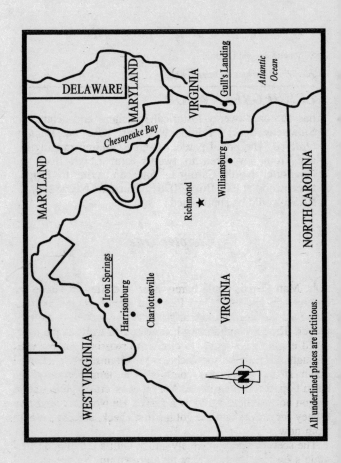

DELAWARE

MARYLAND

VIRGINIA

Gull's Landing

Atlantic Ocean

Chesapeake Bay

MARYLAND

Williamsburg

Richmond ★

NORTH CAROLINA

Iron Springs

Harrisonburg

Charlottesville

WEST VIRGINIA

VIRGINIA

N

All underlined places are fictitious.

Chapter One

Dr. Matt Dennis could barely hear Rod Stewart above the moaning of his 1980 Ford Fairmont station wagon as it labored up the steep mountain grade. He snapped off the tape player. The air-conditioning had ceased to work as the overtaxed engine gave its all to climb the twisting, narrow road through Virginia's Appalachian Mountains. Matt glanced down at the dashboard controls. The temperature gauge wasn't in the danger zone. Yet. It was crucial the station wagon not overheat. Or blow a gasket. He wouldn't have any money for repairs until he got his first check, at least a month from now.

The scenery was completely unlike Gull's Landing on Virginia's Eastern Shore, where he'd grown up. He was unused to mountains that rose five hundred feet into the air, or chasms that dropped a thousand feet. Instead of gnarled sea oaks and scrub pine, the narrow, two-lane road wound its way through a forest of oak, hickory, walnut, cedar, maple and more kinds of pine trees than he ever knew existed.

But the mountain was just as devoid of human life as the

flat, sandy, windswept peninsula between the Atlantic Ocean and Chesapeake Bay where he spent his childhood, shuffled from one foster home to another, living with many families, belonging to none.

Matt shoved his finger inside his collar and prayed for a flat piece of road to ease the strain on the engine so the air conditioner would kick back in, but all he got was another hairpin curve and more road that seemed to climb the mountain at a forty-five-degree angle.

Suddenly the ascent flattened out. The engine stopped groaning. Gradually the temperature inside the station wagon dropped. Matt hadn't grown up with air-conditioning. Even in the eighties, people in Gull's Landing did without it. He could remember sweltering summers when the humidity competed with the temperature to see which could go higher. He had gotten used to air-conditioning in medical school. That's where he started wearing a suit and tie. He liked it. It was his image of what a doctor should be, of what he wanted to be.

Without warning, Matt's battered station wagon plunged down the other side of the mountain, the grade as steep as the one coming up. As he skidded around the first hairpin curve, his right rear tire spewed gravel into the treetops below. All that stood between him and an airborne trip to eternity was a pair of worn brake shoes. He wished he'd taken Dr. Andrews's advice and had them replaced before he left Charlottesville.

Matt took another curve to the accompaniment of grinding brakes and squealing tires. He'd have given his whole first month's salary for a guardrail. Perspiration that had nothing to do with heat popped out on his forehead. He whipped the wheel around to negotiate a third curve, felt his tires bump over a rock as he skidded dangerously close to the edge.

He might not live to reach the damned clinic.

A few minutes later, the road turned abruptly, crossed a stream and flattened out. Matt's pulse gradually returned to normal as he drove down a narrow hollow that lay between ridges rising several hundred feet. Nowhere did he see any sign of recent life, only overgrown driveways, vine-covered, decaying houses and barns long abandoned, fence rails sagging or broken. Trees crowded the narrow road, their leaves blocking out the sunlight, their roots cracking the pavement. Even the moist, cool air seemed green and moss covered.

He wouldn't be going through any of this if he hadn't been in the way of Dr. Reichenbach's favorite nephew getting appointed to a plum residency position. The committee decided Matt needed more one-on-one experience. Then a week ago the doctor assigned to Iron Springs got married and backed out, and Dr. Reichenbach had Matt's assignment changed to this hellhole deep in the mountains. Matt would have enjoyed breaking Dr. Reichenbach's neck just above the cervical vertebrae. He was furious over being sucked back to a small rural community, everything he'd tried to escape.

The road meandered through a narrow valley alongside an empty meadow, past a sign that told him Iron Springs was two miles ahead. Where? On top of the next mountain? The road had begun to climb again.

He didn't intend to stay more than a week. A month at most. His mentor, Dr. Andrews, had assured Matt he'd have him back in Charlottesville inside two weeks. The things Dr. Andrews said about Dr. Reichenbach were exceeded only by what he said about Dr. Reichenbach's nephew.

Matt negotiated a curve and a sharp dip in the road, crossed another stream—probably the same one he'd crossed twice already—and entered another belt of trees. About a hundred feet later, he emerged to see the first occupied house since starting up the mountain fifteen miles back.

Slowing to the required fifteen miles per hour, Matt crept down Iron Springs's main street. Its only street. All the houses were white-shingled, two-story bungalows set about thirty feet from the road. None of them were numbered. How the hell was he supposed to find anybody in this place?

He pulled his station wagon to a stop under an oak that must have been around when Thomas Jefferson wrote the Declaration of Independence. He opened the door, and heat and humidity clamped down on him like a mask. The air felt thick and spongy, too dense to be drawn into his lungs.

He crossed the road to the tiny store that declared itself to be Hannah's Drugs. A rusty, antiquated gas pump next to the building and a shiny, modern soft-drink machine on the porch stood in stark contrast to one another. The wooden steps up to the tilted porch sagged under his weight. The weathered floorboards squeaked at each footstep. The door was propped open with a ladder-back chair. A sagging, wood-framed screen door hopefully kept the flies out.

Matt removed his sunglasses before he stepped inside. The tiny store appeared to be a drugstore, general store, post office and tourist trap all at once. Aisles almost too narrow to allow passage separated black metal racks bent under the weight of junk food, T-shirts and motor oil. A modern, glass-fronted refrigerator containing everything from milk to beer stood next to an ancient cooler filled with soft drinks submerged in ice water. An air conditioner rumbled somewhere behind the banks of merchandise.

"Could you tell me where I can find Mrs. Elizabeth Rawlins?" he asked the woman behind the counter.

She was short, stout, on the far side of fifty, her short gray hair mostly hidden under an Atlanta Braves baseball cap. Small, clear gray eyes returned his gaze. "What would you be wanting Liz for?"

Matt was a little startled. He wasn't used to people asking his business. "I've rented her rooms."

"Are you the new doctor?"

"Yes."

She stepped out from behind the counter, brazenly inspecting him, front and back, before breaking into a broad grin. "Liz sure will be surprised to find *you* on her doorstep."

Matt had been undressed by women before, both with their eyes and their hands, but never so blatantly by a woman probably old enough to be his grandmother.

"I'll wager that passel of women up at the hotel will soon be coming down with all sorts of complaints. Artists, you know. No morals at all. They'll be on you like chickens on a June bug. The men aren't as pushy as the women, but you'll want to watch out for them, too. No good getting that kind of reputation. You got yourself a wife?''

Matt never discussed his personal life with anyone, certainly not a stranger. ''No.''

''Too bad. You might as well put up a sign declaring open season. Oh, well, I expect Sadie and Salome will hold them off. Be careful how you say her name,'' she warned. ''It's Sa-*low*-me, not like that harlot in the Bible. The boys used to call her that just to tease her. They stopped it after she broke Shamus Birdbright's arm. She doesn't look to be that strong, but she'll fool you. You been to the clinic yet?''

''I just got here,'' Matt replied, dazed by the unstinted flow of information.

''So that's why you're looking at me like you're simpleminded. Stay in your office. Leave them to Salome.''

''Just tell me how to find Mrs. Rawlins,'' Matt said, feeling an urgent need for fresh air. No one had ever called him simpleminded.

''Third house on the right as you head out of town,'' said a man who'd been leaning on the counter. He looked to be at least a hundred, thin as dental floss, his head covered with a battered brown hat. He wore creaseless brown pants and a faded blue shirt of coarse material. His face was brown and deeply wrinkled. ''That gal is pretty as a sixteen-pig litter. Don't know why she came back here. She could catch any man she wanted.''

''Be quiet, Solomon. I won't have you talking about Liz like that.''

''It's God's own truth.''

''Maybe so, but she's had troubles enough without an old coot like you telling everything you know and some you don't.''

Solomon cackled. ''Go see for yourself, young man. Something's wrong with you if a good look don't make you randy as a billy goat.''

''Solomon Trinket, you get on out of my store.''

''Don't you order me about, Hannah Coleman.''

Solomon pushed off the counter. He gave Matt nearly as thorough an inspection as Hannah had. "A hot-blooded young man like you is bound to cause trouble," he said as he shuffled toward the door. "You keep your pants zipped, or some husband's liable to come after you with a shotgun."

"Go on with you," Hannah said, practically shoving Solomon out the door. "Don't seem right for your mind to be taken up with such wickedness and you a great-grandfather."

Thoughts of escape filled Matt's mind. If he had believed his car could have made it back over the mountain without blowing up, he'd have tried. "Thanks for your help," he mumbled to Hannah before hurrying outside.

"You come back," she called after him. "I'm open from ten till ten with an hour off for lunch."

Matt was relieved to see old Solomon was not heading in his direction. He didn't think he was up to another brutally frank conversation about his appearance, his sexual appetite or the reaction of the male population to his expected pursuit of their wives and daughters. Matt was no different from any other healthy man of thirty, but he knew better than to get involved with a woman in a small rural community.

He got in his car and pulled onto the empty road. The third house was white, like all the others, but it proved to be considerably larger with a porch on three sides. Avoiding a large pothole that still contained rainwater, Matt pulled to a stop in the unpaved driveway. He wondered if Liz Rawlins was as outspoken as everybody else he'd met.

Liz stood at the kitchen counter, shelling some late English peas. Zip! She tore the green string off the spine of a pea. Her thumb pushed through the hull, sending peas bouncing into the pan. While her right hand discarded the empty shell, her left reached for a fresh pea.

Liz could remember her mother standing in the same spot, doing the same thing, when Liz was a little girl. Her father had died when she was seven. Her mother hung pictures of him in every room. She said he was watching Liz, that she would never be alone. When she grew older, Liz realized the pictures were more for her mother than for herself.

Liz loved her home. Even growing up, longing to get away from the stifling confinement of a small mountain town, she had always imagined herself living in a house like this. Its polished oak floors and faded rugs were as dear to her as the tin roof and windows that stuck when it rained. She never climbed the stairs without remembering sleeping in the rope bed her grandfather had made out of a hickory tree a storm blew over onto the back porch.

Liz washed the peas and put them into small plastic bags. They would soon be joined in the freezer by other packages of vegetables from the garden. She believed vegetables were good for growing children.

Liz threw out the pea hulls, dried and put away her pan and headed upstairs. She wanted to make sure the rented rooms were ready. Her new boarder, Dr. Jane Lumas, would be arriving today. Liz didn't mind renting her rooms. She liked the company, and she needed the money for her kids' college fund. They were only three and four, but those days would come sooner than she wanted.

"Mama, there's a car in the yard," Rebecca called from the front hall.

Liz came to the top of the stairway.

Rebecca had her nose pressed against the screen. "It's a man I never saw before."

"Get away from the door," Liz called as she headed down the stairs. "It's rude to stare."

Ben, wearing nothing but training pants, ran to the door, chubby legs churning so fast he careened into his sister. When Liz reached the door, he pointed at a man getting out of his car. "Big man," he announced proudly.

Liz picked up her son and looked out. She was surprised to see the man was wearing a suit. It was rare for anyone in Iron Springs to wear a white shirt or tie, especially in the summer.

She hardly had time to settle her wiggling son on her hip

before the stranger climbed her steps and was at the door, looking at her with big brown eyes.

"Are you the lady with the rooms for rent?" he asked.

Liz liked the sound of his voice. It was soft, easy, comforting.

"Sorry. My rooms are already taken."

His look turned to annoyance.

"I'm Matt Dennis, the new doctor at the clinic," he said. "I was told the county had rented your rooms for me."

Liz's casual curiosity turned to unpleasant shock. "But I was expecting a woman."

"She got married. I was appointed at the last minute."

"You can't stay here. I'm a single woman."

"I have to stay somewhere."

"Try the hotel." She stepped out onto the porch. Ben wiggled out of her arms. "It's at the end of the road on the left. You can't miss it."

Matt shifted his gaze to Ben and Rebecca, who peered up at him from either side of their mother. He smiled. Ben promptly tried to hide behind Liz. Rebecca timidly smiled back.

"Looks to me like you've got a full bodyguard." He indicated the children.

"Who man?" Ben asked.

"He's a doctor," Liz said.

"Who doctor?"

"He sticks you with a needle," Rebecca informed her brother.

That effectively dried up Ben's curiosity.

The doctor looked at the children with a softened gaze. "Do you take them to the clinic?"

"Yes."

"Then I'll look forward to seeing them." He tousled Rebecca's blond hair. "Probably not very often. They look remarkably healthy."

"Will you give Ben a shot?" Rebecca asked.

"Maybe."

"He'll cry."

Matt knelt down in front of Ben. "Do you cry?"

Her son looked a little scared. He reached for a handful of her skirt. "I don't like shots. They bite."

"I promise I won't let the needle bite you." He poked Ben's stomach with his finger. The boy giggled.

The doctor stood up. Liz watched him change back into the frowning man who resented her preference for female boarders. "It won't be for long," he said. "I was assigned by mistake. I ought to be gone in a week or two."

She was caught. She didn't want a strange man in her house, but the health department *had* reserved her rooms for the clinic doctor. She'd already put the money into the kids' accounts. With a fatalistic sigh of acceptance, she opened the screen door and stepped inside.

"You'd better have a look at the rooms before you decide. They're at the top of the stairs. There's a bedroom, a sitting room and a private bath," she explained, leading the way up the wide stairs. A carpet with faded floral design muffled their footsteps. "Unfortunately you can only enter the bathroom from the hall."

They reached the wide hall at the top of the stairs. Windows in the front and back guaranteed a breeze and plenty of light. She opened the first door on the left.

"This is the sitting room."

It was a large, airy room with a low ceiling. Cream curtains, wine-colored carpet and floral-print slipcovers made it look like a room for a woman, which she had meant it to be. "The rooms come with meals. Three on weekdays, breakfast and lunch on Saturday and supper on Sunday."

"Do you rent those rooms, as well?" Matt asked, indicating the two doors across the hall.

"They're the children's bedrooms."

Everything about him changed, his posture, his expression, the tone of his voice.

"I need complete privacy."

"You'll have plenty," Liz said. "I come up only to clean."

"It won't work," Matt said. "Can you tell me where I can find some other rooms?"

She couldn't help but feel annoyed with him. She'd bent over backward to be obliging. He repaid her by being stiff-necked and obstinate. "I don't know of any, but you can ask Dr. Evans."

"Where would I find him?"

"At the clinic."

He looked as though his patience was just about gone. "Where do I find the clinic?"

"Take the road past Hannah's store. The clinic's on the left, about a quarter of a mile. You can't miss it. It's the only road going south out of town."

"I've already noticed the scarcity of escape routes."

Liz bit her tongue to keep from returning a rude reply. She followed as he almost ran down the steps, watched him hurry down the walk with a ground-eating stride. She reentered the house and locked the screen door, started toward the kitchen.

"Is he going to live here?" Rebecca asked as she hopped down the hall on one foot ahead of Liz.

"No," she replied.

"I like man," Ben said, pointing at Dr. Dennis's retreating form. "Want apple."

"How about a banana instead?" Liz followed them into the kitchen. She put Ben in his high chair, sliced half a banana on a plate and set it in front of him. Rebecca ate her half from the peeling.

Liz sat down at the kitchen table. After her last boarder left, she had agreed to hold her rooms for the new doctor only because she'd been assured she would be a single woman. Matt was clearly not a woman, and unless she was badly mistaken, he wouldn't find any other rooms.

The phone rang. She wasn't surprised to find it was Hannah. She knew everything at least five minutes before anyone else.

"Yes, he arrived.... Yes, I did notice he wasn't a woman. It would be hard not to since he's the best-looking man I've seen all summer.... You didn't tell him that, did you? Amos will have your head. You know he loves his artists best of all.... Oh, no! Not even Solomon would say something like that!.... Good Lord, no wonder he looked like he thought I might bite him. You tell Solomon I'm going to give him a black eye.... No, he's not going to stay here.... I have no idea where he means to stay, but he's gone to the clinic. You can be sure Salome will know if anybody does.... He's a grown man. I imagine he can take care of himself.... I've got to go, Hannah. It's time for the children's nap.''

She hung up. Nobody would have to worry about Matt Dennis. He wouldn't be around long enough for that.

Matt put the key in the ignition. Solomon Trinket was right. Liz Rawlins was a damned fine-looking woman, but he'd seen prettier, certainly more sophisticated. She had met him at the door wearing a low-necked blouse and a tight jean skirt, her thick blond hair in a ponytail. A redneck yuppie— that was his first thought, but her bare feet didn't fit the image. She should have been wearing some fancy jogging shoes, at least white socks and tennis shoes.

Matt started the engine. Remembering to avoid the pothole, he backed into the road. The less he saw of Liz, the better. Redneck or yuppie, he sensed she was the kind of woman who could work her way into a man's dreams. When that happened, wedding bells threatened. Matt had sworn wedding bells would never ring for him.

Chapter Two

The Shenandoah County Medical Clinic was a long, low, cinder-block building situated on the edge of a meadow. Brown trim and maroon, plastic-covered furniture made the cramped waiting room look garish. Matt expected to find that the examining-room lights were fly-specked, sixty-watt bulbs suspended on wires from the ceiling. The young bleached blonde sitting behind the reception desk eyed him in what he could only describe as a predatory manner.

"You want something?" she asked, her bright orange fingernails drumming on the counter. Matching lipstick clashed violently with her green eye shadow. "You don't look like you need a doctor to me." She accompanied that remark by a wiggling movement of her shoulders that thrust her breasts forward.

Matt had already noticed that particular attribute. And that her uniform was at least two sizes too small. "I'm Matt Dennis."

"So?"

She clearly wasn't impressed. "I'm the new doctor," he said, hoping for a more positive response.

"You must have the wrong clinic. We're expecting a lady doctor."

"She got married. They sent me instead."

A squeal beyond his ability to describe escaped those orange lips. She turned and yelled down the hall behind her, "Sadie, get your behind out here this minute! You won't believe the hunk who's going to be our new doctor. Those women up at the hotel will go ape."

Matt heard the soft squishing sound of crepe soles.

"Salome Halfacre, if anybody from the health office ever hears you talk like that, they'll fire you in a..." Her voice trailed off. "I'm Sadie Whiteside," she said after a pause. "I'm the nurse. Salome is the receptionist."

"How do you do? I'm Matt Dennis. Is Dr. Evans in?" Sadie was an improvement on Salome, but her faded blue sweater and pink knit slacks made her look too much like a civilian. He felt an urgent need to talk to somebody who looked like a professional.

"He's been expecting you. Follow me."

A wolf whistle echoed down the hall after him.

"Ignore Salome. She does a wonderful job on the desk, but she's sure got a mouth on her."

"I bet she's related to Solomon Trinket," Matt mumbled before he realized he was thinking out loud.

"His great-granddaughter," Sadie said. "How did you guess?"

Deciding it would be best to keep his thoughts to himself, Matt silently followed Sadie into Dr. Evans's office.

Dr. Evans didn't fit Matt's image, either. At least forty pounds overweight, he wore a yellow knit shirt open at the throat, shapeless blue slacks, and crepe-soled shoes. Cigarette butts spilled from an ashtray on his desk.

"How do you like your rooms?" Dr. Evans asked as soon as the introductions were completed and Matt had settled into a chair upholstered in cracked vinyl.

"I don't," Matt replied. "I was hoping you could help me find something else."

"You won't find any rooms within twenty miles," Dr. Evans assured Matt. "It took me three months to find my house. The closest apartments are forty-five minutes away. Unless you've got a four-wheel drive, you'll never get over that mountain in winter. If you stay at the hotel, you'll have to pay for it out of your own pocket."

Matt didn't know which unsettled him more, the prospect of going back to Liz Rawlins's, or of working every day with Salome Halfacre.

"I was hoping for more privacy."

"There's no such thing in Iron Springs. Everybody's related to everybody else and knows everybody's business. They'll know yours before the week's out."

"I don't expect to be here long. I'm only here because of a mix-up."

"That may be how you got here," Dr. Evans said, offering Matt a cigarette he refused, "but I'll lay odds you'll still be here this time next year. Know anything about the mountains?"

"No. I grew up on the Eastern Shore."

Dr. Evans made a face. "You'll like the people if you give yourself a chance to get to know them. Now, I suggest you hurry back to Liz's and make your peace with her."

"When are you leaving?"

"In two days. The moving van is at the house right now."

"Can't I rent your house?"

"The landlady's son is getting married. He's already rushing me out."

"May I use your phone?"

"Sure."

Dr. Evans left the room, and Matt quickly dialed a number.

"Dr. Andrews? This is Matt. I don't care what you do— promise them money, promise them my organ-donor card— but you've got to get me out of here."

Liz swung slowly in a wooden swing suspended from the limb of an ancient oak. It was her favorite spot in the world.

Behind her the yard ran down to a small creek that gurgled noisily in its rocky bed as it skirted the base of Spencer Mountain. Timber-covered slopes rose more than a thousand feet. Crisp air from its pine- and hardwood-covered flanks drifted down to cool hot, sultry summer days and nights. Liz remembered as a child spending the afternoon playing with her dolls under this oak. As a teenager, she had spent hours swinging and dreaming of what she would do when she grew up.

Maybe if her mother hadn't died the summer between Liz's freshman and sophomore years of college, she wouldn't have fallen in love with David. Aunt Marian had tried to fill the void left by her parents' deaths, but it was too big.

David had stepped right in.

It was flattering to have the attention of such a smart, handsome senior. She had tumbled into love in less than a week, had gone through that spring with her head in the clouds. She couldn't blame him for her quitting school to support him while he got his MBA. She had suggested it.

Liz picked up her glass of fresh lemonade from the white-painted oak table her father had built around the trunk of the tree. She wondered how many glasses of lemonade she'd drunk under this tree since she left David. She'd spent the first three months here, swinging, trying not to think, trying to put her heart back together. The squeaking of the chain as she slowly swung back and forth, the sound of water rushing over the rocks after it rained on the mountain, the croaking of frogs when the creek was low and the water slowed to a trickle, the sounds of campers playing somewhere on the slopes, the rustling of leaves as they stirred in the breeze— they all helped to ease the pain, to dim the memories, to bring back some of the peacefulness she had known as a child. It had taken her two years to heal, but she had recovered. The town, the oak, her children had all done their part.

She saw Matt when he came around the side of the house, his gaze searching the lawn until he spied her. She stilled the swing as he crossed the rough grass toward her, his face set in a smile that said he was going to be pleasant if it killed him.

He reminded her so much of David it was unnerving. They both had the same coldness she had at first mistaken for confidence. Yet there was something different about Matt. The children liked him, and they never liked strangers. Then there was that buzz she'd felt standing close to him. She didn't know what else to call it. It was like an adrenaline rush, a tingle of excitement.

"Dr. Evans tells me there aren't any other rooms for rent this side of the mountain," he said when he reached her.

Even though she knew she was going to let him have the rooms, she couldn't resist tweaking his pride just a bit. "I didn't think there were."

"You're going to gloat, aren't you?"

"Maybe, but only a little."

His smile was almost genuine, Liz thought. "I don't expect to be here long. There was a mix-up in the assignments. In two weeks, you could be showing your rooms to a little old lady who only comes out to go to church."

It was a good thing. She wouldn't like feeling this way for a whole year. "I do have two children," she reminded him.

"It's hard to miss kids that cute."

"They do talk, you know, and laugh and run."

"And cry and scream occasionally, I imagine."

His smile was positively dazzling. She'd have to be mush brained not to know he was oozing charm because he had nowhere else to lay his handsome head. She slid out of the swing. "Let me give you a hand."

"I don't have much."

When they reached the station wagon, he opened the back. "You see before you everything I own."

What she saw was at least a dozen boxes of books. She was amazed the car had made it up the mountain. "Don't you have any clothes?"

"In the front seat."

Everything else he owned was crammed into one suitcase and a clothes bag. It was comforting to know the doctor thought it more important to spend his money on medical books than on himself.

"I'll take the bag," she said. "I'll leave you to wrestle with those books. What did you think of the clinic?" she asked as she started back to the house.

"It's a disaster," Matt said as he hefted a box of books to his shoulder. "Small, dingy rooms, no decent equipment, barely basic supplies. I don't know how Evans put up with it."

"The clinic mostly does family practice. Emergencies are sent to the hospital in Woodstock. It's just twenty miles away." She held the door open for him, then followed him up the stairs. "Was Salome at the clinic?"

"Yes. If she and a woman named Hannah are to be believed, the female artists at the hotel are man-eaters."

Liz laughed, laid the suit bag down. "I'm afraid their reputation is well deserved."

"Hannah said it was unfortunate I had no wife to protect me, but she seems to believe Salome—sorry, Sa-*low*-me—can hold them off."

Liz laughed again. "Salome can handle just about anybody."

She stood by the door while he unpacked the books and put them into piles. "How did you come to be here? Everybody's going to want to know," she said when he looked up at her, a chill in his gaze. "It's easier to tell them right away and get it over with."

She watched his expression harden.

"We've all known each other since birth," she explained. "We're hopelessly curious about any outsider." She guessed that's what he'd feel like the whole time he was here.

"I went to medical school on scholarship," he told her as he resumed unpacking his books. "In exchange, I have to work for the public-health service for three years."

She had intended to leave, but her curiosity was too great. "Tell me about your family."

He had his back to her, reaching inside the box for another

book. "That's really no one's business. It can't possibly have any effect on my medical abilities."

Liz flushed. The rebuke was deserved. She didn't have to ask questions just because everybody else did. "Sorry," she said. "I didn't mean to appear nosy."

He turned, but his look wasn't forgiving.

"I'll leave you to your unpacking. Dinner's at six. Let me know if you need anything."

She walked back downstairs, scolding herself under her breath. She was just as bad as everybody else in town. There was no reason to let this strange reaction to his presence cause her to ask questions about things that didn't concern her.

Matt thought the house was empty when he came downstairs. Then he heard sounds coming from the kitchen. He didn't want to talk to Liz. He didn't like her questions, but it was Liz herself who affected him. Her combination of lush maturity and country innocence didn't fit into one of his neat categories. He didn't trust the anomaly, but it intrigued him.

He decided on a walk. He'd talked to more people this afternoon, divulged more about himself than in any year of his life. He paused on the front porch. The quiet reminded him of the mind-numbing monotony of Gull's Landing. Hell, he could even hear the bees buzzing around the tiny pink flowers on the shrubs growing on either side of the porch steps. The thick grass of Liz Rawlins's yard merged into the yards on either side with no more interruption than a couple of rock-bordered flower beds filled with the green foliage of daisies not yet in bloom.

The gray-painted boards of the steps bent under his weight. A narrow strip of concrete walk cut through a small yard bounded at the street by a white picket fence. He reached the sidewalk and paused. He'd seen everything beyond Hannah's Drugs, so he decided to have a look at the rest of town, if a place this small could be called a town.

Hannah Coleman emerged from the store as he passed. "You find Liz's house?" she shouted at him.

"Yes."

She waved at a passing car. It stopped. "That's the new doctor." She pointed at Matt. "Handsome enough to start a fight in a henhouse, ain't he?"

The people inside—a couple and three children—craned their necks to get a good look. Matt kept walking. People waved and spoke as he passed, but no one else shouted at him or pointed.

Lawns were green and thick. Late tulips and baby's breath obscured the browning foliage and dead heads of daffodils and narcissus. The heavy blooms of white peonies sagged from their own weight. A climbing rose, thick with deep red blossoms, scented the air. Matt recognized the blue iris. They had bloomed in the yard of one of his foster homes. Lilac and mock orange formed hedges between gardens and barriers to hide abandoned barns and chicken houses. Towering oaks covered the street for almost its entire length. Here and there, an enormous stump provided evidence that the canopy had once been unbroken.

He reached the hotel and stopped to stare at the huge building that rose higher than the massive oaks. It looked at least a hundred years old. He passed a small lake and an open common before reaching the entrance to a camp. More than a dozen large, white, rambling summer homes clustered around a circular driveway. The camp had its own nurse, but they depended on the clinic for anything serious.

He turned back and looked down the length of the street. He could see all of Iron Springs at a glance. Twenty-seven houses, two stores, a church, a fire station and the clinic. He thought of Charlottesville and the enormous hospital where he had expected to spend the next three years. Things had been going so well, and now this. It was like starting all over again.

Just as Matt started back to the house, he saw Ben and Rebecca emerge from their driveway on bikes with training wheels. They made a beeline for him.

"I'll beat you," Rebecca called to her brother.

Ben didn't answer, just pedaled faster. He was younger, but his better coordination enabled him to keep up with his sister. Matt could tell their competition was so fierce they wouldn't give a thought to the possibility of running into him.

He jumped off the sidewalk just in time.

"I win!" Ben shouted.

"No, you didn't! I won!"

Matt couldn't help laughing. "It was a tie."

"Mama said it's time to eat," Rebecca said, breathing hard.

"She said come get you," Ben added.

"Did she tell you to run over me if I wouldn't come?"

Rebecca giggled. "We weren't going to hit you."

"You could have fooled me." Matt helped Ben turn his bicycle around. "Looked like you were going to smash me flat."

"We can't smash you," Ben chirped. "You're too big. Mama says you're bigger than granddaddy." Ben looked up at Matt. "Will I grow as big as you?"

"Bigger," Matt said, giving the bicycle a push. "Especially if you eat all your vegetables."

"Do I have to eat asparagus?"

"You'll have to ask your mother."

"Mama says it's good for me. Do you like asparagus?"

"Mama just cut it," Rebecca said. "She says it's fresh as a daisy."

"What's a daisy?" Ben asked.

"It's a flower, dummy," Rebecca said. "Everybody knows that."

"I didn't," Matt said. He figured a little white lie wouldn't hurt.

"We've got lots of them," Rebecca assured him.

"You'll have to show me. Ben, too."

"He knows. He just forgot."

"Boys do that when it comes to flowers."

They had reached the front porch. "What do you do with your bicycles?"

"Just leave them," Rebecca said.

The kids scrambled up the steps and through the door. Matt

started to call them back. Then he realized nobody in Iron Springs would steal a bike.

"It's too much for a man who's used to salads or a quick steak," Matt said, refusing the chocolate layer cake.

Liz was so relieved that dinner had gone well she didn't mind his refusal.

He seemed a little more relaxed. He had been smiling when he came in with the children. They had chattered away to him during the meal, telling him all the things they usually told her. She was amazed at the change in him. She didn't understand why he was far more open with them than with her.

Liz helped Ben down from his chair. "You two run and get ready to go to Aunt Marian's."

"Can the man go with us?" Ben asked.

"Yes, please," Rebecca entreated, dancing up and down. "Aunt Marian gives us ice cream."

Liz saw the sparkle disappear from Matt's deep brown eyes.

"I imagine the doctor's tired," she said. "He's had a long trip and a busy day. He can go with us another evening."

"Will you?" Rebecca asked.

"Sure. I need to go over to the clinic," Matt told Liz. "I'd like to get familiar with the office before I start seeing patients."

"Sadie would love to show you around. I'll give her a call. It won't take her a minute to get there."

"I'd rather do it by myself," he said.

Liz got the impression he liked doing everything by himself. She wondered what had made him want to be so alone.

She watched him walk down the hallway, Ben chattering on to him about ice cream. A shiver of excitement raced through her. There was no way she could look at that man and not feel his attraction.

As she put away the food and washed the dishes, she listened to the muffled sounds coming from upstairs and realized Matt was in Ben's room. When Ben came tumbling down the staircase a little while later, he had changed clothes. Matt must have helped him. Ben couldn't tie his shoes yet, and he wouldn't let Rebecca do it for him.

''Where's your sister?'' she asked.

''The man's brushing her hair. He said she looked like she'd been out in a hurricane. What's a hurricane?''

''A big storm with lots of wind and rain,'' Liz replied. ''Run up and tell your sister we need to hurry,'' she told Ben as she closed the dishwasher and turned it on. ''If we don't, your cousins will eat up all the ice cream.''

Matt Dennis was becoming more of an enigma by the minute. It irritated her he liked her children more than he liked her.

Don't be stupid, she told herself. With his looks and being a doctor, probably every female he meets makes a grab for him. Most likely he's perpetually poised for flight. That made her all the more determined to get to know what made him shy away from her. After all, she wasn't exactly burned toast herself.

Chapter Three

"Do you think the new doctor's going to be happy in Iron Springs?" Marian, Liz's aunt, asked.

Liz watched the five children playing on the lawn while she, her aunt, uncle, cousin and her cousin's husband relaxed on the screened porch. "No, I don't," she answered, "but it won't matter. He doesn't expect to be here more than two weeks. He said there was a mix-up in the assignments."

"Salome is delighted with him," Marian said. "She dropped by the camp office on her way home. She couldn't stop talking about him."

"He's a man. Have you ever known Salome to talk about anything else?"

Her aunt laughed. "Not for long."

"Everybody's dying to see him," her cousin Naomi said. "Hannah has told everybody who set foot in her store about him."

"They'll be disappointed."

"You know something?" Naomi asked.

"No, except he seems wary of adults. I don't know what

he's afraid of, unless it's women grabbing at him his whole life."

"Is he as good-looking as Hannah says?" Naomi asked.

Liz nodded.

"Maybe I'll walk you home this evening." They laughed together.

"Leave the man alone," Naomi's husband, Amos, said. "You women start plaguing him, and he's liable to head back to where he came from."

"His being all that good-looking could be a problem," her aunt said, turning serious. "It's a shame he's not married."

"Being married wouldn't make any difference," Liz said.

Aunt Marian directed a searching glance in her niece's direction. Liz hoped no one could see her heightened color in the darkness of the porch.

"You'll understand when you see him," Liz explained. "But I doubt he'll be here long enough for anybody to catch him, even if he wanted to be caught, which he clearly doesn't."

Liz took a deep breath. Her aunt wouldn't be fooled if she kept talking like this. She would have to show better control in the future.

"Ethan told me he'd invited you to the firemen's picnic," Aunt Marian said.

"He invited the whole family," Liz replied.

"That's sensible," Amos said. "He'll be marrying a whole family."

"I wish you'd stop talking like that," Liz complained. "Ethan Woodhouse hasn't asked me to marry him."

"He would if you'd give him half a chance," Naomi countered. "Everybody knows he's been in love with you since high school. Why do you think he never married?"

"He's had plenty of chances," Amos said. "With his business going great guns, near 'bout every female in three counties has had a go at him."

"But he never got over you," Naomi added. "He says he always knew you'd come back to Iron Springs."

"I'm not ready to think about getting married," Liz said.

"You can't still be getting over David," her aunt said. "You've been divorced two years."

"Leave Liz alone," her uncle ordered. "If she wants to marry Ethan, she'll do it in her own good time."

"I know that," Naomi said, "but there aren't many men around here, certainly not who love Liz like Ethan does. Besides, he can afford to send her kids to college, along with any others they might have."

Liz got to her feet. "I can take care of my own children, thank you. I most certainly won't marry a man just so he can send them to college." She kissed her aunt and uncle. "I'd better get the kids in bed. Me, too."

But as Liz walked back to her house, she had to admit it would be difficult to send Rebecca and Ben to college, even with a full-time job. Rent from her boarders hadn't added up to much yet. She didn't know what she would do if she had to buy a new car or make repairs to the house. She wanted to go back to college when Ben started school, but the nearest college was an hour away. She didn't know how she could commute and still work.

She could sue her ex-husband for the child support he'd never paid, but she didn't think she could stand the strain of a court battle. She wanted to keep as far away from him as possible.

What she needed was a boarder who could help with the children in exchange for reduced rent. Then she wouldn't have to wait until Ben started school to go back to college. As soon as Matt Dennis left, she'd put an ad in the papers.

Matt virtually tumbled down the stairs, his coat over his arm, his tie thrown around his neck. He had overslept his first day on the job. He didn't want to know what Liz would think of him, but it couldn't be worse than what he thought of himself. He prided himself on being professional, and a professional was never late.

The house was silent, the kitchen empty. Everybody had gone.

He spied a note on the table anchored between the salt and

pepper shakers, stepped closer and saw his name on it. He opened it.

> I knew you'd be tired after your trip so I let you sleep. The cereal is in the cabinet above the mixer. Milk in the refrigerator. Fruit is in a basket next to the sink. Coffee is in the pot. All you have to do is heat it.

Matt didn't even consider taking time to eat. He hurried into the front hall, tied his tie in front of the mirror and ran out the front door. He could walk to the clinic, but driving would be quicker. He backed into the road, carefully looking both ways before he realized there was no traffic in Iron Springs. He didn't know why he was hurrying. Most likely nothing more serious than a cold or chronic allergies awaited him. He pulled into the gravel-strewn parking lot, parked behind the sign that read Doctor.

"Morning, Beefcake."

Salome's color of the day was a bright apple green, but the fit of her uniform hadn't changed. Matt didn't know how she breathed.

"Please address me by my title," Matt said, determined to start on the right foot with his staff.

"Sure, Dr. Beefcake. You got a roomful of patients waiting, but no need to rush. It's mostly colds and curiosity."

Matt had never encountered a receptionist who showed such a lack of respect for his professional standing. But as he opened his mouth to tell her she would cease calling him Beefcake or look for new employment, Liz came around the corner.

"Is one of the children sick?" he asked.

"No."

"Then what are you doing here?"

"I work here. I'm the office manager."

He didn't know why he was so surprised. Somebody had to manage the office. It just never occurred to him it might be Liz.

"You weren't here yesterday."

"I'd taken the afternoon off to help the new doctor settle in."

Dressed in a blue suit with a cream-colored blouse open at the throat, she didn't look at all like she had yesterday. Heels, stockings and small gold earrings completed her outfit. Only her ponytail, a concession to the inadequate air-conditioning, prevented her from looking as businesslike as Georgia Allen, an old friend who'd gone on to great success in the corporate world.

"She's a wiz," Salome assured him. "Dr. Evans would have screwed up everything without her."

"I'm sure she is," Matt said. "Now I'd better start seeing patients. I wouldn't want them to die of curiosity."

"They're more likely to die of frustration from not being able to wrestle you down right there in your office," Salome said.

Matt decided the only way to control what Salome said would be to cut out her tongue. Since that wasn't a viable option, he admitted defeat and retreated to his office.

The room smelled of mildew, strong soap and Dr. Evans's cigarettes, but it was a haven from Salome. And Liz. It wouldn't be easy, but he could put up with Salome for the short time he would be here. He wasn't so sure about Liz. There was something about seeing her in that suit that told him she was a lady he hadn't even begun to know. It told him just as clearly that he wanted to change that.

As the morning progressed, his suspicions were confirmed; he hadn't seen anyone who couldn't just as easily have consulted the nurse. Or their grandmother, for that matter. Even the woman wearing a dashiki and giant hoop earrings who'd declared that no modern artist painted with anything but acrylics, and who'd invited him to make a thorough examination of her chest, couldn't summon up more than a few shallow coughs.

He got up and walked over to the filing cabinet. This was a good time to start studying patient records. He'd be much better able to help his patients if he knew something of their medical history, even if it consisted of nothing but mumps, measles and an occasional bout with bronchitis. He'd no sooner opened the first chart when the door flew open.

"Lunchtime," a pair of green lips announced.

"I know."

"Well, come on."

"Come on where?"

"To Sadie's office. We always eat in there."

"I don't have a lunch," Matt said. "Besides, I intend to spend the time studying charts."

"Liz packed your lunch," Salome said in a stern voice.

"Then I'll eat it in my office."

Salome marched over, took the open file from his hands, closed it and put in on the pile with the others. "You're having lunch with us. I have a thousand questions I want answered."

Matt fully intended to tell her he would do no such thing, but she clamped her hand around his wrist and pulled. Maybe it was the sight of apple green fingernails encircling his wrist. Maybe it was the hypnotic effect of seeing words emerge from between apple green lips. Whatever the reason, Matt found himself following Salome down the hall.

"People are going to expect me to know everything there is to know about you," Salome said.

"I can't imagine why anybody would be interested in hearing about medical school," Matt protested, wondering why he didn't give up and go AWOL.

"Nobody gives a hoot about that stuff," Salome said, shoving him into a room where an obviously embarrassed Sadie and a serene Liz waited.

Liz had said she went home for lunch, but she seemed to be waiting for something before she left.

"I want to know about your love life," Salome continued. "You seeing anybody serious? You a great kisser? Are you any good in bed?" She patted him on the behind. "You may be a dud, but you'd sure look mighty good spread out on a sheet."

Matt's temper snapped. "I'm a good kisser, but I'm better in bed. I'm not serious about anyone, but I'll be damned if anyone is going to spread me out on a sheet. Now, where is my lunch, or did you just get me in here to ask X-rated questions?''

Matt was shocked by his own response. He'd never reacted like that before. Salome's insanity must be contagious. Something had to account for it.

Liz chuckled all the way home. She would never forget the look on Matt's face when Salome told him he'd look good spread out on a sheet. It had been all she could do not to snicker at him. She didn't know why Matt was so stiff, but if Salome couldn't take the starch out of him, no one could.

Still, he *would* look nice on a sheet. Liz had been thinking about him since she'd first seen him. Now that Salome's remark had focused her imagination on one particular image, she doubted she would be able to get the picture out of her mind. Its being a very agreeable picture made it that much more difficult.

Liz stopped in the middle of the gravel path. She was as bad as everybody else who couldn't stop speculating about each stranger who came to town. That's exactly what she'd run away from so many years ago.

She picked up her pace. If she didn't hurry, she'd be late fixing lunch for Rebecca and Ben. She'd made that part of her agreement when she took the job. Today was the first time she wished she could have left the children to Naomi. She would love to have taken Sadie up on her oft-extended invitation to have lunch with them.

Liz didn't fool herself that it had anything to do with Sadie or Salome. No, it had everything to do with one very handsome ''Dr. Beefcake.'' She laughed aloud. She had to agree with Salome's opinion he could have his own calendar if he wanted.

Liz gave herself a mental shake. Just minutes ago, she'd decided not to indulge in idle speculation, and now she was imagining Matt sprawled out for a calendar photo shoot. She should be appalled at herself. Instead, her mental images made her slightly warm all over. Maybe she should marry Ethan. She was definitely in need of some male attention.

Only Ethan never made her feel like this. But if he loved her, and she liked him an awful lot, why should he leave her cold while a virtual stranger shifted her imagination into overdrive?

For the same reason movie stars and rock singers had been driving women crazy ever since Rudolph Valentino. Charisma. It was nothing more. She would be over Matt Dennis three days after he left. She was certain he would go. A man like him would never spend a minute longer in Iron Springs than he had to.

She thought of the fax she'd found in her machine that morning, a belated notification that Dr. Matt Dennis had been assigned to replace Dr. Jane Lumas. If it had come sooner, she would probably have withdrawn her offer of rooms, she would never have met Matt, and she wouldn't now be worried about his effect on her. Though she was certain her life would have been much smoother without this interruption, she couldn't entirely regret it. Matt might stay no more than a few weeks, but his presence promised to give the people of Iron Springs something to talk about through the long winter.

And her? Well, a daydream now and then didn't do any harm. Besides, if she thought very much about that calendar, she might not need her electric blanket.

"I'm hungry," Ben announced.

"Me, too," Rebecca said. "How long do we have to wait?"

"Just a few more minutes," Liz told her children as they stared hungrily at food getting cold. "If he's not here by six-thirty, we'll eat without him."

Where could Matt be? She'd told him dinner was at six. She was certain there hadn't been an accident. In a community this small, she'd have heard about it in less than five minutes. No, he was just plain late. There was no point in waiting any longer.

"We'll eat now," she said.

Ben immediately started spooning mashed potatoes into his mouth.

"Aren't we going to wait?" Rebecca asked.

"I've changed my mind. He's too late already."

"I think we ought to wait. He might come in."

Now that she'd been given permission to do what she'd been begging to do for the past twenty minutes, Rebecca didn't want to begin eating. Ben looked up, a spoonful of potatoes halfway to this mouth, a worried expression on his face.

"You can wait if you want, but Ben and I are hungry. He might be very late."

Matt didn't come in until thirteen minutes of seven. Liz didn't have to tell him he was late. The children did it for her.

"You're very late," Ben announced. His *very* sounded more like *worry*.

"We didn't wait," Rebecca announced. "Mama said maybe you didn't like to eat with children."

Liz felt herself blush. Someday she'd learn not to say anything to the children she didn't want repeated within five minutes. "I did tell you dinner was at six."

"I was studying patient records and lost track of time." He tousled Ben's hair. "Did you leave me any food, sport?"

"Lots of food," Ben chirped. "Everything cold."

Liz flushed again as she got to her feet. "It won't take but a minute to heat it in the microwave."

"That's all right. I can eat it cold."

"You can't eat cold potatoes or peas," she said. "Sit down. It'll be ready in a minute."

"I'll wash up."

He was back down just seconds after the food came out of the microwave.

"Where are the children?" he asked as she served his plate.

"Getting ready to go to Aunt Marian's."

"I was looking forward to talking to them."

"Then you'll have to get home earlier. They go to bed as soon as we get back."

"Sorry, I didn't mean to mess up your schedule."

Why couldn't he be fat and ugly? Liz thought. That would make it easier to stay mad at him for being so thoughtless. Instead, he sat there looking like he'd just stepped out of that calendar she'd been thinking about all afternoon, and she couldn't do anything but smile back at him.

"It's not that," she said. "I can fix your dinner separately, but I can't if you don't tell me when to expect you."

"That won't be necessary."

"It will if you mean to come in at all hours. The children need to keep to a regular schedule. I like to feed them at six."

"Then I'll be here at six."

"You don't have to. I can fix you something cold."

"After a cold breakfast and lunch, I look forward to a hot dinner."

"I fixed a hot breakfast." She wasn't going to let him push the blame for this off on her. "If you want a hot lunch, you'll have to go to the hotel."

He looked reproachful, even angry, but he forced himself to smile. He was going to be agreeable if it killed him.

"Being late twice in the same day is unpardonable. I promise I won't do it again."

"It doesn't matter to me," she said. "But if you want hot food—"

"Tell me when I'm to be at the table, and I'll be here."

"Seven-thirty for breakfast, and six o'clock for dinner. If you can't make it, let me know. I'll try to—"

"If I can't make it, I'll get my own. Now, don't let me make you late to your aunt's. If you'll leave the water in the sink, I'll wash my plate."

"We got dishwashers in Iron Springs years ago." Did he think they were still bagging their dinner in the woods and dressing it in the backyard? "Just put your plate in and turn it on."

Ben and Rebecca came running into the kitchen. "Is the man going to Aunt Marian's with us?" Rebecca asked.

"Tie shoes," Ben said, and thrust his foot at Matt.

"Ben, you can't—"

"I'll be happy to," Matt declared. He got up from the table and knelt down on the floor.

"Can't tie shoes," Ben announced.

"Then I'll teach you," Matt said. "Give me your other foot."

Ben put his foot on Matt's knee. Liz started to say something, but Matt calmly tied the shoe.

"We'll have to see about getting you some shoes with Velcro straps," Matt said.

"What's 'well-crow'?" Ben asked.

"Magic shoes," Matt said.

"Can I have magic shoes, Mommy?" Ben asked.

"We'll see. Now, we'd better hurry or we'll be late." She hoped he would forget the *magic* shoes. Shoes for three-year-olds cost more than thirty dollars.

"You never said if you were coming," Rebecca said to Matt. She might be only four, but she never forgot anything.

"Maybe next time."

"Aunt Marian wants you to come. She says she wants to see what all the panting is about."

Liz silently vowed that in the future her children would be locked in their rooms the minute Matt set foot in the house.

"Salome's been talking," Liz explained, hurrying Ben and Rebecca out of the house before they could say anything else to embarrass her.

She started to ask them to be careful what they said, then realized it would be impossible. Besides, it wasn't their fault if adults didn't know any better than to utter every foolish thought that came into their heads in front of them. Maybe this would help her think before she spoke.

But what could anybody do about Salome Halfacre?

Chapter Four

"I ought to run around the mountain before I go to the clinic," Matt said. "If I eat this much every morning, I'll soon need a complete new wardrobe, and I can't afford that." He pushed his chair back from the table, which had been laden with dishes of scrambled eggs, sausage, grits, toast and warm peaches in milk.

"The children need a big breakfast," Liz said.

"I know. I just have to learn not to try to outeat Ben."

"I hope they didn't bother you too much."

"Nothing I can't get used to."

They had been boisterous but well-behaved. Ben had been too concerned with eating to pay much attention to Matt. Rebecca had asked him if she'd have to take out people's insides if she became a doctor. When he said no, she'd asked about the brain. She'd laughed merrily when he said she had a gruesome imagination.

Liz sent the children off to wash up and get ready to go to Naomi's.

"I've talked about everything from dissecting cadavers to

bowel resections over breakfast, lunch and dinner,'' Matt said to Liz. "This morning was the first time I realized they didn't make very suitable table conversation. Do they always stay with your cousin?''

"There's no day care in Iron Springs.''

"Surely other women work. Who keeps their children?'' She looked slightly uneasy. He wished he hadn't said anything.

"I'm something of a scandal in Iron Springs. A divorced woman. The only one.''

"Surely they don't think…'' Unsure of what he wanted to ask, he swallowed the last of his sentence.

"I know exactly what they think. You always do in a place this small. They didn't approve of my marrying a Yankee and moving to New York. But having made my bed, as the saying goes, I was expected to lie in it.''

"But it had too many lumps?''

"That's one way to put it. Now that I've let you stay here, they'll have more food for gossip. They'll probably decide I'm chasing you.''

Matt set the coffee cup he'd just raised to his lips back down.

Liz laughed. "Don't look so startled. People have to have something to talk about. Besides, there's something predatory about divorced women. Everyone knows it takes virtually nothing to turn us into man-eaters.''

The tension eased, and Matt felt himself grin. "What about big-city doctors? Are we wolves in sheep's clothing?''

"They haven't made up their minds about you, but generally they blame this sort of thing on the woman. If she chases a man, she's a tramp. If he chases her, he's just doing what she wanted him to do. Really, you men have no will of your own.''

He didn't know why this amused him. "You'll have to keep me up on the latest.''

"Speculation will probably die out in a week or two. Since we both work at the clinic, people will get used to seeing us together. After they realize Sadie and Salome have nothing to tell them, they'll find something else to talk about."

"That reminds me," Matt said, "who hires the staff at the clinic?"

"I do."

"Do you replace them, as well?"

Any appearance of friendliness vanished from Liz's expression. "If necessary, but I haven't had to consider that. Things have gone very well since I hired Salome."

"So you did hire her?"

"Yes. Is anything wrong?"

"Do you think she's a proper receptionist for a public clinic?"

She gave him a look that had bulldog determination written all over it. "Are you talking about her liking for brightly colored lipstick?"

"That, and her calling me Dr. Beefcake in front of the patients."

"Anything else?"

The steely look she directed at him didn't encourage him to be entirely frank. "I'm used to a more professional atmosphere."

"Does that include Sadie? You might as well tell me now, because I hired her, as well."

"Why didn't Dr. Evans do it?"

"Because it's my job." Her gaze narrowed dangerously. "Or don't you think I'm qualified?"

Matt opened his mouth, then shut it. How could she be expected to know how to staff a public medical facility? She hadn't even finished college, much less had any medical training.

Liz regarded him with a penetrating look that made him uneasy.

"Answer me."

"No." There was no point in evading it. It had to be said.

Her gaze didn't waver. "And I don't think you have the experience to know what kind of staff a clinic like this needs to run smoothly."

He couldn't have been more shocked if she'd said she wanted to have sex with him in the middle of the kitchen floor. "Are you questioning my medical knowledge?" No one ever had, not in college or during his residency.

"No. I know you graduated at the top of your class at the University of Virginia. I also know you won the most prestigious residency in the state, that you're considered a brilliant surgeon, and a bright future in some great hospital is widely forecast for you."

Surprise caused him to momentarily forget Salome. "How do you know all that?"

"This may be a tiny town in a tiny valley in the mountains, but we have telephone lines. And faxes. I had your complete history in my hands before lunch yesterday. How did a wunderkind like you ever get sent to a place like Iron Springs? You must have made someone really mad."

Matt didn't know what made him more angry, that she questioned his knowledge, that she had found out his whole history without his permission or that he was in this dead-end village in the first place. It hardly mattered. Each was enough to cause him to blow a gasket.

"Did you find out what I like best for dinner, my hobbies, the age at which I reached puberty?"

"No, but I'm sure if I ask...you're not making a joke, are you?"

"No." How could having his entire life history at the fingertips of the rest of the world be a joke?

"I didn't get any information that isn't available to everybody else in the medical community. I felt I needed to know something about you. After the way you clammed up the day you arrived, I didn't expect you'd tell me."

He wouldn't have, but now it seemed like wasted effort. "How long have you had this job?"

"Two years."

"So you've only worked with Evans. As far as you know, every doctor could be exactly alike."

"I know enough of human nature to know that will never be the case."

She was a slippery character, one not easily gotten around.

"But you don't know whether another doctor would mind working with Salome."

"No. I just know that Dr. Evans didn't."

"Did he say so?"

"Not in so many words. He did say he didn't want to pay for fancy degrees as long as I could find somebody willing and able to do the work. He wanted all available money used for supplies he could hand out to people who couldn't afford them."

Matt's collar suddenly felt too tight. He had been climbing on his medical high horse only to have it knocked out from under him by Dr. Evans's humanity.

"I wasn't aware that patients couldn't afford to buy what they needed."

"You would be if you looked at the price of the drugs you prescribe."

It had never occurred to Matt to think of the cost of the drugs he used, just their effectiveness. It had been someone else's job to see that the patients got them.

The children raced into the kitchen.

"I got here first," Rebecca said, flashing an ear-to-ear grin. Everything they did seemed to be a competition.

"Make sure you put all the toys you want in your bag," Liz said to the children. "I'll be ready in a minute." She turned to Matt. "Anything else you want to say?"

"No." He had to admit that his first day in the office had gone without a hitch. Everyone had been cheerful, the patients had been on schedule and properly prepared, charts and equipment ready and waiting for him. He'd never gotten the wrong chart or equipment—not even the wrong room.

"Are you going to the clinic now?" Liz asked.

"I think I'll stay here and work on charts until about eight forty-five. That'll keep me out of your way while you get things ready." It would also keep him out of the range of Salome's tongue. The mere word *beefcake* was enough to set his teeth on edge.

* * *

Matt didn't like mountains, but he had to admit they made an idyllic backdrop rising behind the clinic, mist curling up out of the trees. But not even the refreshing fifteen-minute walk from Liz's house could make him feel the least bit idyllic. He wanted to punch each doctor in the nose who'd voted to send him here. No, he'd rather force them to work here instead. He couldn't think of a more suitable revenge.

He came up to the clinic from behind, paused with his hand on the door. He didn't relish facing Liz. He hadn't meant to get her so upset by criticizing her work. He'd come to the office thirty minutes early because he wanted to talk to her before Salome and Sadie arrived. Even though he knew he was right, he wished he'd never said a word about Salome. He was sure Liz had done the best she could. He wouldn't do anything right now, but when the time came, he'd show her the proper way to go about staffing a medical office.

But the minute he stepped inside, all thought of staffing problems left his mind. In the hallway between all the offices and the examining rooms, he saw Liz kneeling over the body of a man, alternating between giving mouth-to-mouth resuscitation and cardiac massage.

"Nobody answers at your house," a frightened woman was saying to her.

"Then let's hope he's on his way here," Liz said as she applied all her strength to the man's chest. "Did you get the fire station?"

"Yes. They're sending the ambulance right over."

"Then you'll have to help me until they arrive," Liz said, and changed to mouth-to-mouth resuscitation.

Matt, coming out of his momentary immobility, hurried forward.

"I'll do heart massage," he said to Liz. "You keep up the breathing."

A look of startled recognition was the only reaction he got. As he worked to restore the man's heartbeat, Liz kept breathing for him. In between gasping breaths, she calmly told Matt what had happened.

"This is Tommy Pruitt.... He was eating breakfast.... He collapsed here.... He's forty-three."

"What's your name?" Matt asked the older woman.

"Edith Pruitt," the frightened woman replied. "I'm his wife. This is our daughter, Doris."

"Liz and I can't stop what we're doing. You're going to have to help us. Can you do that?"

"Edith never panics," Liz said between breaths.

"Go into that first room on the right," Matt directed, keeping his voice as even as possible despite the tremendous exertion required to give cardiac massage, "and bring me the cart with the red toolbox." He hoped Liz's estimation of Edith's character was accurate. Her husband's life could depend on it. "Doris, find me a blanket. Look in any examining room."

Edith returned with the cart faster than he'd expected.

"Good work," Matt said. "Now open the top drawer. Look for a 2-cc syringe. Find it? Good. Now look for a bottle of the epinephrine. It should be right in front."

Tommy Pruitt was very fortunate in his wife. She found the unfamiliar objects with no trouble.

"Liz, take over while I give this injection and get the paddles ready for cardiac shock."

He hated to involve her. She looked exhausted. He didn't know how she'd managed it this long, but she took over without a moment's hesitation.

Matt could hear the sound of the ambulance. They'd be here in a few minutes. He filled the syringe and gave the shot in the man's arm. The clinic wasn't equipped to give shots into the heart. Tossing the empty syringe aside, he took the paddles off the cart, greased them and slapped them on the man's chest.

"Move back," he told Liz. "I'm going to shock him now."

Matt flipped the switch, and the man's body convulsed. Grabbing up his stethoscope, Matt listened intently to his chest. "I've got a pulse," he said. "It's not regular, but it's there."

Matt started to take over the breathing—he knew Liz was too exhausted to continue—but just then the ambulance crew poured in through the office door. The first man slipped an Ambu bag and mask over Tommy's face which took over his breathing.

"He's as stable as we can get him here," Matt told the ambulance crew. "Get him to the E.R. You probably saved his life," he said to Liz as he helped her to her feet and over to Salome's chair.

The look she returned was expressionless. He wanted to take the time to tell her what a great job she'd done, how extraordinary she had known what to do and had kept doing it as long as necessary. Nothing had thrown her off stride. It took guts not to panic when you're suddenly faced with a dying man and no one to help you.

"Would you like me to drive you to the hospital?" Liz asked Edith Pruitt.

"You're too tired to do anything but go home and lie down," Matt said to Liz. "I'll drive Edith to the hospital. Her daughter can bring their car."

He hated to leave Liz just now, but he had no choice. "Promise me you'll let Salome take care of everything."

He got a faint ironic smile. "You think she can?"

He hoped Salome was as good as Liz thought. She was going to have to rearrange his entire schedule, and the patients weren't going to like it.

It required most of the morning to admit Tommy Pruitt to the hospital, so Matt didn't get back to the clinic until nearly noon. Salome was the first person he saw.

"How's Tommy doing?" she asked, anxiety replacing her usual bubbly good cheer.

"He'll be all right, but he's going to have to take it easy for a while. He'll need to change his eating habits, too. No more vegetables seasoned with pork fat."

Salome grinned. "He'll starve. There's nothing Tommy likes better than fatback."

"I think he's decided he likes living even more."

"Good." Salome handed him a fistful of charts and batted

her navy blue eyelashes. "Your office is full. There can't be a single artist up at the hotel. Don't forget you're due at the camp at four. Amos is anxious for the campers to meet you."

Just what he needed. A waiting room full of women who weren't sick, and a camp full of kids who would do everything in their power to break something before their two weeks were up. He wanted to talk to Liz, but he had the feeling she didn't want to speak to him.

Liz had not gone back home to lie down. She had spent the better part of the morning at the clinic trying to convince herself she didn't care what Matt Dennis thought of her professional ability, or lack of it. She was foolish to devote even two thoughts to a man who was going to be gone in a matter of days. And any woman who let herself get carried away by one tiny compliment needed to have her head examined.

It was obvious Matt Dennis held everyone and everything in Iron Springs in contempt. He saw only its smallness, its limits. He had no idea of the huge heart that beat in this small town. It was that heart, the caring, the feeling of belonging that had drawn her back home from New York despite having once run away from those very things that now repelled Matt.

And when he did see something admirable, he had the effrontery to look surprised. What was she supposed to do, wring her hands in helpless dismay while Tommy Pruitt died in front of her? She didn't have a medical degree, but she knew a few things. Matt had been even worse about Salome. She wanted to tell him that behind Salome's wild colors was an encyclopedic knowledge of the medical needs of every person within thirty miles of the clinic. Whenever the clinic had free samples to give away, Salome knew who needed what most. She could make people feel like they were doing her a favor by taking it.

But people from big cities didn't value things like this. They were concerned only with how much money you made, the size of your house, whether you drove a BMW or Mercedes. David had driven a Jaguar and bought her a Volvo station wagon. He'd also cheated on her. Liz had been happy to trade it all for her parents' house and a beat-up old Ford. It pleased her to know Dr. Dennis drove an even older car.

She'd been startled to find him kneeling beside her over Tommy, but she'd been relieved to know he was there. She wanted to ask if she'd done the right things, but she hadn't seen him for five minutes all day. First he'd been at the hospital. Now he was trying to catch up on the backlog of patients. He might be a snob, but she had to give him credit. He was a stickler about seeing every patient. She glanced at her watch. Three-thirty. He'd be here until late. She'd have to hold dinner. She stepped out into the hall to tell him she'd been able to get Amos to reschedule his visit to the camp. The clear, penetrating voice of Josie Woodhouse stopped her in her tracks.

"Hannah says she couldn't tell me a thing about the new doctor," Josie was saying to Salome. "She said he hadn't set foot in her store since that first day."

"I don't know about that," Salome said. "He doesn't take me into his confidence."

Liz could hardly believe her ears. Salome was being circumspect.

"I didn't expect he would, you being just a receptionist," Josie said. The woman was the worst snob in Iron Springs. "But you have to know something about him. You're around him all day."

"I can tell you he's the best-looking hunk of man flesh I've ever set eyes on," Salome confided.

"I'm not interested in what you think," Josie said. "I just wanted to know something about him before I decided whether to consult him. My indigestion is acting up again, and Dr. Kennedy can't seem to do anything about it."

Liz had heard all about Josie's indigestion. She used it to get her way when nothing else worked. She didn't have to use it often, since she made a habit of getting her way.

"The doctor's overbooked," Salome said, "but I'll see if he can work you in."

That meant Josie would go into the first examining room that came open, Liz realized. She would never consent to wait. Josie wouldn't understand why she should. Liz waited until Matt finished with a little boy who was suffering from severe allergies.

"Could I speak to you a minute?" she asked.

"If it's about this morning…"

"It's not."

He looked like he wanted to say something. Then he stepped back to allow her to precede him into her office.

"It's about one of your patients, Josie Woodhouse," she said as she closed the door.

"I haven't seen anyone by that name."

"She just came in, but she shouldn't be here. She has a private doctor—Dr. Isaac Kennedy. He'd have a fit if he knew you had looked at her."

Matt frowned. "That doesn't prevent her from changing to the clinic if she wants to."

"Josie would never become a patient at a public clinic. She'd consider it beneath her. Besides, I heard her questioning Salome about you. Her indigestion isn't troubling her. She's just here to satisfy her curiosity. She has to know more about everything than anybody else or she's miserable."

Matt's frown became deeper, actually quite unfriendly. He looked like a teacher about to chastise an errant pupil. She hoped he would be careful what he said to Josie. It wouldn't do to get her back up. Josie was basically harmless, but she could cause a lot of trouble.

"I don't know what kind of working relationship you had with Dr. Evans," Matt said, his tone as unfriendly as his look, "but this sort of thing won't wash with me. You've overstepped your bounds. I don't discuss my patients with my staff, and I don't expect my staff to bother me with gossip and innuendo."

Liz felt like she'd been slapped. It never occurred to her that Matt would interpret her remarks as gossip. She had merely wanted to warn him about Josie's habit of using her complaints of indigestion in a manipulative manner. She'd also wanted to warn him against giving Dr. Kennedy a reason to complain about him to the medical board. Every doctor within a radius of fifty miles knew to keep well away from Dr. Kennedy's patients.

Liz forced herself to look Matt in the eye. "I apologize. I won't do it again."

She walked over to the door, held it open for him. For a moment, he just stared back at her. She could feel the tears begin to gather at the back of her eyes, and it made her furious. She refused to cry in front of this pompous know-it-all. Nor would she allow her chin or lips to quiver. She would face him just as he was facing her, her body erect, her head high, her gaze direct and unwavering.

"It's very unprofessional to discuss patients with a doctor," he said, "even when you know them very well."

"I said I wouldn't do it again."

He waited as though he expected her to say something, but she had said all she meant to say to Dr. Matthew Dennis. He could find himself in the middle of a sticky investigation for all she cared.

Matt waited a minute longer, then left her office without saying anything else.

Liz remained standing. She felt like a cardboard figure, stiff, unable to move. Yet her insides were churning. She was mad and embarrassed at the same time. Mad that Matt thought she would do something as petty as spread gossip about his patients. Embarrassed that she had done something he considered unprofessional. It probably was, in the strictest sense, but she thought she'd acted for the best. The energy that had sustained her all day left in a sudden whoosh, and she collapsed into her chair.

Confess it. She was also upset because Matt had seen her in a bad light. She was being just as silly as all the rest of the women in Iron Springs over a handsome man, but she wouldn't do it again. She would keep her mind on her work and her nose out of other people's medical histories.

"I can't prescribe anything until I examine you more thoroughly," Matt said to Josie.

"Dr. Kennedy says it's indigestion."

"Then you'd better see him."

"He doesn't like to see patients today," Josie said. "It's his golf day. Besides, it's my body. I know what's wrong with me."

Matt hated to admit it, but he should have listened to Liz. Every time he tried to discuss Josie's medical history or her present condition, she responded with a series of personal questions that made Hannah Coleman and Solomon Trinket look like disinterested bystanders.

Matt stood. "Then I suggest you make an appointment to see him tomorrow."

Josie remained seated. "I may want to switch to you."

"I don't expect to be here more than a few weeks. It would be better to stay with a doctor who's familiar with your constitution."

"Why are you leaving?" Josie asked as she stood. "You just got here."

"My assignment to Iron Springs was a mistake."

"Of course it was if you're any good. Are you any good?"

Matt didn't think he'd ever get used to such direct questions. However, he decided to meet Josie's bold approach with one of his own. "I'm very good. So good, in fact, several major hospitals are angling to have me on their staff."

"You probably aren't that good," Josie said as matter-of-factly as if they had been discussing his shoe size. "Brilliant doctors are small and nearsighted. But you've got the confidence of a man who knows his ability. You're probably good. Maybe even very good. We shouldn't hope for brilliant. Not that it would make any difference. You wouldn't stay in Iron Springs in any case."

Matt only wanted to escape. Josie was worse than Liz had said. He opened the door. "Let me say again that you should see Dr. Kennedy as soon as possible."

But Mrs. Woodhouse didn't appear to hear him. She was staring at something at the end of the hall. Her entire body seemed to swell with indignation.

"I see she's still working here," she said, her tone hard as ice.

"Who?" Matt asked.

"Liz Rawlins."

"Of course she is," Matt said. "She's the office manager."

"She's a hussy and a harlot," Josie hissed, "a stealer of men's affections."

Matt was all at sea. He didn't know if Josie had a husband or a boyfriend, but he couldn't imagine Liz being involved with a man of Josie's age. He realized he didn't really know anything about Liz, but his instincts told him she was not a woman to compromise herself.

"I don't enter into the private lives of the people who work for the clinic," Matt said. "I'm sure that—"

"You're living in her house."

Matt wouldn't have stated it exactly in those words. "I rent a room there."

"You watch out, or she'll have you in her snare, as well. She can't stand to see a man indifferent to her. She'll weave her spell about you, hypnotize you until you can't see anything but her. I've seen her do it. She's bewitched my poor Ethan until he won't even listen to his mama. He can't see any wrong in her even when it's under his nose."

Matt began to understand. Ethan was interested in Liz, and Josie didn't like it.

"Leave my poor Ethan alone!" Josie called out to Liz. "You can have anybody you want, even this doctor here."

She'd warned him against Liz, but she was ready to sacrifice him to save her son. This woman would bear watching.

"Please give him back to his poor mother," Josie continued dramatically. "Release him from your spell."

"I don't have Ethan under a spell," Liz said, her calm voice returning a sense of reality. "He's welcome to date anyone he pleases."

"You know he can't," Josie wailed. "You've bewitched him. He's forsaken his family for you."

"I'm sorry about that, Josie," Liz said as she approached the woman, "but I have cast no spell over Ethan, nor do I have any desire to do so." She turned to Matt and handed him a folder. "I canceled your visit to the camp. Amos said to reschedule whenever it was convenient. Unless you have an objection, I'm going home. Bye, Josie. I hope your indigestion is better."

"You don't care about my indigestion," Josie called after Liz. "You hope it kills me. Then you could have Ethan all to yourself."

Matt couldn't stand any more. It was disgraceful that this woman should have so little self-control she'd stand in the middle of the clinic screaming accusations at Liz. He took Josie by the elbow and propelled her into the lobby.

"Call Dr. Kennedy's office and make an appointment for Mrs. Woodhouse tomorrow morning," he said to Salome, who'd followed the exchange with an amused eye. "You can tell his nurse her indigestion is acting up again."

"It always does when she doesn't get her way."

"You, young woman, are a disgrace to—"

"She's a very efficient receptionist," Matt smoothly finished, deciding it would be best to usher Mrs. Woodhouse out of the office altogether. "She never gets upset, no matter what happens."

"She doesn't have a son," Mrs. Woodhouse said.

"If I did, I wouldn't want him tied to my apron strings," Salome flung after Mrs. Woodhouse. "You've practically castrated the poor man."

Matt closed the door on Mrs. Woodhouse and turned back to the waiting room. Only then did he notice the four grinning faces of waiting patients. Salome and Mrs. Woodhouse had played to a nearly full house.

He thought longingly of the huge, impersonal hospital in Charlottesville. Nothing like this ever happened there.

Chapter Five

Matt knew he ought to apologize to Liz—no, he *had* to apologize—but all through dinner that night the words wouldn't come. He was not used to being in the wrong. The part that rubbed the hardest was that he was also right. It *was* unprofessional to talk about patients. Yet it was sometimes necessary to know some background when you had a patient like Josie Woodhouse. He was right about Salome, too. And he was wrong.

"Wanna get down," Ben told his mother the minute he swallowed the last of his apple cobbler with vanilla ice cream. "Wanna play."

"I want to play, too," Rebecca said. "Joe and Eddie want to come over."

"Danny, too," Ben added.

"You can have as many children over as you want, but don't leave our yard," Liz said. "And stay out of the creek. You got a cold the last time you got wet at night."

The children scrambled out the door. The sudden quiet made his being alone with Liz feel more intimate; it gave him

a heightened consciousness of her presence. It also gave him
an opportunity to become aware of the clothes she was wearing, the faint aroma of her perfume as it wafted in and out
among the food smells.

Liz had changed from her business suit into shorts and a
sleeveless blouse. She probably wasn't conscious of the impression she made, but he was. He found himself staring at
her with the open-eyed wonder of a teenager. He'd seen better
figures—well, not much better—and he'd smelled perfume
that cost a hundred dollars an ounce, but somehow they
hadn't made quite the impression Liz made on him.

Or his body. His arousal had almost reached the point of
being embarrassing. He'd been celibate for too long. "I'd
better go, too," he said, pushing back his chair. "I've got
charts to read."

She didn't say anything. She hadn't spoken to him except
when necessary since she warned him about Josie.

He stood. "I'm sorry about Josie," he said. "If I had
known she was going to attack you like that, I wouldn't have
let her into the hall until you were out of sight."

Liz didn't pause in clearing the table. "She acts like that
every time she sees me. I'm used to it."

"It can't be pleasant."

"It's not."

He stood there, waiting, trying to push the words past his
lips. "I apologize for speaking to you the way I did. It's
usually not a good idea to talk about patients, but in this case
it would have been better if I had listened to you."

Liz paused, a slow smile curving her mouth. "I didn't
think you'd apologize. I didn't think you could."

He felt anger, but he repressed it. "I almost didn't."

"I suppose I shouldn't have said anything. I can see what
you mean about it being unprofessional. It's just that I know
Josie and Dr. Kennedy. I didn't want you to get in trouble
with him."

Matt wasn't used to having anyone worry about him. It
wasn't a factor he'd ever had to put into the equation of how

he dealt with people. It left him feeling unsure of how to proceed.

"About Salome..."

All amiability vanished to be replaced by a look that said she was ready to fight.

"She's not at all proper, but she does get the work done."

"Then you don't want me to fire her?"

"I never did." But hadn't he? He wasn't sure now. Nothing in this town worked like it ought to. He didn't feel nearly so sure of himself.

"I thought she handled everything today rather well," Liz said.

So did he, but he didn't feel like he needed to give so much ground all at once.

"I also wanted to compliment on your work today."

She looked surprised. "Helping Tommy? That was nothing."

"It was quite a lot. He wouldn't be doing nearly so well without you. That showed great courage to tackle a job like that. Most people would have waited for the ambulance."

"But he couldn't wait. He—"

"I know. That's why it's so remarkable. You're a gutsy lady."

Matt didn't know whether he'd ever made such a long speech in his life. He certainly didn't remember anything making him so uncomfortable. "Well, I'd better get to those charts."

He left the room with Liz still staring at him. As he washed his hands and brushed his teeth, he couldn't shake the feeling of dissatisfaction with himself, the feeling that he'd done something wrong. He didn't understand it. He'd always known exactly what to do, how he would feel about it afterward. He couldn't understand why he felt so dissatisfied now.

He guessed it came from Liz. Somehow he felt he'd hurt her feelings, and he didn't like that. But that was silly. They were both mature adults, both professionals. They could discuss a situation, even disagree, without getting their emotions tangled up in it. Or if she couldn't, it was time she learned.

But he was the one still chewing on this. Maybe he wasn't as objective as he thought. Or maybe Liz was getting in the way of his objectivity.

But that was ridiculous. She was attractive, but certainly not enough to cause him to make a fool of himself. Besides, he didn't like her very much.

No, it couldn't be Liz. It must be his assignment to this wretched speck on the edge of civilization. He couldn't think straight with all this quiet, among people who had known everything about each other since the moment of their birth. You needed distance to be objective. Everybody in Iron Springs might as well live in the same house for all the privacy anyone had.

On reaching his room, Matt settled into a comfortable armchair and picked up a handful of charts. He wouldn't be here long enough to worry about it. But as long as he was here, he had patients to care for. He opened the first folder and started reading.

Less than an hour later, he put the charts aside. The sounds of children floated in through the window, but that shouldn't have affected his concentration. The noises of Charlottesville never had.

He got up and walked to the window. The children were playing dodgeball, and Liz was playing with them. She was the only one left in the circle. Most of the children were screaming and shouting encouragement to Liz or to the older children who dominated the ball handling. Matt could see the looks of determination on their faces as they tried to get her out. Rebecca and Ben urged their mother on with loud, shrill voices. He could hear Liz's laughter as she dodged one ball after another. After the day she'd had, he didn't know where she found the energy.

Then Liz slipped on the damp grass, and one of the boys managed to hit her. She made a big production of pretending to be mortally wounded. All the kids laughed and ran to her. They collapsed into a wiggling mass of arms and legs, laughing and shouting with happiness.

Matt found himself feeling like an outsider peeping

through a keyhole at a world he wasn't allowed to enter. He'd never cared in Gull's Landing, but tonight he didn't want to be excluded. He wouldn't have known what to do if he'd been down there, but the yearning to be in the midst of all that happiness was suddenly intense.

It was so strong he left his room and went downstairs and out onto the front porch. He stood at the corner, leaned against the post. He could see the children in the backyard. They had formed another circle with some of the bigger children inside this time. They had an easy time avoiding Ben's throw, but they shrieked and pretended to barely make it out of the way. Ben thought he was great stuff.

Liz got one out, and all the children cheered.

"Good evening, Dr. Dennis."

Matt turned. A man and woman were passing along the sidewalk in front of the house. He'd seen the woman in his office yesterday afternoon. She had kidney stones. He'd given her a medicine he hoped would dissolve them and eliminate the need for an operation. "Good evening, Mrs. Gaddy."

"Nice evening for sitting on the porch," she commented.

"A good walk would do you better," her husband said.

"I've got too much work," Matt replied. "I'm just taking a break."

"Make sure you use something for the mosquitoes if you mean to say out much longer," Mrs. Gaddy said. She waved, and they passed on down the sidewalk.

The woman across the street called out, and Mr. and Mrs. Gaddy crossed the street. While the women chatted, the men leaned against the fence, speaking occasionally, but mostly watching their wives.

A family came out of Hannah's Drugs and got in their car. They stopped and Mrs. Gaddy and her friend went over to talk to them. They just stood there in the middle of the road, moving when a car came but more often talking to the occupants, as well. The drivers seemed more anxious for a chance to join in the conversation than to get on with their business.

Matt tried to imagine such a thing happening in Charlottesville. Traffic would be backed up a dozen blocks in less than fifteen minutes. Somebody would call the police.

Matt looked up and down the road. The scene was the same everywhere, people sitting on porches, visiting over fences, calling out to neighbors as they passed. Several spoke to him. He didn't know who they were. It made him want to go inside. Yet he stayed on the porch, watching, speaking to everyone who spoke to him.

"You should have played a game with us. The kids would have loved trying to get you out."

Liz had come around the corner of the porch. Beads of perspiration glistened on her neck and shoulders. Ringlets of blond hair stuck to her forehead. Exercise had given her face added color. She rubbed the back of her neck with a towel, but Matt thought she looked just fine. She wore a halter top and shorts—not Bermuda, *real* shorts—that left no question in his mind that Liz was a woman in her physical prime. He didn't know why her husband had left her, but it couldn't have been because he found someone more attractive. Matt revised his earlier evaluation and moved Liz up several places on his all-time-best list.

"Too much work."

"Why aren't you doing it?"

"I'm taking a break."

She started up the steps. "Is that a nice way of saying we're making so much noise you couldn't concentrate?"

He grinned in spite of himself. "Maybe it means you were having so much fun I was jealous."

He hadn't wanted to criticize, but he hadn't meant to say that, either.

"You could change your clothes and join us. They're good for another half hour or so."

"I'll pass this time."

She stopped drying her hair, gave him a penetrating look that made him uncomfortable.

"I can't decide whether you look down on us for being country bumpkins, or you're just afraid to let yourself go and have a little fun."

Despite having survived Salome, Josie Woodhouse and

Hannah Coleman, he was caught unprepared by this frontal attack. It made him furious.

"I've been too busy working my way through college and medical school and trying to build a career to have time for fun. But when I get back to Charlottesville, I'll make certain to get a membership in the YMCA."

"Your mind needs the fun as much as your body needs the exercise."

She wasn't backing down. She wasn't even the slightest bit embarrassed that she'd strayed into areas that were none of her concern. She stood there, waiting as if she expected him to offer an explanation. Well, it would be a cold day in Hell before he did that.

"Maybe, but I'll stick with my old habits. I've gotten along fine so far."

"I don't know. You ended up here. And as far as I can tell, you think that's as close to Hell as you've ever been."

He wanted to agree with her. He wanted to say mean and spiteful things about Iron Springs, its people, its single street, its gossipy network of relationships, but he wasn't really angry at her or the people of Iron Springs. He was angry at the medical board who sent him here.

"I'm more comfortable keeping my distance," he said. "I'm not very good with relationships."

"You won't get better until you try."

"I have tried. It only got worse."

Ben came tearing around the corner of the porch. He pounded up the steps, ran over to Matt and thrust out his foot. "Tie shoe," he said in between gulped breaths.

"Ben, it's soaking wet. You can't ask Mr. Dennis to—"

"It's also covered with grass clippings," Matt commented as he knelt to tie Ben's shoe. "But I've handled worse things than a wet shoestring."

"Becca says you're to come play," Ben said, watching Matt intently. "She says you can get out Jeremy."

One of the big boys, Matt presumed.

"Hurry," Ben said when Matt didn't work fast enough for him. "Gotta go back."

"There," Matt said. Ben turned and headed off.

"What do you say?" his mother called after him.

"Thank you." Ben raced down the steps and tore off around the corner of the porch.

"So much for your being rotten with relationships," Liz said.

"What do you mean? Oh, that? He just needed someone to tie his shoes."

"Ben is ashamed of not being able to tie his shoes. Generally he won't go to anyone but me. He went to you that first day."

"He's a little boy. He'd naturally go to a man."

"Not Ben. He even avoids his uncle. And Rebecca never invites adults to do anything with her. She's invited you to go to Aunt Marian's twice and play ball once."

"I don't see… That doesn't mean… I like kids. Yours are especially nice. You've done a great job raising them."

"Thank you, but you're trying to ignore what I'm saying. You can be good with people if you want. Everybody likes you, even Salome."

Matt thought of what Salome called him and decided what she liked had nothing to do with his personality.

"You can go on being a hermit if you like," Liz continued, "but don't excuse it by saying you can't handle relationships. Maybe you don't want to handle them, but I imagine you could do it extremely well. Now, before I make you so angry you'll pack up and live in a tent before you'll spend another minute in my presence, I'm going to take a shower."

Matt woke early the next morning. He didn't want to. It was his first day off. After studying charts until well past midnight, he'd intended to sleep late. There was nothing to do in this miserable excuse for a town, this bump on the backside of the Appalachian Mountains. No reason to get up.

Yes, there was. The sounds of children poured in through the window. He looked at the clock—7:43 a.m. What kind of parents let their children out of the house at this ungodly hour? A parent like Liz Rawlins apparently. She'd probably driven them outside so she could sleep late.

He looked outside. At least a dozen kids filled Liz's backyard. Just his luck to have taken rooms adjacent to the community playground. He closed the window, cut on the air conditioner and got back in bed. It didn't work. He was awake. He might as well get up.

But he didn't want to go downstairs where he might run into Liz. He was still angry at her for offering advice about personal relationships. He'd been to dozens of "counselors" and "attitude adjusters" when he was growing up.

His mother had stopped in Gull's Landing long enough to have her baby and die. The townspeople had felt compelled to do their duty by him, but they didn't feel compelled to like him. They said he was ungrateful and mean. They said he was sullen and uncooperative, a loner with no social skills. He was like a mongrel cur they were afraid would bite. They were glad when he won a scholarship and left for college.

Now Liz was telling him people in Iron Springs liked him. Let them get a whiff of his background, and that would be the end of that. He got up and pulled on a T-shirt and jeans. He couldn't hide in his room. He never had, and he wouldn't start now. Besides, he was hungry.

Liz tried to calm her voice. She didn't want David to know how much his call had upset her.

"Of course I'm surprised to hear from you," she said to her ex-husband. "You haven't bothered to contact me since I left New York."

"I was in the middle of very sensitive negotiations," David said. "They took every minute of my time."

"I realized that when you didn't show up in court for the divorce decree."

"I didn't need to be there. Everything had already been decided."

Liz didn't know why she was bringing this up. She knew how unimportant she was to David. His infidelity had proved that. His neglect had proved he didn't care much about his kids, either. So why was she so upset at the sound of his voice?

"My business is a real success," David said. "Everything worked out just like I said it would."

"I'm glad for you, David."

And she was. She couldn't have loved him as much as she did, lived with him as long as she did, feel as betrayed as she did, and not still feel some of what drew her to him in the first place.

"I thought you might have been happier if I'd failed."

"I may have said some terrible things to you, David—I'm not sure, since I was too upset at the time to remember—but I've never hated you. You've wanted this all your life. I'm glad you have it. Maybe you can have some time to yourself."

"I doubt that. Owning your own company is even more work."

She didn't understand men. They seemed to think building things—companies, bridges, even writing books—meant they had made a contribution to the world, had left a mark, had done something worthwhile. Couldn't they see that children were their only real legacies?

"I'm sure you'll make it," she said. "If that's all you've got to tell me, I've got to go. I'm in the middle of making a dress for Rebecca. I've got to finish it in time for her to wear it to church Sunday."

"Wait," David said. "The children are the reason I called."

Liz stiffened with alarm. The only thing she'd wanted from the ashes of their marriage was her children. She'd waived alimony, given David the house and everything else in exchange for sole custody of the children. He'd never shown any interest in them. Why should he develop an interest in them now?

"What about the children?" she asked.

"I want you to send them up for a visit."

Visions of David kidnapping her children and running off with them to another state exploded in her mind. She told herself not to be foolish. David had given up his family for his company. He wasn't about to change his mind now.

"That's a little hard for me to believe after you've ignored their existence for three years."

"I am their father."

"You're also the man who left his children alone in a house to go visit his mistress."

"I told you I was sorry about that. You can come so there won't be any question about their being left alone."

"The last time we were together, you hit me."

"For God's sake, Liz, must you remember everything?"

"That's rather hard to forget."

"I was stressed out. You were calling me names. I got mad."

"I was mad, too, but I didn't hit you."

"Okay, so maybe you and I were never any good together. That doesn't mean I don't want to see my kids. Now that the company is doing so well, I'm sending you a check for all the back child support."

Liz didn't understand how David could put his company before his children. She would have supported her children if it had cost her everything she had. She guessed that was the difference between her and David. Now he had his company, and he wanted his children, as well. Well, he wasn't going to get them that easily.

"You'll have to do more than that before I can trust you with the children," Liz said. "I couldn't—"

She broke off. She was certain she heard somebody on the stairs.

"Rebecca? Ben? What are you doing inside?"

No answer, but Liz was certain she heard the soft squeak of a stair.

Matt! My God, he could have heard everything she said. Her face burned just thinking about it.

"Someone's here, David. I've got to go."

"You haven't answered my question."

"I'll think about it, but I can't decide anything now."

She hung up. In the silence, she heard the sound of footsteps going into Matt's room.

Chapter Six

Matt came down ten minutes later. Liz examined his face closely, but she could see nothing that would indicate he might have overheard her conversation.

"Are you ready for breakfast?" she asked, laying the dress aside.

"I can fix my own," Matt said. "Go back to your sewing. I wouldn't want Rebecca to be without her dress."

"How did you know I was making it for Rebecca?" Had he heard her after all?

"You can't fit into it, and I doubt Ben would let you put it on him."

She couldn't help but smile as she laid the dress aside. "You want your eggs fried or scrambled?"

"Fried."

"I have bacon, grits, toast and orange juice. Is that enough?"

"It's more than enough."

He had on Top-Siders, an emerald green polo shirt and faded jeans that fit his body with tantalizing snugness. She wondered what he did to keep so trim. There was no place to work out within an hour's drive. If he jogged through Iron Springs, every woman in town would be hanging out the window. Knowing how he felt about people's curiosity about him, he'd probably rather get fat.

"Can I help?"

"You can fix your coffee."

They talked about nothing important while she fixed his breakfast. She took up her sewing again while he ate. By the time he settled back with a second cup of coffee, she was fairly certain he had gone back upstairs as soon as he heard her on the telephone. She didn't know why she was so anxious he not know about David. Everybody in town knew. He'd find out sooner or later.

"I realize you've only been here three days," Liz said, "but how do you think things are going at the clinic?"

"Better than I expected, though I'll never get used to Salome's lipstick. Where does she find that stuff? I don't know how you had any idea she would handle the job so well. I wouldn't have hired her to direct cars into the parking lot."

The casual way he couched his apology enabled Liz to relax enough to laugh. "You'd let yourself be distracted by her nail polish. I knew her before the long nails and tight uniform. I knew there's nothing that walks on two feet Salome can't handle. She and Sadie have been best friends since grade school. When you live and work in a place as small as Iron Springs, that's important."

"I hadn't thought of it like that. I guess I should consult you when I have any questions about my patients."

"I wouldn't dream of saying a word." She thought he looked a little embarrassed.

"Normally I wouldn't consider such a thing, but I don't know how to attack it."

"Attack what?"

"Everybody seems to be afraid of me."

She raised her eyebrows. "Even the artists?"

His eyes twinkled. "I was talking about the locals. They come into the office, then sit there with their mouths closed."

"You're new. It takes people in a small town a while to accept newcomers."

"I can't help them if they won't talk to me. I had a woman in yesterday asking me about something that was wrong with her sister. It took me nearly ten minutes to figure out she was talking about a female problem. I still don't know her sister's name."

"Who was it?"

"Idabelle Ray."

"She doesn't have a sister. You sure she didn't say sister-in-law? She has six."

"I'm positive."

"Then it was Idabelle herself."

"Well, I can't really help her if she won't talk to me."

"Have you ever had a woman give you a complete exam?"

The look on Matt's face was priceless. She wished she had a camera.

"No."

"Do some time. Then you'll understand. You've got to meet people outside the office, let them get to know you as a person."

"How do I do that? Hang out in Hannah's store, sit on the front porch and stop everybody who walks by?"

"That's one way. Another would be to go to church with them. We have only one church. Everybody would be there."

"I'm going to Charlottesville this afternoon. I won't be back until late Sunday."

"Then you could accept some of the dinner invitations you've already gotten."

"I don't believe in doctors mixing socially with their patients. I don't think it makes for good medicine."

For a moment, Liz couldn't think of anything to say. She'd never heard anything more ridiculous in her life, but she could tell that Matt Dennis was the kind of man who, once he made up his mind, wasn't likely to change it.

"I don't agree with you," she said. "In fact, I think the best medicine comes from doctors who have known their patients and their families over a number of years. People aren't automatons. They respond to feelings and emotions.''

''That's exactly what I mean,'' Matt said. He leaned across the table toward her, his expression completely serious. ''Emotion has no place in medicine. It's a science. A doctor needs to have complete objectivity so he can consider problems without being confused by having to consider the patient, as well.''

''How can you possibly look at a broken toe and not see the boy who's going to miss his championship game?''

''I was thinking of something a little more important than that.''

''Okay, how about the man with a young family who has cancer? Or the old woman without any family who is an invalid?''

''There are people whose job it is to deal with those things. The doctor shouldn't have to be concerned with anything but the illness and how best to treat it.''

''You sound like you'd rather not have to see a patient at all.''

''I didn't say that. I just said we'd have better medicine if we could eliminate emotion.''

''But how can you look at a child in pain and not feel compassion for it?''

''I can't. Nobody could. But if half of your mind is taken up with sympathizing with the patient, that's half of your brain that's not concentrating on the medical problem. If you're too concerned about the patient's feelings, you might start making decisions based on those feelings and not on sound medical practice.''

''That's the most inhuman thing I've ever heard.''

He looked shocked, like he really didn't believe what he'd heard.

''How can you say that? All I'm talking about is delivering the best possible medical care so the patient can go home sooner, recover faster, lead the fullest possible life.''

''I have no argument with that. I just can't see how anybody can look at patients and not feel anything for them.''

"I didn't say I could, only that I thought it would be ideal."

"I can't see how you'd even want to do such a thing. It's inhuman."

"You said that already."

"I'm sorry, but I think your attitude is appalling. I sincerely hope that's not what they're teaching in medical schools these days."

"Actually it's a widely held belief, but I reached that conclusion long before I reached medical school."

Liz knew Matt was a private person who didn't want to be in Iron Springs a minute longer than necessary. She had assumed that was the reason for his standoffishness. She didn't want to believe he really felt this way about people. She had to convince him that knowing people, caring for them would enable him to be the best possible doctor. But she'd no sooner marshaled her argument and prepared for battle than she heard a knock at the back door.

"Good morning," Ethan Woodhouse said, not waiting for her invitation to let himself in. "Can a lonely bachelor get a cup of coffee?"

Matt backed out of the driveway, headed his station wagon toward the mountain and breathed a sign of relief. He was headed to Charlottesville, civilization and a liberating degree of anonymity. Even the prospect of crossing the mountain ridge again didn't dampen his excitement. He felt like he'd just been let out of prison. He had only a little more than twenty-four hours, and he meant to enjoy every minute of it.

He was also relieved to have escaped an argument with Liz. He could tell she was winding up to try to convince him his ideas about doctor-patient relationships were wrong. He didn't care that she thought he was wrong, but he did care that she felt she had to convert him. What did she know about doctors and medicine? She wasn't even a nurse. She was an office manager. Important, yes, but it didn't qualify her to know how doctors worked.

It certainly didn't qualify her to know anything about him.

He doubted they would ever be able to see things the same way. It was a good thing her boyfriend had come in when he did.

Thirty minutes later, he had crossed the mountain, was headed south on I-81 and he was still thinking about Liz. He couldn't understand that. He had a little black book with names and addresses of young women who appreciated the same kind of no-strings-attached relationship he enjoyed.

So why was he still thinking about Liz? He'd known her less than a week.

He couldn't stop thinking about that heart-attack patient. She thought what she did was nothing out of the ordinary, but he'd seen experienced medical personnel freeze when faced with an emergency they weren't equipped to handle. She'd just dug in and done what she could, all the while calmly telling his wife whom to call and where to find the telephone numbers. He had to admire that kind of courage no matter how much he might disagree with her on other matters.

Also, despite their differences, he could identify with her. She had no parents, no brothers or sisters, no husband. She might have a few relatives close by, but Matt knew from firsthand experience nothing replaced a family.

At least she had children.

But they were a worry, as well as a blessing. She was fighting for the kind of life she wanted for them and herself, knowing all the while she probably couldn't earn the kind of money necessary to educate them and still stay in Iron Springs.

She wasn't asking anybody to solve her problems. It would have been easy to blame her husband, to make him pay through the nose. But if the little scrap of conversation Matt had overheard meant what he thought it did, she had even refused that. Liz had made mistakes. But she had accepted responsibility for them and settled into the job of doing something about them.

He didn't know anything about the situation, but he thought Liz ought to do everything in her power to see that her children had as much of a normal relationship with their father as possible. Nothing in the world was more important than having parents, than belonging. Without it, all the success in the world didn't mean much.

Matt cursed. Thinking about Liz made him start feeling sorry for himself. He turned onto the approach ramp for I-64 east. He'd spend the rest of the trip planning his weekend. It had to be a good one. He wouldn't get to leave Iron Springs for another seven days.

"Ride over to Timberville with me," Ethan said to Liz. "A man over there's got a '67 Mustang I want to look at."

"There's nobody to keep the children," she said. "Besides, I've got to finish this dress for Rebecca."

She wished Ethan hadn't come over. She was still irritated at Matt's attitude. She was also upset over David's telephone call. She needed time to herself.

"Naomi will keep the kids," Ethan said. "Or they could go up to the camp with your aunt. You can do your sewing in the car."

"Naomi keeps them all week, and Aunt Marian has her hands full with the camp. If I tried to sew this dress in the car bouncing all over that mountain, there wouldn't be a straight seam in it."

"Then bring the kids along, and I'll buy Rebecca a dress."

That was Ethan all over, generous to a fault. He had adored her since high school. Ten years, a broken marriage and two kids hadn't changed anything. She was certain he would make a good husband and be a kind father to her children. With his thriving business, there wouldn't be any worry about their education. But no matter how hard she tried, Liz couldn't feel any passion for him.

When she'd first returned to Iron Springs, she had been desperate for friendship and support. Ethan had taken her and the kids to dinner, brought them treats and often dropped by unannounced wanting her to join him on some spur-of-the-moment trip. It had been so wonderful to have someone so attentive to her needs, ready to do anything he could to make things easier for her, to make her happy, that she had hoped her fondness for him would turn into love. It never had. Now she found herself wanting to pull back and not knowing how to do it.

Liz let her sewing drop in her lap and looked up. "I can't let you give Rebecca a dress. You've given the children too much already."

Ethan pulled out a chair and sat down at the table next to her. "Marry me, and it won't matter how much I give them." He reached out and took her hands in his. "You know I want to take care of you and your children."

Liz carefully disengaged her hand. "I know, Ethan, and I appreciate everything you've done for me, but I can't think about remarrying yet."

Ethan got to his feet and swung away from the table. "Hell, Liz, it's been two years since you divorced that bastard." He stopped at the sink and turned to face her. "When are you going to forget him?"

"It's not that easy. He called this morning. He wants me to send them for a visit."

Ethan dropped in the chair and gripped both her hands in his. "Marry me. I'll send him packing in short order."

Liz disengaged her hands, picked up her sewing again. "You've been a wonderful friend, Ethan, but this is something I have to do myself."

"To hell with this *friend* business. I want to be your husband."

"I've already told you I'm not ready to fall in love again."

"You will be. And sooner than you think. Now how about that ride to Timberville?"

Liz sighed. There was absolutely no way she was going to get out of this without hurting his feelings. Besides, the kids would enjoy the drive. With Matt in Charlottesville, she had no responsibilities here.

She wondered what Matt was doing. She hadn't dared ask, not after telling him his patient approach was inhuman. She wondered whom he planned to see? An old girlfriend, she was certain. A man like Matt Dennis would have girlfriends wherever he went. Beautiful women without ex-husbands or children, women who wanted to have fun with no promises about tomorrow. Women a lot more beautiful than she was.

What he did was none of her business. She should stop thinking about him and concentrate on what she was going to do about David and Ethan.

What a mess. She had two men in her life and she was spending all her time thinking about a third. She needed to see a psychiatrist.

"How about twelve-thirty?" she said to Ethan. "That'll give me time to get the children cleaned up and feed them lunch."

"Make it twelve. Lunch is my treat." Ethan bent over and kissed her on the cheek. "Wear something sexy. I want every man in Timberville to know I'm with the best looking woman in Virginia."

Matt's fellow doctors laughed until they held their sides. "It sounds like something out of a Jerry Lewis movie," Terry Owens said. "No wonder you're screaming to get out."

"My favorite is Sa-LOW-me," Brad Pfeiffer said. "When can I meet her?"

"Maybe you can get Melanie to paint her lips and nails green," Terry said. "That might put life into some of the geriatric cases."

"Melanie with green lips and a uniform two sizes too small would give them heart attacks."

The men laughed again. Matt found it wasn't as funny as he thought it would be. He hadn't told his friends about Salome to have them laugh at her. He just wanted to share his experience with them. But somehow it hadn't turned out like he'd expected.

"Did you get in touch with Georgia?" Terry asked Matt.

"She's tied up right now," Matt said. "She promised to call the minute she could get away."

"What are you going to do until then?"

"Hang around here."

"I'd wait with you, but I've got the graveyard shift." Terry stood. "Dr. Allison gives me the worst shifts he can."

"I've got a date," Brad said, getting up and tossing his beer can into a trash can sitting in the middle of the room. "I don't expect to be back before tomorrow afternoon."

"Don't worry about not getting out of that Podunk mountain town right away," Terry said. "If Dr. Andrews said he's working on it, he's doing all that can be done."

"He didn't have any idea when he could get you out?" Brad asked.

"No. Dr. Reichenbach makes all the assignments, and he's against changing them."

"Then you'd best sit back and keep a low profile," Terry said. "Let Dr. Andrews do the dirty. If he can't get you out, remember it's only a year."

Maybe, but a year's lost momentum could take five years to regain.

After his friends left, Matt busied himself straightening the apartment. He didn't expect Georgia to call. She enjoyed the time they spent together, but her career came before anything else—and that included Matt.

But the thing that bothered him most was he kept thinking about Liz, wondering what she was doing, wondering if she was out with Ethan, if she was kissing him, if she was going to marry him. Matt told himself he was getting desperate when he had to wonder about the dating habits of a stubborn divorcee in a hick town in the mountains.

He picked up his coat and headed out. He knew of at least two bars in town where the action never stopped. If he couldn't participate, at least he could watch. Maybe that would keep his mind off Liz Rawlins.

Chapter Seven

"If it doesn't slow down around here, I'm going to quit," Salome announced when she marched into Liz's office to hand her the morning mail. "If I'd wanted to work myself to death, I could get a job over at the local diner."

"Things will slow up soon," Liz said. "Everybody's trying to do all the things before summer starts that they've put off since last summer."

The past two weeks at the clinic had been brutal. Their patient load had nearly doubled. It seemed like everyone within a thirty-mile radius had suddenly come down with a cough or a mysterious rash. They had been so busy Liz had had to take over reception while Salome helped Sadie with patients. If things didn't ease up soon, she was going to have to hire extra staff.

"It's all Beefcake's fault." Salome dropped down into a chair and whipped out her compact. One glance and her eyebrows flew up in dismay. She took out her lipstick and began to do repairs. The color today was a pink so vivid it made Liz's eyeballs ache.

"Why do you say that?" Liz asked as she quickly sorted the mail. She'd given up trying to convince Salome to call Matt by his proper title.

"You don't see droves of men crowding in here, do you? It's the women."

The phone rang. Salome jumped up. "I'm starting to feel like a racehorse in a starting gate."

She had hardly disappeared when Matt stuck his head in Liz's door.

"I need the Baywater family history," he said. "I've just seen Ray Baywater, and I think he's got heart disease. I remember from his charts that his father and grandfather had it. I'd like to review their treatment and the results. I'd like to know anything you can find out about their diet, too. People here seem to think they ought to live to be a hundred eating chicken, pork and enough grease to give a whole city high cholesterol."

"Solomon Trinket nearly has."

"I don't understand it. Getting blood through his veins must be harder than hacking through a bamboo jungle."

His head disappeared, and he was gone. Liz smiled. She had recently come to the conclusion Dr. Matt Dennis was a great big fake. He pretended not to care about his patients. He scowled enough to scare little children. He occasionally made patients so furious they stormed out of his office.

But he cared. And the patients knew it. Those who stormed out invariably came back. Those who liked him—and most did—went home and promptly phoned every relative within twenty miles. Within a couple of days, the whole tribe usually managed to think of some reason to drop by the clinic.

Liz had known Matt was smart. His string of scholarships proved that. But after he virtually memorized every chart in the office, she decided he had to be a genius. Even Salome and Sadie had remarked that he seemed to know more about the patients than the patients themselves.

She'd asked him about it a couple of days earlier.

"I'm just trying to be professional," he had said. "The

more information I have about a patient, the better I can di-
agnose him.''

But that didn't account for the hours he spent studying
charts. He might call it being professional. Liz called it going
the extra mile to make sure his patients got the best care.

Liz noticed with relief that the clock said seven minutes
after five. She had gotten off work seven minutes ago. She
felt a little guilty about leaving when everybody else had to
stay until six, but not guilty enough to stay. She looked at
her desk, decided not to straighten it. Salome would cover it
with charts before she left tonight. Liz cut off the window air
conditioner and went out. It was time to go home and spend
a little time with the children before she started dinner. She'd
have more time tonight. Matt had already told her he'd be
late.

"Can't we wait a little longer?" Rebecca begged.

"Yeah, can't we wait?" Ben echoed.

"He's already forty-five minutes late. The meat loaf will
be dry as a bone.''

"I like dry meat loaf," Rebecca said.

"I like dry meat loaf, too," Ben echoed.

"If we don't wait for him, he won't come to Aunt Marian's.''

That's what Liz suspected. Matt had taken to going to her
aunt's with them most evenings, though he never sat on the
porch with the adults. He played with the kids—tag, football,
hide-and-seek, anything they wanted. He seemed at ease with
them, happy, more like a normal human being. But let one
of the adults come near him, and he turned into a silent sen-
tinel, stiff and uncommunicative. Liz didn't know why he
liked children and disliked adults, but it was clear he did.

"If we wait any longer, we won't have time to go to Aunt
Marian's," Liz said.

"I don't care," Rebecca declared. "I don't want any ice
cream.''

That was too much for Ben. "I want ice cream.''

Liz sighed. "I'm sorry, but we can't wait any longer.

Sometimes Dr. Dennis has a lot of patients in the office when I leave. He can never tell—''

The children weren't listening. Liz heard a car come to a stop in the driveway.

"Here he is!" Rebecca cried. She jumped down from her chair and raced to the front door.

"Want down!" Ben shrieked. "Wanna see Matt!"

Liz didn't approve of the kids' calling Matt by his first name. But he insisted upon it, and they insisted upon waiting for him. She heard the excited greetings as he came in the front door.

"Be down in a minute," he called to her from the hall as he headed up the stairs two at a time like he always did. The children pounded up the stairs behind him. She knew they would. They always did.

While she took pots from the stove and put vegetables into dishes, she listened to the babble of voices from above—the high soprano squeak of Rebecca, Ben's husky alto and Matt's resonant baritone. As far as she could tell, all three of them were talking at once. She had no idea how anybody knew what anybody else said.

She didn't know how Matt stood it. He wouldn't have from adults. He was forever telling them to calm down, speak slowly and lower their voices. He never once said that to Ben or Rebecca. Now that she came to think of it, he didn't say that to the kids at the office, either.

She couldn't help smiling despite her irritation over his being so late. He was kind to her kids, two fatherless children who desperately wanted a man around to play with and look up to. She couldn't help but be grateful for that. Neither could she help but like him for his kind heart. He didn't think he had one—in fact, gave every indication of not wanting one—but he was becoming an integral part of her children's days. She didn't know what they were going to do when he left.

Matt hadn't said anything about leaving in nearly two weeks, but it hung over Liz's head like a rain cloud waiting to dump on her. No matter who followed him in the clinic, it would be an awful jolt for the patients. It would be a terrible jolt for the kids. And if she was perfectly honest, she wouldn't like it very much herself. He didn't include her in his good humor and smiles, but she'd grown comfortable with having him around.

She took the meat loaf out of the microwave and sliced it.

It did irritate her that he was cold to her. The tension caused by their differences over Salome and Ethan's mother had eased, but she still couldn't penetrate his reserve. A tumbling sound on the stairs told her Ben and Rebecca were racing to see who would be first to the table. Apparently Matt was ready for dinner.

Ben won. Liz suspected he got a head start. He was very competitive, always looking for chances to beat his sister at anything. Rebecca would rather talk a minute longer, but she hated to lose. She always tried her hardest. This time she knocked the chair into the table. Aware that she'd gone too far, she quickly sat down and dropped her gaze to her lap. Ben took one look at his mother's face and decided not to crow about beating his sister.

"Here you go, sport." Matt lifted Ben into his chair. He'd given up his high chair when Matt brought home two thick medical catalogs for him to sit on. Ben took great pride in being able to sit at the table like everyone else.

"Sorry to be so late," Matt said, "but at the last minute they brought in a boy from the camp with a broken arm. It didn't take long to set, but I had trouble with the cast. I never had to use plaster before."

"You should have let Sadie do it. She's done dozens."

"The medical board sent me here to get some family-medicine experience. I imagine plaster casts were one of the things they had in mind."

He had that gritted-teeth look he always got when he spoke of the medical board, but it was an opening she couldn't ignore. "Have you heard from them, I mean about when they're sending your replacement?"

"Time for the blessing."

He was stalling. He told her he'd never said blessings until he came to her house. She told him they always did at her table. They held hands. It was Rebecca's night to give the blessing.

It took them several minutes to serve the children. Fortunately they were hungry and didn't bombard Matt with news of what they'd done that day.

"You didn't answer my question," Liz said once everyone was served.

"I haven't heard anything," he replied without looking up.

"What does that mean?"

"I don't know."

"The longer they wait, the more disruptive your leaving will be." It wouldn't do any good for her to worry about that. She had nothing to do with who was sent to the clinic or how long he stayed.

"Are you leaving?"

Both children had stopped eating, anxious expressions on their faces. Liz was ashamed of herself. She'd let her curiosity make her forget how the news might affect the children.

"All the doctors leave," she said. "They come here for a short time and then they're sent somewhere else."

"I don't want Matt to go," Rebecca stated.

"Me, neither," Ben said.

"I'm afraid it's not up to us. He was supposed to go somewhere else. They sent him here by mistake. As soon as they get things straightened out—"

"I'm not going anywhere anytime soon," Matt said. He was looking at Rebecca, but Liz got the feeling he was speaking directly to her. "The medical board doesn't like to move people around too quickly, even when they've made a mistake. I imagine I'll be here for at least the rest of the summer. Probably a good deal longer than that."

Rebecca's grin went from ear to ear. "Can you play kick ball with us tonight?"

"Only if you eat in a hurry," Liz said. "You know bedtime is eight o'clock."

She got the usual chorus of groans, but Liz was firm about that. Her children needed their rest.

"Don't eat so fast," Matt said to Ben. "You'll have meat loaf all over the floor."

"Hurry up," Ben said, ignoring Matt's words of caution. "Wanna play kick ball."

"If you get sick at your stomach—" Liz began.

"They'll have a doctor at hand to take care of them," Matt said.

Nobody asked for seconds. In no time, the kids were up from the table and racing upstairs to brush their teeth.

"I'm sorry about spoiling dinner," Matt said as he got up to follow them.

Liz looked at the remains of a dinner she'd worked nearly an hour to prepare. Bolted in ten minutes. It was enough to make her want to nail the kitchen door shut and take out a lifetime's lease on a booth at a burger joint.

"It's okay," she said. "I don't suppose a doctor can turn his back on a kid with a broken arm, not even at dinnertime."

She didn't envy the woman Matt Dennis married. She'd never know when they could sit down to dinner.

What was she talking about? When he married, *if* he married, he'd choose a career woman. They'd both have secretaries to work out their dinner schedules. They'd probably eat in restaurants. They wouldn't see their own kitchen in daylight except on weekends.

"You should have eaten without me," Matt said.

"I was willing, but the children weren't. I don't know what you've done to them, but you've turned them into loyal disciples."

"It's being good at kick ball," Matt said with a grin Liz was certain had already melted a million female hearts before he turned it on her and her daughter. "I'd better change, or I'll be late."

Liz looked at the table. Except for the meat loaf, there wasn't a thing on it that couldn't wait an hour. She put the meat loaf in the refrigerator and headed toward her room. She was going to play kick ball tonight. As she remembered, she used to be quite good at it.

* * *

"You never told me you were such an athlete," Matt said to Liz. They were headed home after a vigorous game of kick ball that ended up involving nearly every kid in Iron Springs close enough to be attracted by the whoops and hollers of the players. It even drew Liz's cousin and her husband off the porch.

"Mama was great, wasn't she?" Rebecca asked.

"Sure was," Matt said. "Next time she plays on our team."

He'd been surprised when Liz came out of her bedroom dressed in a T-shirt and old cutoffs. He'd known she had a really good body, but he hadn't seen it so well delineated since the day he arrived. The effect on his groin threatened to embarrass him.

"Mama's gooder than anybody," Ben said.

Liz hoisted Ben off the ground for a quick kiss. "It'll be you and me against Matt and Rebecca. Do you think we can take 'em?"

"Yeah," Ben said with a wide grin. "Matt gotta play on Mama's team, too."

Rebecca took hold of Liz's and Matt's hands. "We can all play on the same team," she amended. "Then nobody can beat us."

All of a sudden, Matt could almost see himself walking down the middle of the road, holding hands with two kids, laughing and joking like he was married to Liz. Like they were family.

It gave him the chills. He couldn't believe he was acting this way. He never had before. As long as he could remember, he'd told himself he didn't need to belong, that he didn't want to be part of a family like this. It had taken years for him to admit he'd done that because he was afraid it couldn't happen, that he'd be rejected again if he tried. He knew relationships like this didn't work. They hadn't for him. They hadn't for Liz. He didn't belong in a place like this. But having come, he should have had enough sense to keep his distance. He had to leave. They had to stay.

But he couldn't draw back. It felt too good. Besides, it

would soon end. Why not let go just this once? What harm could it do?

Liz patted both children on their bottoms when they reached the steps of the house. "Rebecca, I want you in my bathtub in two minutes. Ben, you be ready the minute Rebecca gets out."

"I want Matt," Ben said.

"He's got work to do. Besides, you've worn him out already."

"I want Matt," Ben insisted.

"I've told you it's rude to—"

"You still have to clean up because I was late," Matt said. "Consider my helping Ben with his bath my apology."

"You don't have to. You've probably never bathed a child in your life."

"Ben's a big boy. He doesn't need my help. I'll just watch."

"If you don't, the only soap that'll get on him will get there by accident."

"I'll see what I can do. How about it, sport? You ready for water polo?"

"Matthew Dennis, if you dare teach him to play games in the bathtub, I'll...I don't know what I'll do, but I'll think of something terrible."

Nobody called him Matthew. It wasn't his name, but he liked it. He was afraid to like it too much because he might start to need it. This whole area—the town, the people, the mountain—was a magical place where the unexpected could happen. It was like an Eden, small and green and friendly.

But no one was allowed to stay in Eden forever. Especially not Matt Dennis.

Several hours later, Matt tossed aside his book, turned out the light and lay down in his bed. He fluffed the pillow, then turned on his side. Moments later he flipped back again. He was warm, so he threw the covers aside. But the pillow or covers weren't keeping him awake. He couldn't sleep because he couldn't stop thinking about the feeling of belonging he had experienced today with Liz and her children. The intensity of his need had taken him by surprise. Despite his attempts to distract himself, that longing had lingered all through the evening. Even now, unwelcome images continued to float through his mind.

Marshaling all his willpower, Matt made up his mind not to think about it. He'd been through this before. There was no need to go through it again. Nothing like this could ever happen to him. He ought to get to sleep. And if he insisted upon lying awake, he could put his mind to work figuring out how he was going to make up for a year lost in the wilderness.

Matt knew something was wrong. His foster parents were often solemn and frowning. He wasn't the little boy they wanted. They had told him so many times. But there was something different about today. His father had come home from work early. He never did that. They were going for a ride in the car in the afternoon. They never did that, either. But what confused him most was that his mother had packed his suitcase, put his toys in grocery bags, his books in a cardboard box and piled them all in the trunk of the car.

He hoped they were going on a trip across the water so he could play on the rides at the beach, but they'd never taken his clothes before. Besides, his mother hadn't packed anything for her and his father.

"Where are we going?" he asked.

"You'll see in a minute," his father replied.

They weren't going to the school. Matt breathed a sigh of relief. He hadn't been in as much trouble this year as last. He had grown bigger than most of the kids who used to pick on him, but his parents had been called to the school twice in the past week. His principal said they'd never had a third-grader give them so much trouble. Matt had given up trying to tell them he wouldn't cause trouble if the other kids would leave him alone. No one listened to him.

His father pulled to a stop in front of a small cinder-block building. Matt didn't remember having come here before, but he had a really bad feeling when his father took the suitcase out of the trunk. This had happened the times he moved from one foster home to another.

But it was supposed to be different this time. Mr. and Mrs. Cooper had adopted him. They said they were his father and mother. They'd insisted he call them Mama and Daddy. They had said they loved him and hoped he would soon learn to love them. All summer long, his mother had kissed him at night and told him she loved him, bought him the books he so loved to read. His father had taken him to the beach, played ball with him, taken him fishing in the creek. After a wonderful summer, Matt had started to believe somebody could love him.

Then school started, and everything changed. Each time he got in trouble—and he got in trouble a lot—their frowns grew deeper, stayed longer. Assurances of their love grew scarcer, then stopped altogether. Then they stopped talking to him. He knew then he wasn't going to find love this time, either.

"Am I going to stay here?" he asked as they entered the building and walked directly into a waiting area. His father put a hand on his back and pushed him toward a vinyl-covered couch. They sat down on either side of him, stiffly erect, the suitcase at his father's side. They didn't have to wait long before a door opened.

"Mr. and Mrs. Cooper, you can come in. Mrs. Osgood will see you now."

Matt recognized Mrs. Osgood. She was the lady who helped him get adopted. She looked as stiff and formal as his parents. They all sat down. Matt got a seat to himself this time.

"You haven't changed your minds?" she asked.

"No."

"You realize adoption is a legal contract. Canceling it won't be easy."

A paralyzing fear gripped Matt. "You can't give me back!" he exclaimed, turning first to his mother, then to his father. "You said you loved me. You said they'd never be able to take me away again."

His parents stared straight ahead at Mrs. Osgood.

"Your parents say you're too much trouble," Mrs. Osgood said. Only her face showed sympathy. "They say you've destroyed the peace in their lives with your fights and constantly being in trouble at school."

"It's not my fault," Matt said, turning to his mother. "Nobody likes me."

"Why should they?" his mother demanded, her icy silence gone. "There's not a parent in Gull's Landing who will let their children play with you. You're a bad little boy. You steal, you—"

"I don't take their things unless they take mine first," Matt argued, but they wouldn't listen to him. They never did.

"You sass your teachers, won't do your work. You're sullen or downright rude when called on to perform in class."

Schoolwork was easy for Matt, but his classmates resented it when he did well. One teacher even accused him of cheating. He found it easier to pretend to be average.

"We're a quiet couple," his mother said to Mrs. Osgood. "We always wanted children but couldn't have any. Matt was such a beautiful little boy. Everybody said he was bright, that all he needed was a good home. We thought he'd be perfect for us."

"He's ungrateful, uncooperative and determined to blame all his trouble on somebody else," his father said. "He's turned our home into a battleground. Margaret and I can't stand it anymore. We don't want him. Take him back! Take him back! Take him—"

Matt awoke, sat up in the bed and massaged his temples to release some of the tension. It had been a long time since he'd had that dream or even thought of the Coopers.

Could it be because he'd been thinking about Liz's family and how much he enjoyed being a part of it? Could this be his subconscious warning him not to let himself hope for something that could never be?

He didn't need the warning. He had grown into a man whose goals precluded a wife and family, especially in such an out-of-the-way place as Iron Springs. One day he intended to work in one of the great hospitals of New York, Houston or Los Angeles.

He couldn't afford the distractions of home and family, the time they consumed or the expenditure of emotional energy. He needed to concentrate on his career. He intended to prove to every man, woman and child in Gull's Landing that, despite their predictions, he'd made something out of himself. He intended for that something to be damned good.

Chapter Eight

Liz couldn't help but smile as she glanced in Matt's direction. She had to give him credit; he was singing the last hymn as manfully as he'd attempted to sing all the others. As far as she could tell from the low rumble that issued from his throat, he was missing most of the notes. Apparently being a brilliant doctor didn't guarantee you could carry a tune.

She couldn't help him. She'd have had to screech to reach the highest notes. She continued to sing the alto part, even though the unfamiliar notes caused him to cast puzzled glances in her direction.

The hymn came to an end. Hymnbooks clunked into the hymnal racks, and the members of the congregation bowed their heads for the final prayer.

Matt had startled Liz when he came downstairs earlier that morning, just as she and the children were about to leave for church, and announced he intended to go to church with them. He was dressed in a navy pin-striped suit, and she'd been almost as strongly affected by his handsomeness as by surprise. All during the service, she'd been aware of heads turning in their direction. There'd be a lot of curiosity that needed satisfying before this day was out.

The preacher said the final amen from the back of the church, and the organ burst forth into the postlude. The congregation burst forth into even louder conversation. Matt hadn't taken a single step toward exiting the pew before a woman in front of him turned and spoke.

"Welcome to our little church, Dr. Dennis," she said. "I'm so glad you could join us."

"Good morning, Mrs. Briggs. It's good to see you, too."

"The Lord have mercy on us!" Mrs. Briggs exclaimed, obviously surprised and very pleased. "How did you remember my name?"

"You brought your daughter, Wynona, in to see me," Matt said.

"That's right. Fancy you remembering."

"How is Wynona?" Liz asked. Matt might remember his patients' names, but Liz could see he wasn't comfortable dealing with them outside the office. "Do you think she'll make cheerleader this year?"

"I hope so. We're sending her to cheerleading camp."

Liz moved as they talked, forcing Mrs. Briggs to move, as well. She stopped in the aisle to let Matt pass in front of her. But all her strategies didn't keep other women from crowding around him. By the time they reached the porch of the church, he looked ready to bolt. When she saw the minister coming his way, she knew she had to do something. The Reverend Pike was a wonderful minister, but he looked upon all outsiders as lost souls.

"Good morning, Mr. Pike," Liz said. "I enjoyed your sermon as always."

"Good to see you in church, Liz. Where are your delightful children?"

"With my cousin. This was her day to keep the nursery. I want you to meet Dr. Matt Dennis. He's the new doctor at the clinic."

"I've been wanting to meet you," Mr. Pike said, "but I've been too healthy."

"That hasn't stopped anyone else," Matt said.

Liz nearly choked. "Everybody's been coming in for all the things they were too busy to do during the school year."

Liz pulled on Matt's sleeve, and they moved on. But getting past Mr. Pike was far from her most difficult task. It seemed nearly every woman in the church was determined to speak to Matt, introduce her entire family and carry on an exhaustive investigation of his dinner plans for the next month. Before ten minutes had elapsed, Matt had been invited to eat enough fried chicken, country ham, hot biscuits and homemade ice cream to keep him fed through the rest of the summer.

"I use my evenings to study and my weekends to relax out of town."

If Liz heard Matt say that once, he said it two dozen times. He was obviously used to people taking no for an answer. He didn't know what to do when nearly every person said, "You can come over to my house. I won't tell anybody." These would-be hostesses didn't seem to realize that by adding the line, "I'll even invite some nice young ladies so you'll have somebody besides us old people to talk to," they ensured the failure of their plans. There was jackrabbit in Matt Dennis's veins, and Liz could see he was ready to use it to remain well out of the clutches of these "nice young ladies."

Liz actually felt a little sorry for him. Despite his size, looks and abilities, the great and wonderful Dr. Matt Dennis was scared to death of all these little country ladies. Just as surprising, Liz found herself feeling protective of him.

She knew the people of Iron Springs had hearts of gold. Their straightforward, frank, open approach augured a real caring about people. Their curiosity about personal and family details was merely an extension of that. Knowing everything about a person allowed them to share that person's life, to make them a part of the community, to feel like they belonged to the extended family. Still Liz could see how, to a man used to the impersonal atmosphere of a big city, it might seem like nosy, even rude, curiosity.

Since no one seemed willing to take Matt's refusal as anything but bashful reluctance, it devolved on Liz to turn down these unwelcome invitations. It taxed her ingenuity to do it without offending anyone.

"They're only trying to be friendly," Liz said when she'd extricated Matt from an invitation to a family reunion.

"I should never have let you talk me into staying here," Matt said. "I should have gone to Charlottesville. Richmond, if I had to."

"You don't have to run from us. Nobody's going to eat you."

Matt gave her a skeptical look.

"They're just interested in you."

"I'm their doctor, not their friend and buddy. I don't think it's a good idea to—"

"You told me. Doctors should keep their distance from their patients. I don't agree with you, but after today, I can see why you feel the way you do. Oh, good Lord! Here come the children with Ethan and Josie trailing behind."

Liz had an understanding with Ethan about his mother. When the three of them were in the same place, he was to stay with his mother and keep his distance. Josie was certain that when Liz tricked her son into marrying her, she wouldn't want any more children and Josie would be denied her own grandchildren. She had announced several times she couldn't possibly accept a Yankee's children.

Liz had tried to point out that being from Baltimore, Maryland, didn't make David a Yankee, but Josie didn't want to hear that.

Liz couldn't decide whom her children were happier to see, her or Matt. Ben wanted Matt to pick him up. Rebecca positioned herself between Liz and Matt. That left Ethan to walk on Liz's other side and Josie to walk next to Matt. Neither was happy.

"Ben and Rebecca seem to like you a lot," Ethan said to Matt. "They don't usually take to strangers so quickly."

Liz guessed Ethan felt nettled. It had taken the children

nearly a year to accept him. Ben still wouldn't climb up in his arms the way he did Matt's.

"It's hardly surprising," Josie Woodhouse said. "With him living in the same house, they must think he's their father."

"My daddy lives in New York," Rebecca announced. "He and Mama are mad at each other."

"Are you going to see your father this summer?" Josie asked Rebecca.

"Mama says Daddy neglected us. She says she can't trust us alone with him."

One of the hazards of trying to explain things to your children was that they were likely to repeat everything you said to the rest of the world, Liz recognized.

"I think they ought to see their father," Josie announced. "I deplore this modern penchant for divorce. I hope you're going to take your children for a long visit."

She meant she hoped Liz was going to get out of town and leave Ethan alone.

"I couldn't leave the clinic just now," Liz said. "We can barely keep our heads above water as it is."

"It won't matter if you're not there," Josie said. "You're not a nurse." She turned to Matt. "Don't you think it's important for children to spend as much time with their parents as possible?"

"Yes, I do," Matt replied, "but I can't spare Liz just now. We'd probably have to close the clinic."

"There, Mother," Ethan said, smiling proudly at Liz, "I told you they couldn't get along without her. Stop trying to chase her out of town. If she stayed gone very long, I'd have to go after her."

"Ethan, you promised me you wouldn't leave Iron Springs," Josie wailed. "This is your home. You can't—"

"This is where we have to leave you," Liz said, thankful Josie lived seven houses away. Matt and the kids turned down the sidewalk.

Ethan put his hand on Liz's arm to detain her. "I came to ask you to have lunch with us."

"Thank you, but I can't leave Matt by himself."

"He's a grown man. I'm sure he's used to being by himself." He sounded irritated.

"This is his first Sunday in Iron Springs. He stayed because I told him he ought to go to church and get to know people. I can't just walk out on him."

"I don't see why not." Now he sounded possessive *and* irritated.

"Don't plague her, Ethan. If she doesn't want to have lunch with you, leave her alone."

"It isn't that," Liz said to Josie, exasperated. "It's just that I don't feel right leaving Matt."

"You seem to be awfully interested in him all of a sudden," Ethan said.

"How could I not be? I work for him. He stays in my house."

"I never did like that," Ethan said. "I don't think it's proper."

"I wouldn't have offered the house if I hadn't thought it was going to be a female doctor, but I can't ask him to leave now."

He reached out and took hold of her arm. "You can if you stop stalling and marry me," Ethan said.

"This isn't the time to discuss it. I've got to go." Liz tried to break his hold.

"Let her go, Ethan. If she doesn't want to marry you, she's a fool. I keep telling you she's not good enough for you. Besides, she's already been thrown out by one man. You can't want another man's leavings."

Ethan released her. Liz turned and walked toward the house. She'd almost become hardened to Josie's insults, but that didn't mean she wanted to stand around and listen to more of them.

"Are we going to visit Daddy this summer?" Rebecca asked the minute Liz walked into the house.

That was another reason for being angry at Josie. She'd upset her children.

"I don't know. We'll decide later. Now go change your clothes while I fix your lunch."

"Matt says he's not going to eat with us. He says you're not supposed to fix his lunch on Sunday."

"Nonsense. Tell him if he's not at the table in ten minutes, I'll turn both of you loose on him."

Rebecca pounded up the stairs, anxious to deliver Liz's message. Liz went to her room to change her clothes and mull over all the ways she might torture Josie Woodhouse.

"I hope you didn't let everybody's determination to get you over to their house scare you out of going to church again," Liz said after the kids had finished their lunch and gone out to play. Matt had remained at the table to finish his iced tea.

"I'm not much on parties and visiting people," Matt said.

"I know. A doctor shouldn't get to know his patients. He should—"

"It's not just that," Matt explained.

He looked up from his tea, his face a mask of irritation. Yet Liz saw something else. He had withdrawn into a shell. This one looked impenetrable.

"You don't have to tell me anything," Liz said, remembering his reaction that first day to her question about his family. "It's none of my business."

"It's probably in that damned computer somewhere."

"There's nothing there except your degrees, honors, scholarships, doctors you've worked with, stuff like that."

"Well you might as well know. I don't have any family. I was a foster child."

"There's nothing wrong with that. Several people in Iron Springs are—"

"My mother arrived in Gull's Landing on a bus. No one knows where she came from or where she was going. She had me an hour later, gave me my name, then died. She wasn't wearing a wedding ring, and she didn't tell anyone my father's name. I'm a bastard."

Liz didn't know what to say. Nothing like this had ever

occurred to her. She'd just thought he was a very private person who felt uncomfortable with strangers asking him personal questions.

"That's not your fault." It was a lame response. People got damned all the time for things that weren't their fault. "There's no reason anybody has to know, but they wouldn't hold it against you."

"Do you have any illegitimate kids in Iron Springs?"

"Well, no."

"Any women who had children out of wedlock?"

"No."

"People who follow the rules don't like those who don't. I know. I was passed from home to home because nobody wanted me. Even my adoptive parents gave me back. Everybody in Gull's Landing was delighted when I got a scholarship and left."

"Okay, so they were narrow-minded and stupid," Liz said. "People in Iron Springs aren't like that."

"What makes you think they're different from everybody else?"

"Because I don't think many people are like the people in Gull's Landing. You may not know your father's name, but you've made something of yourself. You're a doctor with a brilliant career ahead of you. People respect that."

"I don't think so."

"Of course they do. They like you."

"Why should they?"

"I don't know. Why do you like Rebecca and Ben or Salome?"

"I don't like Salome. She—"

"Of course you do. You wouldn't let her call you Beefcake if you didn't."

"Could I stop her?"

"Of course."

"How?"

"Speak to her the way you spoke to me that first day."

He looked startled.

"Salome might wear lipstick bright enough to blind you,

but she likes you. To paraphrase one of her remarks into repeatable form, you're sexy as hell with a body to die for.''

Liz couldn't believe her eyes. Unless she was badly mistaken, Matt Dennis actually blushed. How could a man who looked good enough to give Don Juan a race for his money appear embarrassed at being called sexy? Now, that was truly intriguing.

''A man likes to be wanted for more than his body.''

Liz would apologize for laughing when she had time to catch her breath, but she'd never thought to hear that complaint come out of a man's mouth.

''You find that funny?'' Matt asked.

''I find it nearly hysterical. Do you know how many times—?''

''Millions.''

''A conservative estimate.''

''Okay, a billion.''

''Closer.''

''Okay, men are pigs. We're the enemy.''

''Yes, but such charming pigs, such a lovable enemy.''

''Are you ever serious?''

''Yes, and never more than right now. David was charming and lovable, but he is a prizewinning pig.''

''David?''

''My ex-husband, but I didn't mean to talk about him. We're talking about you and the fact people in Iron Springs will continue to like and respect you, regardless of your origins. I tell you what, why don't you come to the firemen's picnic?''

''Why, so you can introduce me as the local bastard?''

''Don't be stupid. Or self-pitying.''

Now she had really made him mad.

''I didn't mean that the way it sounded, but that's how you sound. 'Poor me, the orphan boy. Nobody likes me.' I know things must have been terrible to have made you so bitter, but that's just the breaks. You've got to get over it.''

''I am over it. I just don't intend to put my head on the chopping block again.''

"So you're going to hide behind your degrees and your professional relationships."

"I'm not hiding."

"Of course you are. I bet you don't even want a wife and family. And if you do break down and bless some woman by letting her marry you, she'll have to be a professional who's just as cold and detached as you want to be. You'll both hide in your plush offices behind your big desks and your very efficient secretaries and never take a human breath in your life."

"Where do you get off telling me what I'll do?"

"I'm one of those nosy old biddies who inhabits tiny mountain villages, pries out every bit of gossip I can sniff out and turns up my nose at people whose birth isn't as good as mine. We specialize at ferreting out and holding up to public ridicule any child whose parents didn't have the foresight to get married before his conception. No, birth. We do have a few who weren't too careful about the conception date."

"Okay, so I may have been too severe."

"My, aren't you magnanimous."

"What do you want, blood?"

"No. I want an apology."

"Okay, I apologize."

"Not in words. I want you to go to the picnic. Ethan is taking me and the children. I can introduce you to everybody."

"No."

"Coward. Everybody will be there. You can announce your terrible secret and let everybody revile you. It ought to make for a fun afternoon. Come to think of it, it's quite selfish of you to refuse. We haven't had a good public reviling in a long time."

"Okay, dammit, I'll go."

"Good, but now that I think about it, I think you'd better not announce your guilty secret just yet. This is the fire department's big day. I don't think they'd appreciate being upstaged."

* * *

Matt stalked back and forth in his room, too agitated to concentrate on his work. He was going to strangle Liz and leave her body in the street as a warning. He didn't want to go socializing with every female who asked. He still thought it was best for a doctor to keep his distance from his or her patients. It made things rather lonely sometimes, but fortunately he was a person who didn't need other people.

He particularly didn't need people poking and probing into his background, his innermost thoughts, his love life—which happened to be nonexistent at the moment. Everybody in Iron Springs could tell every secret they knew, chew over every scandal until it was threadbare, whisper over back fences until their dinners burned to crisps, but they wouldn't be talking about him.

He had a right to privacy. His life was his own, and he didn't intend to hand it over to every Joan and Jennifer to gossip about. More likely, every Beulah Mae and Anna Belle. Or Prudence and Charity. They did give women the damnedest names in this place.

But it was Liz he was angriest at. She was the one who'd taunted and baited him until he agreed to go to that damned picnic. She was the one he was fool enough to trust with his secret, who accused him of indulging in self-pity.

She ought to have tried growing up in Gull's Landing. She ought to have heard all the taunts when no adult was around, seen the looks when they were. Even the kind ones couldn't forget he was illegitimate. He wasn't indulging in self-pity. He knew how people reacted.

He had no intention of putting himself through that again.

But he'd agreed to go to that picnic. He could back out, but Liz would call him a coward again. And he would be. He might not like to have to fend off curiosity seekers, but he could do it. And he would.

But he would get even with Liz. He didn't know how just yet, but it was beginning to look like he would have a full year. That would give him plenty of time to think of something truly diabolical.

Chapter Nine

‘‘David, why are you doing this to me? You never cared about the children before.’’

Her ex-husband had called for the second time in two weeks to insist that she send the children up to New York. This time he’d called Liz at the office, upsetting her routine and the composure she needed to handle her job properly.

‘‘I always did, but I never had the time until now.’’

‘‘I can’t let you work your way back into the children’s lives, let them start to depend on you, then have you forget them when things get a little rough.’’

‘‘I’ll never be late with the check again.’’

‘‘It’s not about money, David. I can support them.’’

‘‘How, with your little job in the clinic?’’

David always belittled anyone who didn’t aim for the top.

‘‘I’m talking about your children learning to love you, David. They may be only three and four, but they have feelings. They can be hurt.’’

‘‘I told you. I’ve changed.’’

"So you've said. But let a crisis rear its ugly head, and you'll forget all about them."

"No, I won't. And if I did, my wife would look after them."

Liz didn't know why that should shock her so much. She had expected David to remarry. He'd played around with enough women to have a wide choice.

"You didn't tell me."

"I didn't figure you wanted to be invited to the wedding."

"No, but I would like to have known."

"Well, now you do."

That was David. Sensitive to the core.

"Who did you marry?"

"You don't know her. I met her on a business trip about a year ago. We got married two months ago."

"You can't expect me to turn my children over to a woman I've never met."

"Look, Liz, I mean to see my kids. Next time I call, I want to know when they can come up so I can send plane tickets."

"David, you can't—"

He hung up on her, didn't even say goodbye. It made her so angry she wanted to slam the phone down. But that would only break the phone, and she'd have to pay for it. She thought of the check David had sent. She could buy a lot of phones with that. She could buy a new car, replace the furnace, recarpet the downstairs and a few other things. It would serve him right if she spent it all on clothes for herself.

But she'd put it in the children's college fund. She didn't know how long David's benevolent mood would last, and college for the children was one of her biggest worries.

She walked to the front screen door and looked out. She had to think of something. She couldn't just turn Ben and Rebecca over to a strange woman for two weeks.

"I won't do it," she said aloud as she stepped out onto the porch. "David can scream all he wants, but I won't do it."

"I don't know what you won't do, but if David screams even once in this town, it'll set everybody on their ears."

Liz's heart jumped into her throat. She turned to find Matt dozing in the porch swing. She hadn't known he was there.

"Sorry, I was thinking out loud."

"The bright pink of your ears tells me those thoughts weren't for my ears. If I remember correctly, David is your ex-husband."

"Yes."

"Is he still in New York?"

"Yes."

"Then don't do it. He can scream all he wants, and nobody down here will hear him."

Liz smiled in spite of herself. "It's not that simple."

"It never is."

The invitation to tell him was there. He wasn't going to say anything. He wasn't that kind of man, but he would listen, and she needed to tell someone. She'd thought first of Aunt Marian, but Matt might be better. He'd never met David, and he didn't know much about her. He was more impartial.

"You don't want to hear my sad tale," Liz said. "You like to keep your distance, remember?"

"That's from patients."

She hesitated a moment, then settled into a rocking chair next to the swing. "David wants me to send the children for a visit. He's remarried, so he's got somebody to take care of them if he gets tied up in the office and forgets about them."

"Anything else in his favor?"

"He sent their child support."

"A big plus."

"This is the first time ever."

"A big minus. Any more?"

"Yes. David's whole life is tied up in his business. For years he never had time for any of us. If he gets tied up again, he'll forget all about them again. I don't want them to get hurt."

"How attached can they get in two weeks a couple of times a year? If his wife takes them to the movies, restaurants and a theme park, they won't even know he's not there."

"There's no point in sending them to New York to spend their time with a baby-sitter."

"Agreed. But if he has visitation privileges, you don't have much choice."

"He hasn't wanted to see them in three years. Why should he want to see them now?"

"What did he say?"

"He said he'd changed."

"Do you believe him?"

"I don't know."

"There's one way to find out."

"How's that?"

"Go up with the children. Rent a motel room for two whole weeks if necessary."

"I'd end up seeing more of his wife than I would of him." He didn't say anything, but she knew he had something to say. "Out with it."

"You don't like his wife?"

"I've never met her."

"But you don't like her."

"No."

"Why?"

"Because he rejected me for her. He told me he didn't meet her until after I'd left him, but it doesn't make any difference. He threw me out because I wasn't any good. He married her because she was."

"But you divorced him."

"I know."

"So you rejected him."

"I swallowed my pride to stay with him and try to make our marriage work. I didn't leave until it became painfully clear none of us meant anything to him."

"So you're still angry at him."

"Yes." She hadn't admitted that before, probably wouldn't have if David hadn't remarried without telling her.

"That won't do you any good in dealing with David."

"I know, but I can't help it."

They rocked in silence for a moment.

"Okay," she said when she couldn't wait any longer, "what do you think I ought to do? I can see you've got an idea."

"I shouldn't be giving advice."

"Why not? Everyone else will."

"You won't like what I have to say."

"Neither of us ever likes what the other has to say. Go ahead."

"I think you ought to let the children see their father," Matt said. "Hear me out before you cut my throat."

She didn't have anything that severe in mind, but she was considering dumping him out of the swing. She hadn't expected him to be her ally, but she hadn't expected him to stab her in the back.

"Unless David is mean and abusive, I think it's crucial for your children to know their father. I didn't have one, and I know what it did to me."

"I don't think he really wants them. I think it's just for his wife."

"I wasn't thinking of David or his wife. I was thinking of Ben and Rebecca. I can't tell you how tough it is for a kid without a father. It's like you don't belong, you don't have a membership card."

"They've got one. He's just a lousy father."

"They'll realize that with time, but it's important for them to know he wants them. There's nothing quite so horrible as knowing you're not wanted."

Liz was caught between sympathy for what Matt must have suffered and irritation at him for recommending she do exactly what she didn't want to do.

"I don't want them to have anything to do with David."

"Then you shouldn't have gotten married and had children."

"I wasn't expecting my marriage to end in divorce."

"Nobody ever does. Relationships are like that. The more people you have in your life, the less control you have over it."

"So you decided to sit out the game."

"You could look at it that way."

"What other way can I look at it? You're not married, not dating, not even interested as far as I can see. You even avoid social contact. That might make you a good doctor, but as a person you're dead."

"Do you always act this way when people give you advice you don't like?"

"No. Sometimes I lose my temper."

His smile was sudden and spontaneous. "Remind me to get out of the way when you do."

"I don't know what happened to you growing up in that town, Matthew Dennis, but it's nearly killed the man inside that doctor's coat. I say *nearly*. You've tried to stamp it out, but little bits and pieces have survived. Enough for just about everybody in this town to like you. Enough for Ben and Rebecca to think you're the best thing that's happened to them.

"If you keep trying, you'll probably trample all the little bits that are left. It'll be a shame because I think you had the makings of a rather magnificent person inside you at one time. You told me you wanted to be wanted for more than your body. Well, you're too late. Your body's about all you've got left."

Liz turned and hurried inside. She knew she shouldn't have said so much, shouldn't have gotten so personal. But it irked her that he could sit there, intentionally cutting himself off from every human emotion, and pass out judgments. He had no idea what it meant to have children, to be worried about what their father might say or do to them, to be scared to death about their future.

But that wasn't the only reason she was angry. She did think he could have been a rather magnificent human being. Everybody liked him, and he hadn't done anything to endear himself to anyone except Ben and Rebecca. He played games with them, told them outrageous stories, helped them get dressed, made them laugh. Most important, he treated them like real people, not just shadowy imitations. Some people just had that knack. It was a shame to waste it.

Besides, he did care. It showed in the way he remembered

obscure bits about his patients' lives, the way he insisted that everything be done thoroughly and systematically. He might call it professionalism or good medicine. She called it caring.

And much to her dismay, she'd started to care about him. She was too disgusted to ask herself how and why. Here she was with Ethan wanting to marry her. First she'd turned him down to marry David. Now she was finding that where Ethan left her cold, Matt warmed her in more ways than she wanted to explore.

Maybe it was just lust. Everybody knew he was too handsome to ignore. She doubted she was the only woman to dream about him. But anything else was insanity. She had to nip this foolishness in the bud before it got out of hand. The last thing in the world Dr. Matt Dennis would do would be to marry somebody like her and spend the rest of his life in a town like Iron Springs.

That's exactly what Liz wanted to happen, exactly the truth she had not wanted to admit, even to herself. She hardly knew the man, yet somehow she knew he was most like his real self when he was with her kids. And that Matt had enough heart and soul for any woman.

It couldn't have been a more perfect morning. Bright sunshine, dry air and cool breezes had turned Iron Springs into a mountain paradise. It would have been a sin to stay inside on such a perfect day. Matt decided it was time to stop fooling himself. He was going to the firemen's picnic because he had let Liz get under his skin, not because of the weather. It was foolish to let her goad him into doing something he didn't want to do because he didn't want to appear small in her eyes. He shouldn't care how he appeared in her eyes, no matter how blue they were.

And that was something else. It was impossible not to be aware of how well she fitted into a pair of white shorts. She was walking just ahead of him. He'd have to be blind not to notice. It was okay to remember the color of her hair—it was such a shimmering blond he couldn't forget—but he shouldn't know the color of her eyes. You had to be paying attention to notice eyes.

He ought to call his longtime friend Georgia Allen and head straight for Charlottesville. She'd called to say she was in town and had the weekend free. He could have told Liz he had business in Charlottesville and couldn't go to the picnic after all. Instead, he'd told Georgia he was busy and he'd try to catch her next time she took a vacation from her high-powered, all-consuming job.

So here he was—Ben on one side holding his hand, Rebecca on the other—on his way to a picnic infested with strangers. He must be crazy. A month ago, just the thought of doing something like this would have caused him to experience shortness of breath. Now he was actually looking forward to it. He didn't understand it, but there was no other reason for the spring in his step or the cheerfulness in his voice.

The only other possible explanation had to be that his body had been taken over by an alien.

"Stick close to me, and I'll introduce you to everybody," Liz was saying.

"He's a grown man, Liz honey. He can take care of himself," Ethan said.

"Not in Iron Springs. You know people here eat strangers alive."

"He's not a stranger," Rebecca said. "We know him."

"Then you can introduce him around," Ethan said. He put his arm around Liz's waist. "I didn't invite you to have you spend the whole day paying attention to another man."

Matt didn't know whether it was wishful thinking, but he got the distinct impression Liz stiffened when Ethan put his arms around her. He wasn't under any misapprehension as to his own reaction. Something coiled tightly in his gut. It was all he could do to keep from telling Ethan to keep his hands to himself.

He was relieved when Ben said, "There's Aunt Marian."

Both children started pulling him toward where she was standing under one of the magnificent oaks that had managed to avoid lightning strikes and cankerworms for more than two hundred years.

"I see Liz was able to get you to come after all," Marian said. "She didn't think you would."

"We brought him," Rebecca announced. "He promised to take us on all the rides."

"Me, too," Ben added.

"You sure you're up to all that?" Marian asked.

"I'm committed," Matt said.

"Then don't eat too many hot dogs or too much cotton candy. It would be a shame to be sick all over yourself."

Since the most exciting ride to make it over the mountain was a small Ferris wheel, Matt felt sure his lunch would be safe.

"I want cotton candy," Ben said.

Matt lifted Ben up and settled him on his shoulder. "And you shall have it. Lead the way," he said to Rebecca.

"I want to ride on your shoulder," Rebecca declared.

"You get to ride next," Matt said, wondering why he suddenly had a small boy shrieking with laughter sitting on his shoulder. He'd never had one up there before. He must have been invaded by a really odd alien.

"Don't let them wear you out," Liz said.

"He's a grown man," Ethan protested. "How can two kids wear him out?"

"It's obvious you've never had children," Marian said. "One can do it. Against two, it's hopeless."

"I've been tying to talk Liz into letting me try, but I can't get her to say the right words," Ethan said.

Matt wanted to tell the guy not to be such a dolt. If he wanted Liz, he wouldn't be dancing around saying please and begging for kisses. He ought to spirit her off to a secluded spot and show her he couldn't do without her. Any idiot could spout a mouthful of pretty words.

"You're not moving," Rebecca complained.

"What?" Matt said, suddenly aware of a little girl at his feet looking up at him impatiently.

"You said we were going to get cotton candy, but you're just standing there."

"So I did," Matt said, coming to his senses, "but I don't know where they've hidden the cotton-candy machine."

"Over there." Ben pointed to where a line of children was already forming in front of a small booth.

"Lead the way, Miss Rebecca, and I'll get you a big batch of the pink stuff."

"I want blue," Rebecca said with a giggle. "It turns my tongue all terrible."

"I want terrible tongue, too," Ben echoed.

"Two terrible tongues coming up," Matt said. "Anyone else?" He looked straight at Liz, but Ethan had his arm securely around her.

"Yell if you need help," Marian said. "Somebody will rescue you."

"Without delay, I hope. I have a feeling I won't last long in hand-to-hand combat."

"What's hand-to-hand combat?" Ben asked.

"Wrestling," his sister told him.

"I like wrestling," Ben said.

"I was afraid you would," Matt said. "Let's get the candy. We'll have to negotiate about the wrestling."

"What's *'gotiate?*" Ben asked.

"Does he ever stop asking questions?" Matt asked Liz.

"Never. I can't wait until he can read."

Several hours later, Matt found Liz, minus children and jealous escort, relaxing in a lawn chair next to the band shell. He'd been down by the lake, recovering from his time with Liz's two demons. The remnants of a hamburger with mustard and onions had been left for the birds, squirrels, ants and anything else that wanted it. "Where's Ethan?"

"He kept after me to let him take the kids to his house for their nap, so I let him." She laughed. "I shouldn't have, but Josie was plaguing me. I knew she wouldn't let the kids inside her front door without being there to protect all her precious antiques."

"Ethan lives with his mother?"

"If he tried to move out, Josie would wail loud enough to be heard across the mountain."

"What's going to happen when you marry him?"

Liz's smile disappeared. "Who says I'm going to marry him?" Her tone was sharp.

"I don't guess anybody has. I just assumed—"

"Then don't. I've told Ethan I'm not ready to consider marrying again."

"He looks plenty ready."

"I know."

"What are you going to do about it?"

"I'll think of something."

"The obvious thing is—"

"I know what the obvious thing to do is."

"Well…"

"Don't you have some cotton candy to eat, some brunette siren to seduce?"

"That was Salome's doing." Matt told Liz about how Salome had found him earlier in the day and loved to parade him around like a prize pig.

"Why?"

"Devilment."

"For a man who's scared to death of strangers, you sure have been playing pigeon among the cats."

"It's safer than the tightrope you're walking."

"I'll make sure I don't fall."

"And I'll make sure the cats don't get more than feathers."

Josie had buttonholed him in the hotel lobby where he'd gone to escape the afternoon sun. She claimed she wanted to talk about her indigestion, but Matt soon learned the only thing upsetting her digestion was her son's determination to marry Liz. It hadn't taken Josie long to get around to her real purpose.

"It's a shame Liz has to remain in such an out-of-the-way place as Iron Springs," Josie Woodhouse lamented. "After living in New York, she's bound to be bored to death here."

"She doesn't seem bored to me."

"She needs a job in some place like Charlottesville. You must know lots of people there. You could put in a word for her."

"I never worked in personnel."

"But you're a doctor. Surely you can do something."

Matt couldn't help but laugh. "When you're first out of medical school, you're little more than an overeducated, underexperienced flunky. You get all the grunt work, the graveyard shifts and anything else they can shove off on you. You don't dare say anything about it or you'll be passed over as hard to get along with when the plum jobs finally come up."

Josie gave him a hard stare. "I've got to get that woman out of Iron Springs before she ruins my son's life. I know you could help me if you wanted to."

"Sorry. Even if I could help—and I promise I can't—I wouldn't get involved. Anything between Liz and Ethan is none of my business."

"Well, it's mine, and you're my doctor. You're bound by that oath you take to give me advice."

"Isaac Kennedy is your doctor. Ask him."

"Shiftless, good-for-nothing! He doesn't come in off the golf course long enough to think of anyone but himself."

"I've got to go. I promised Ben and Rebecca one last ride on the Ferris wheel."

"If you like her children so much, why don't you marry her?"

The question startled Matt so much he couldn't answer immediately. He'd never even thought of Liz in that way. Nor the children, for that matter. But that wasn't the part that rendered him speechless. He could easily see himself as part of Liz's family, and that scared him senseless.

"I'm not in love with her."

Maybe not, but his feelings were very far from the cold, professional attitude he'd intended to maintain.

Chapter Ten

"Another picnic so soon?" Liz was saying to Ethan.

"It's summer. You have nothing to do on the weekend."

Matt didn't enjoy having to listen to this conversation. They were walking home from the firemen's picnic just as they had walked to it—Liz and Ethan walked ahead, Ben and Rebecca holding Matt's hands. Ben tried to step on every crack. Rebecca tried to avoid them. Since the pavement was old and of poor quality, she jumped around like a puppet on a string.

"Nothing except rescue my garden from weeds and can and freeze as much as possible," Liz said.

"How about next Sunday? The devil will get you if you work on Sunday."

"How about it, kids? Do you want to go on a picnic with me and Ethan?"

"Yeah," Ben said, pulling so hard on Matt's arm he nearly pulled him off balance.

"Can we go to the lake?" Rebecca asked.

"Sure," Ethan said.

"Then I want to go."

The kids turned their attention back to the cracks in the sidewalk while Liz and Ethan discussed where to go and what to eat. Matt tried not to be jealous of Ethan's attention to Liz, tried not to think of the feelings she aroused in him. He wasn't successful on either score.

Matt had never been ruled by his physical passions. He liked women, and he'd never denied himself the pleasure of their companionship, but his energies had always been focused on his career. Everything else was secondary.

Maybe it was just the heat. Maybe it was all those hot dogs and cotton candy sloshing about in his stomach. Maybe it was the sight of Liz's long bare legs, tightly molded backside, tapered back and bare arms—all just a few feet ahead of him. He felt like the donkey and Liz the carrot. He followed because he couldn't do anything else.

He couldn't remember when he'd been so aware of a woman's body. Or his own. Her nearness seemed to turn the sensitivity of his nerve endings up tenfold. He could feel the slight friction created by his shirt as it moved against the hairs on his chest, his suddenly sensitive nipples. The breeze seemed to activate every hair on his legs and thighs, creating a network of sensation that didn't stop until it had worked its way up to his groin.

He stubbornly refused to let his mind go further. Since he had chosen to wear cutoffs today, his inflamed condition would be clearly visible. Given the frank nature of everyone in Iron Springs, he could expect to have at least half a dozen people demand to know what *and whom* he was thinking about. He'd lusted after women before, but nothing like this had ever happened.

But he had more to contend with on this sultry summer afternoon than lust.

He liked Liz, although he wasn't quite sure why. She didn't hesitate to disagree with him, attack his philosophies, bully him into doing something he hated. At the same time, she bent over backward to make sure the clinic ran smoothly, didn't complain too much when his constant lateness interrupted her schedule and seemed quite happy to let her children make a pet of him. She even cooked dishes he liked. For a man alone in a place he hated, that was very important.

He looked down at the two kids blissfully cavorting beside him, and he felt a great sense of loneliness sweep through him. He liked her kids. He even liked her aunt, and he liked being with them. Even being introduced to what seemed like hundreds of strangers hadn't been as bad as he'd anticipated. He was pleased he'd managed to handle Salome and Josie Woodhouse without making them furious with him.

Maybe the medical board had known what it was doing. Still, he warned himself not to expect too much, to steel himself from wanting Liz's family to like him too well. Even if he had any intention of staying around, which he didn't, small communities didn't accept outsiders.

"I want Matt to give me my bath," Ben announced when they turned into Liz's yard.

"You can't ask a stranger to give you a bath," Ethan said.

"Matt's not a stranger," Rebecca replied.

It was obvious Ethan didn't like the situation, Matt realized.

"What does he know about bathing little boys?"

"Not much," Matt said. "Mostly I keep him from splashing all the water out of the tub. The soap takes care of the rest."

"You've done this before?" Ethan asked.

"Lots," Ben chirped with an ingenuous smile.

"I hope you don't let him give Rebecca her bath."

"For goodness' sake, Ethan, Matt's a doctor."

"I don't see that makes any difference," Ethan argued.

"Mommy gives me my bath," Rebecca said. "She says there are some times when girls have to stick together."

"Boys stick 'gether, too," Ben added.

"Fine, just don't touch anything on your way inside," Liz said, "Or you'll stick to it and Matt will never get you loose."

Ben laughed when Matt grabbed him up and held him out

at arm's length. "Think we ought to put him under the hose first?"

"Yes!" Rebecca said.

"Noooooo!" Ben squealed.

They headed toward the house, each child trying to convince Matt to use the hose on the other.

"I don't think it's right for him to be so familiar with the children," Ethan said. "What will they do when he leaves?"

"I don't know, but it's the first chance they've had to have a man around, and they love it."

"I'm around," Ethan said.

Matt knew that wasn't the same as having their real father. He also knew Ethan didn't have the same feeling for Liz's children that he had for Liz. The man who married Liz had to want to be Ben and Rebecca's father just as much as he wanted to be Liz's husband. Matt knew what it was like to be unwanted. He didn't want that to happen to anyone if he could help it.

Liz locked the door to the clinic and headed home at a fast walk. She had to relieve the emergency baby-sitter. Her cousin had had a crisis that morning and couldn't keep Ben and Rebecca, so Liz had left them with a sleepy-eyed Matt. She hated to ruin his Saturday morning, but all he had to do was keep one eye open until the camper Aunt Marian was sending over arrived. After that he could go back to bed.

Things had been hectic at the clinic. It had taken all her people skills to convince patients to see the substitute doctor rather than cancel and make an appointment to see Matt the following week. She wondered if he had any idea how much faith people had in him.

No. He saw himself as delivering good medicine, but he was oblivious to the people. She thought she'd mistaken him, that he was a real softie after all. She'd been wrong. He wasn't the granite pillar he thought himself, but neither was he the marshmallow she wanted. He was good, he was concerned, he cared, but he wasn't getting involved. It was obvious that when the time came to leave, he wanted no ties with this town.

She worried about the effect his leaving would have on her children. She hadn't wanted them to become so attached to Matt, but it had happened before she realized it. One minute he was a stranger at her door; the next, her children couldn't eat a meal, get ready for bed or play a game without him. She admitted she'd been too happy for the kids to want to stop it. Now she wondered if she had made a big mistake.

Despite knowing Matt didn't mean to stay in Iron Springs a minute longer than he had to, Liz was finding it harder and harder to think of his leaving. She had gotten used to having him around. They didn't seem able to agree on much, but they liked each other anyway. It was an odd thing to say, but they were comfortable together. She wondered why.

She wasn't as comfortable with Ethan these days even though they had much the same interests, likes and dislikes. She was even less comfortable since he proposed to her after the firemen's picnic. It must have been the dozenth time. She hadn't kept count. He had poured out his heart to her, telling her all the reasons they ought to get married, what he wanted to do for her, what he wanted to do for her children. Much to her chagrin, she kept wondering what Matt and Ben were doing in the bathroom.

When Ethan had pressed her for an answer, she'd said she had to settle things with David before she could even think of getting married again. When he offered to handle David for her, she told him she wasn't helpless, that she could handle her own affairs.

But as Liz turned into her own yard, she realized there was something more here than not being ready to think about marriage. She had started comparing Ethan unfavorably with Matt. She'd better set herself down and figure out exactly what was happening before she did something stupid. She'd better make up her mind about Ethan. If things were going in the direction she feared they were, she would have to tell him right away. After all his kindness, it would be unthinkable to let the first hint come from someone else.

Liz expected to hear loud noises from the yard, to see toys scattered all over the house, to find a frazzled teenager struggling to keep up with her two little terrors. The yard was empty, and the living room and hall were clear of stray toys, clothes, and shoes.

Just as she decided Aunt Marian must have taken them up to the camp, she heard voices coming from the kitchen. She walked in to find Ben, Rebecca and Matt seated at the table having lunch.

"Hi, Mommy," Rebecca called with her mouth half-full. "We saved a place for you."

Four places had been set, complete with napkins. A sandwich and potato chips on one plate, apple slices on another and a glass of milk made up almost exactly the kind of lunch Liz would have fixed.

"I didn't want Aunt Marian to do this," she said as she went to the refrigerator to get herself a glass of water. "I told her I'd feed you when I got home."

"Matt fixed lunch," Rebecca said, "and I helped."

"Me, too," Ben said.

"You did not," Rebecca said. "You spilled your milk, and Matt had to clean it up."

"I helped," Ben insisted.

Liz couldn't help staring at Matt.

"How hard can sandwiches be?" he asked.

"Where's the camper Aunt Marian sent?"

"She never came," Rebecca said.

"Why not?" Liz asked Matt.

"I didn't see any point in it since I was going to be here already," Matt explained.

"Your eyes weren't open when I left."

"They were the minute the door closed behind you. Faced with being alone with the Terrible Tyke, it was pay attention or suffer the consequences."

"I'm the Fabulous Female," Rebecca announced. "That's a good name. Matt didn't have to open his eyes for me."

Liz felt like she'd better sit down while she was still able to control her limbs. This stubborn man had just spent the morning with her children, fixed them lunch, for God's sake, virtually had them eating out of his hands, and he thought people wouldn't like him, would reject him because of his birth. This after she'd spent a whole morning trying to get his patients to see another doctor.

Why couldn't he see everybody was crazy about him!

Because he'd convinced himself otherwise. Or the people of Gull's Landing had done it for him. It may have even continued in college and medical school. She didn't know, but after thirty years of believing he was a social reject, a few weeks of acceptance in a nearly invisible town deep in the mountains wasn't about to change his mind.

Yet here he was, the personification of the kind of man any sensible, red-blooded American girl would gobble up in one swallow. He was handsome, smart, had a great career ahead of him, and her kids adored him. For that matter, she was rather fond of him herself.

But she had to call a halt before things got out of hand. She didn't want her kids—or herself—to become attached to a man who was going to leave at the first opportunity, who had little understanding of the values that made her love Iron Springs and the people in it. It was crazy to let her liking for him go one step beyond wanting him because he was so impossibly good-looking.

She poured a glass of water and came to the table, her place directly across from Matt. "If I'd known you could get along so well without me, I'd have taken Salome up on her invitation to go shopping. Maybe even taken in a movie."

"Take me to mobie," Ben said.

"Why don't you?" Matt said.

"Because I can't leave you here with Terrible Tyke, even if you do have Fabulous Female to help you."

She took a bite of her sandwich. It tasted delicious. He'd heated slices of the picnic ham, melted cheese over it, used mayonnaise and lettuce. She'd let him fix lunch more often.

"We'll be just fine. We've got plenty to do."

"I wouldn't think of it. I've got the garden to pick and—"

"We already picked it," Rebecca announced.

"I picked cu-cumbers," Ben managed to get out.

"It's better to pick vegetables while it's still cool," Matt said.

"I helped shell the beans," Rebecca related. "I don't like it. It's hard."

"They're in the refrigerator," Matt said when Liz turned her surprised gaze on him.

"Can I hire you?" Liz said, unable to think of anything safe to say. "Picking and shelling is the part I hate."

"Matt had to bend way down," Ben said.

She dreaded going to look at her garden. She was sure every bush was broken, every row trampled down.

Liz leaned back in her chair. "What else did you do? Or were you too exhausted from your labor in the garden to do anything else?"

"Show Mommy your surprise," Matt said to Ben.

The little boy lifted his leg and put his shoe on the table. "Matt teached me."

The knot in his shoelace was in danger of falling out any minute, but it had definitely been tied.

"Did Matt really teach you to do that?" she asked.

"Yes." He put that foot down and brought up the other one. "See."

"How did you do it?" she asked, turning to Matt. "I've been trying for months."

"He's left-handed. So am I. In effect, you were trying to teach him to tie his shoes backward."

That explanation had never occurred to Liz.

"He promised to teach me how to play paddle ball," Rebecca said.

Liz considered it a silly game, but Rebecca had wanted to learn ever since one of the campers who was a wiz with a paddle and ball baby-sat them early in the summer.

"He said he would buy me one as soon as Hannah gets one in her store. She's all sold out. We went over this morning and looked."

"You shouldn't have asked Matt to buy you a paddle ball," Liz said, embarrassed.

"She didn't. I volunteered," Matt clarified.

"You still shouldn't have."

"It's a small thing."

"Small things add up."

Now, why had she said that? Was she talking about him or herself? "I don't mean to sound ungrateful. I just feel guilty imposing on you."

"Don't worry. When I get tired, you'll know. Now I've promised the kids a game of football if they take their naps without a fuss."

"Is Rebecca going to play?" Rebecca hated football. She always refused to play.

"Sure. She's our quarterback. Did you know she's got a wicked arm? I asked her to throw an overgrown cucumber into the compost pile. She pitched it thirty yards without even trying."

Liz turned to Rebecca, who grinned with pride.

"Quarterback, huh?" Liz said.

"I have to play," Rebecca explained. "You can't play football with just two people."

"Your Dr. Andrews had better get you recalled soon," she said to Matt. "If you stay here much longer, I won't know my own children."

"Are you sure you didn't mind coming with us?" Liz asked. Josie had had one of her attacks of indigestion at the last minute and had insisted Ethan take her to Dr. Kennedy. Ben and Rebecca had begged Matt to go with them to the Wolf Gap Recreation Area for their picnic.

"That must be the tenth time you've asked me the same question," Matt said. "I didn't mind an hour ago, and I don't mind now. Why do you keep asking?"

"I guess I feel guilty taking up your Sunday like this. You could be sleeping, or visiting friends in Charlottesville, or wherever you go when you disappear."

The children were now playing by themselves on the swings. After wearing both Liz and Matt out with games of tag, hide-and-seek, kick ball and general roughhousing, they'd been forbidden to utter their names for at least an hour. Matt and Liz relaxed in the shade of an old maple, the remains of their lunch long since abandoned to a pair of brazen cardinals.

It was a peaceful, lazy summer afternoon. An overnight rain had cooled the temperature to the low eighties. A light breeze wafted through the trees, rustling leaves overhead. The surrounding woods were noisy with the chattering of greedy squirrels searching for food and arguing over favorite resting spots.

"I'm glad you came," Liz said. She sat up, her arms around her knees, which were drawn up under her chin. Matt sat next to her, their shoulders almost touching. "The kids would have moped for days." She looked to where they were now chasing each other around the car. "Well, hours at least."

"Do they ever get tired?" Matt asked. "If I kept going like that, I'd be dragging for at least a week."

"They'll collapse into bed tonight, sleep for twelve hours without turning over, then be as good as new tomorrow."

Matt shuddered. "I can't imagine I was ever like that."

Liz wondered what his life had been like as a little boy, shuttled from one foster home to another, shunned by some, wanted by none. Had he been quiet, a loner, or had he been boisterous and outgoing? He must have been cute. Nobody could grow up to be this handsome and not have been a darling little boy.

She was certain all the little girls had had crushes on him. It wouldn't matter that he was illegitimate, a foster child or constantly in trouble. That would only have added to his attraction. She wondered if even now some young woman, happily married to her safe and dependable husband, didn't occasionally remember a handsome little boy and wonder what had happened to him.

She would have.

"Did you play football in high school?" she asked. He never talked about his past.

"Sure. We were a small school. It took everybody we had just to field a team."

"What did you play?"

"Quarterback."

"Were you good?"

"Not particularly. I was too worried about my hands. Even then I knew I wanted to become a surgeon."

"Did you date the head cheerleader or the homecoming queen?"

"No."

"Why not?"

"I didn't have money or a car. Other boys had both."

That was thoughtless. Common sense should have told her that.

"I'm sure they were sorry. You must have been twice as smart as anybody on the team and three times as good-looking."

Matt chuckled. It was a delicious sound, the first time Liz could remember anyone other than the kids making him laugh. It pleased her greatly that she had.

"Maybe, but it never worked to my advantage. People don't like to be around somebody who's able to outdo them in everything."

"I don't see why not. I would. I mean, what's the point of having a husband who's average, or even below? I'd want a man who was better than I was, at least in most things. Then when something came up I couldn't handle, I'd feel confident I could turn it over to him and he wouldn't screw it up worse than I would."

This time Matt's laughter came from the belly, full and totally spontaneous.

"I wish I'd thought of that argument. It would certainly have improved my social life."

"You shouldn't have had to come up with any kind of argument to convince those girls to go out with you. They must have been remarkably silly. Did they wear glasses? Probably too ignorant to go to the doctor and get them adjusted. They probably saw two of you and figured you'd have twice as many hands they'd have to fight off.''

"Would you have gone out with me?"

"Certainly. I have very good eyesight, and I've fought off boys with more hands than an octopus.''

Without warning, Matt leaned over and kissed her.

Chapter Eleven

Startled, Liz pulled back. It wasn't because he'd kissed her but because of her reaction to his kiss. She wanted him to kiss her again, and that realization shook her very badly. It had been a quick kiss, almost innocent, yet it made her want to forget every restraint, every scruple that kept her from kissing him back. Liz couldn't understand how one kiss could affect her so profoundly. Yet in the space of a moment it had caused the basis of their entire relationship to shift.

"Why did you do that?" she asked.

"Every beautiful woman should be kissed."

"You think I'm beautiful?"

"Everybody in Iron Springs thinks so. Solomon Trinket told me so the day I arrived."

"I'm not asking about everybody. I'm asking about you."

"Yes, I think you're beautiful. I think you're beautiful when you're dressed in your power suit, being the efficient manager of a very small county medical clinic. I think you're beautiful when you pull out your frills to go to church and risk another encounter with Josie Woodhouse. But I think you're most beautiful right now, when your hair is up in a ponytail and you're wearing a halter top, very skimpy shorts and tennis shoes without socks. That way I can see the absolute most of you.''

Liz felt a warmth spread through her that had nothing to do with the sunlight peeking through the maple leaves. For the first time since learning David had been cheating on her, she actually *felt* beautiful. She wanted to stretch and preen and lie languid before him like a Siamese cat. She wanted to luxuriate on satin sheets, to lie nearly submerged in scented bathwater, to wash with soft sponges. She felt wholly sensual and alive.

She wondered why Ethan couldn't make her feel like this. He constantly told her she was beautiful, but he hadn't touched her half as deeply as Matt had with a simple kiss.

"You'll get into trouble if you make a habit of kissing every attractive woman you meet," Liz said. "Some of them are bound to have husbands who wouldn't understand you were just paying homage to Nature's handiwork."

"In your case, they'd be right."

Liz got to her feet. She wasn't exactly running away, but she was afraid to let herself stay, afraid of what she might do if she did. Matt followed.

"I shouldn't have kissed you," he said. "It was unfair. I didn't mean to upset you."

"Not unfair, just unexpected."

"You're dating Ethan."

"Yes."

"I should have known that put you off limits."

It did put her off limits, but she knew with total certainty she didn't want to be off limits to Matt.

"Let's walk," she suggested.

"You don't have to run away."

"I'm not running away." She was, but not from him. "The children are playing in the stream. I want to be close to them."

There was barely enough water in the stream to cover their ankles.

"I never asked you what you wanted to do," Liz said, trying to think of something to defuse the tension, something to give her time to think. "You said you hoped to be appointed to the staff of a very famous surgeon, but you didn't say what you wanted to do after that."

"I want to become a rich and famous surgeon and work in one of the great hospitals of New York, Los Angeles or Houston."

His remarks surprised a laugh out of her. "When you dream, you dream big."

"Aren't dreams supposed to be big?"

"I guess so. But why do you want so much?"

"For most of my life, people have done their best not to see me. I want to be so important I'll never be invisible again."

Liz didn't know what to say. His goal was enormous, his reason for wanting it so painfully naked. She wondered again about his experiences as a child, how cruel and powerful they must have been to convince a man who had so much that he deserved so little.

"Now tell me about yourself," he said. "How did a beautiful and intelligent woman end up divorced with two small children to raise by herself?"

"The usual, a bad marriage."

"You've got to explain better than that."

She felt a moment of hesitation, then it vanished.

"I wanted to get away from Iron Springs."

"I don't believe you. I thought you were connected to this place by an umbilical cord."

"I grew up here. I thought it was the end of the world. I don't know what I thought I was going to do after college, but I was certain I'd never come back here."

"What changed your mind?"

"You're getting ahead of the story. I left for college, majored in business, met David and fell in love. I couldn't wait to marry him and quit school to support him while he got his MBA."

"What happened to your degree?"

"David got this wonderful job offer in New York. Before I could get us settled and look into colleges, I got pregnant with Rebecca. I've always thought a mother should stay home with her children if she could, so I settled back to await the baby. Little did I know that while I was getting fat, David was making the rounds of the female staff in the office. I found out after Rebecca was born, and I threatened to leave him."

"I gather you didn't."

"David swore on his knees that he must have been crazy, that he'd never look at another woman again. I must have been just as crazy because I believed him. Even worse, I got pregnant again.

"David covered his tracks better this time. After Ben was born, I started working out at a gym, trying to get my figure back, trying to get to know the wives of his friends, trying to fit into his world. One day, while I was at the gym, he left the kids in the house alone while he went to visit his mistress. One of my new 'friends' told me about it."

"Kind of her."

"David didn't ask for forgiveness this time. He said he didn't have time for a clinging wife, that he needed to devote all his time and energy to building his company. I asked about the *time and energy* he was devoting to his mistress. He said she was fun, that she didn't pull him down. That's when I left him."

"And came back to Iron Springs."

"I didn't know what else to do. I traded alimony for an uncontested divorce and custody of the children. I had a house and a job here if I wanted them."

"But you could have found that in other places. Why did you come back here?"

"Because as much as I sometimes feel stifled, I wanted to live among people who have values I respect and trust. People here may stick their noses into your business, criticize you, give you unwelcome advice, but they won't hesitate to help you the minute anything goes wrong. Josie Woodhouse hates the idea of my marrying Ethan, but she'd take me and my children into her home if we had nowhere to go.

"People here believe in the importance of family, in their commitment to each other. David cast me aside when I got pregnant because I was fat and unattractive. He pushed the children aside because they took up time and money he wanted for his business. But everyone in this town would jeopardize his own business if it was the only way he could help me or anybody else in Iron Springs."

"You'd make a wonderful spokesperson for the Iron Springs Chamber of Commerce."

Liz laughed. "If we had such a thing. But you can see why I came back, why I'm determined to stay."

"What about your degree? You can't finish it here."

"I can't finish it anywhere until the kids start school."

They walked a moment in silence. "So you're as determined to stay in Iron Springs as I am to get out," Matt said.

"I like it for all the reasons you don't. It's—"

She broke off. A car had driven into the park. Instead of staying in the gravel area, it swerved around the curb and came toward them across the grass.

"Mama, the car's driving on the grass," Ben shouted, running toward them.

"I know."

"That's bad. Tell the car to stop."

"I intend to," Liz said, angry anyone would drive into an area where children were playing. But when she recognized Salome at the wheel, she knew something was wrong.

"There's been an accident at Ethan's shop," Salome called to Matt through the open window.

"Who is it?" Liz asked.

"Bill Bennett."

"Is he badly hurt?"

"Bad enough."

"I'll come, too," Liz offered.

"No need. Sadie's with him. Hurry up," Salome said to Matt.

"She can drive herself home," Salome directed. "Hurry. Sadie says he's bleeding pretty bad."

"Just leave me your keys," Liz said.

Matt dug the keys out of his pocket, handed them to Liz and jumped into Salome's car. She tore out of the park, sending a spray of grass and dirt in her wake.

"Where's Matt going?" Ben asked. "Doesn't he like us anymore?"

"Of course he likes you," Liz said, kneeling down to give her son a hug. "A man got hurt. He has to go help him."

"Can't somebody else help him?" Rebecca asked. "I want Matt to stay with us."

"He's a doctor," Liz explained. "They have to help people when they get hurt."

"Who makes them?"

"Every doctor makes a promise to take care of people who are sick or hurt."

"I won't if I become a doctor," Rebecca said.

"Wouldn't you want a doctor to come if you were hurt real bad?" Liz asked.

"I guess so."

"Well, that man wants Matt to come. That's why Salome came for him."

"I don't think I want to be a doctor when I grow up," Rebecca said.

"Why?" Liz asked.

"I don't want to leave my little girl at the picnic. She'll be sad."

"You shouldn't be sad. We've had a very nice day. It was almost time to go home anyway. I'll collect the cooler and throw the plates and stuff away. You and Ben can fold up the blankets and put them in the station wagon."

But no matter what Liz said or did, the children's light-heartedness had gone from the afternoon.

Once again she found herself worrying about the effect Matt's leaving would have on them, but she had waited too long to do anything about it. They wouldn't understand if she tried to separate them.

Neither would he.

She wondered if Matt could ever have a normal home life, if any family-practice doctor could. Maybe in the city where they had office hours and partners to help cover evenings and weekends, but not in the country. Not in a place like Iron Springs. When somebody got sick, he had to go. His family would have to come second.

But more than Matt's absence troubled Liz. She had to come to a decision about Ethan. It was unfair to everyone to go on mindlessly drifting, not making up her mind, leaving hope without a promise.

She'd never thought there could be anything between Matt and her. They were too different. Then, against long odds and common sense, deep feelings had developed between them. But his goal of being rich and famous, of living in a big city and working at a great hospital, had effectively put an end to any chance they could be more than a fleeting dream.

What he wanted sounded like life with David all over again. She wouldn't risk that. She and her children had already been placed second, behind a career and being seen with the right people at the right places. That's what Matt would have to do to get where he wanted to go. He might not realize it yet, but he would soon.

And he would do it. She could just see him smiling while he remained separate and lonely. Doing that would kill any softness that hadn't already been beaten out of him in Gull's Landing, but she couldn't tell him that. He wouldn't believe her. And what if he did? What did she have to offer him? Iron Springs and picnics in the state park during the summer, Josie Woodhouse and Solomon Trinket all year round.

That kind of life might appeal to her, but it wouldn't to a man like Matt.

Salome had fallen silent. Matt would have liked to believe it was to allow her to concentrate on her driving. The way she took the curves convinced him she couldn't be looking where she was going. Otherwise, she wouldn't be breathing, either.

"Am I driving too fast for you?" she asked, looking in his direction.

"Hell, yes, and don't take your eyes off the road."

"Don't worry. I know this road like the back of my hand."

"The only way I can not worry is for you to let me out of this car."

Salome laughed. "You'll get used to it."

Matt doubted it, just as he doubted he would get used to the feeling that had started to hit him every time he was around Liz. It was almost like being a teenager, getting excited just being around certain girls. Only he wasn't a teenager anymore. He knew what that kind of excitement meant, what it led to. Only it wasn't leading anywhere, and he was incredibly frustrated.

He kept telling himself she was Ethan's girl, that if she wasn't going to marry him, she still hadn't told anybody. He kept telling himself she was the mother of two kids. And as adorable as they were, they represented the kind of commitment he didn't want. He kept telling himself she was a small-town girl with small-town values. She might say she didn't care about his birth, but did she really mean it? Could anyone brought up in a place like this not care about something like that?

She was tied to this town, if not physically, at least spiritually. She would hate it where he wanted to go. She would hate the kind of people he had to work with, no doubt the same kind of people David worked with, people willing to sacrifice anything for the success they craved.

Was he any different?

He'd always thought so, but now he wasn't sure. He hadn't walked over any bodies to get ahead; he hadn't abandoned any responsibilities. He simply had given up any idea of having the kind of life everyone else seemed to want—a wife, family, friends. For him, success was enough.

But every time he looked at Liz, every time he thought of her—and he thought of her a lot—he began to wonder if there was some way to have both. He knew there wasn't, but he couldn't stop asking.

He kept asking himself why he liked her so much. He recited his usual litany, which answered nothing. Why?

Just because.

He'd never thought he'd find himself accepting that as an answer, but it came as close as he could get to the truth. He liked being around her. He sometimes didn't even mind that he probably wasn't going to get out of Iron Springs for a whole year. He didn't mind not going to Charlottesville. He didn't mind helping with the kids. He almost didn't mind dealing with people like Josie Woodhouse.

He chuckled. Wouldn't Georgia Allen love to hear that? After the long talks they'd had about how they weren't going to let anything interfere with their careers, she'd be certain he'd lost his mind.

"What's so funny?" Salome asked.

"Somebody once told me that St. Peter had a list of everybody in the world. Beside each name he had the date they were supposed to arrive at the Pearly Gates. I was wondering what happens when you arrive early. Does he make you wait?"

"You think I'm going to kill you?" Salome said, taking a curve with the wheels on Matt's side of the car on the shoulder.

"The odds seem to favor it."

"You ain't seen nothing yet."

Matt shuddered. "I thought I was a courageous man. I was wrong."

Salome laughed, skidded around another curve and suddenly slammed on brakes. Before the tires stopped squealing she turned into a driveway and gunned the engine. Fifty yards up the dirt track, she braked again and spun half around to the right. The car came to a stop directly in front of the entrance to a wood-frame building that looked like a barn.

"He's inside," she said. "Sadie sent someone to the clinic to fetch your medical bag."

Matt stumbled out of the car muttering a prayer of thanks he was alive. If the injured man had to go to the hospital, he was going to make damned sure Salome wasn't driving the ambulance. No point in patching up external injuries only to have the patient die of heart failure.

"I can't marry you," Liz told Ethan. They were in his office. She hadn't wanted anybody to overhear what she had to say.

"What are you talking about? We're practically engaged. The whole town is expecting us to announce the date at any moment." He looked like he'd been hit in the face with a wet fish. Not hurt, just stunned. He obviously couldn't believe she meant what she said.

"Only because this is such a small town we're always turning up at the same places. You know as well as I do if a man talks to a woman more than twice, that means they're going steady according to people around here."

"We did a lot more than just talk," Ethan said, getting a little angry now. "At least, I did. I told everybody I wanted to marry you."

"I know."

He'd made her take a seat, insisted he fix her some coffee. He handed her a foam cup.

"You let me go around expecting—"

"Ethan, I've told you over and over again I wasn't ready to think about marriage. It may seem like I led you on—I can see how you would feel that way—but I never once said I was even thinking about getting married...to anybody. I've tried to get you to see other women."

"I don't want to see other women. You know I've never loved anybody but you."

"Ethan, you can't spend your life waiting for me to fall in love with you. What if I never did?" She sat her coffee down untasted. "You know I've always liked you, but you also know I never loved you. I told you that."

"I know, but—"

"You thought I'd get tired of waiting, or desperate, and marry you anyway, didn't you?"

"That's not fair. I love you. I'll take you on just about any terms."

"I'm sorry, Ethan, but it just won't work. If I haven't fallen in love with you by now, I'm never going to."

He came around the desk toward her. She motioned him back.

"How do you know? You might—"

"Ethan, when I came back here, I was hurting. I needed a friend. I needed someone to like me, to help me feel worthwhile again. You were willing to do that, and I let you, but that's all it's ever going to be. I'm sorry I didn't say something before now. It was cowardly of me, but I didn't want to lose your friendship."

"You wouldn't have."

"Maybe, but it would have strained things between us."

She could tell he was still angry, but he was less angry than she had expected. She wondered if he was as disappointed as he thought he was. Ethan had told himself he was in love with her for so long he probably hadn't asked himself if his teenage crush endured only because she seemed out of reach.

"I'm not the same woman you used to know," Liz said. "I don't even know what I want anymore. I need room to experiment, make mistakes, go in different directions. I'm going to go back to school in a few years. I don't know what I want to do after that."

"I can wait." He sat down on his desk, but his confidence was shaken.

"You've waited too long already. You know who you are, what you want, what you plan to do with your life. You'll be a lot happier with someone who can fit into your life."

"That's you."

"We've argued about one thing or another since we were in high school. I don't think you want to keep doing that for the rest of your life. I know I don't. Look around you. There are lots of nice girls who'd love to take care of you, spoil you rotten. You might even find one your mother can like."

"I'm not marrying to please my mother."

"I know. I was just teasing, but I'm serious about all the rest. It's over, Ethan, really over."

* * *

"Don't try to put me off, Liz," David said. "I've hired a lawyer. I know my rights."

Liz watched her knuckles turn white as she gripped the table. Things had been so busy at the clinic, she'd brought home some forms to request additional budget. David's call had driven all her arguments out of her mind. She'd have to start all over again later.

"I'm not trying to put you off. I just—"

"You are. You know I have visitation rights."

"Which you've never exercised."

"I still have them, and I'm exercising them now."

"I need time to prepare the children. This isn't like a trip to the grocery store."

"Look, I'm not going to put up with this. I'm actually in a better position to have custody of them than you are."

"How can you say that when you've never—"

"I'm married, and you're not. I've got plenty of money to support them. You don't."

David had apparently decided to ignore his behavior of the past three years. He'd always been very good at ignoring things he didn't want to hear.

"Let's face it. I can give the children a better life."

"You!" Liz could hardly control herself. He thought all he needed to be a perfect father was money and a wife to baby-sit his kids. "You don't know a thing about children, especially your own."

"I won't learn with you keeping them in that mountain backwater. Listen, Liz, if you don't agree to let the kids visit me, I'm going to sue for custody. With things the way they are now, I'll get it."

Chapter Twelve

The rat, her ex-husband, had threatened to take her kids. She would kill him if he tried.

Liz dropped into the chair and leaned against the table. What was she going to do? What could she do? She didn't know what came over her, but all of a sudden she started to cry. She tried to stop. She was mad, not ready to throw her hands up and wail in despair, but the tears kept flowing. The harder she tried to stop, the worse it got. Soon she was bawling like a child. She put her head down on the table and gave in.

Liz didn't know how long she'd been crying when she suddenly felt certain someone was in the kitchen. She heaved a gusty sob and raised her head. She didn't see anyone, but the feeling wouldn't go away. She pushed her hair back from her face and turned around.

Matt stood in the doorway to the hall.

Mortified, she turned away and wiped her eyes. "I thought you were in Charlottesville," she said when she could command her voice sufficiently to speak.

"I came back early."

She didn't know what to do. She couldn't hide. He'd already seen her. But she couldn't keep on sitting here, no doubt looking like a drowned rat with red eyes.

"We've already eaten, but there's some leftover casserole in the refrigerator."

"I stopped on the way back."

"There's dessert."

He walked around where she could see him. "Are you going to tell me what's wrong, or are we going to keep talking about food?"

She looked away. "It's my problem. You can't do anything about it."

"I can listen."

"That won't change anything."

"It might make you feel better."

She looked up. "But you'd have to get involved in somebody else's problems, and you wouldn't like that." That was mean of her. This wasn't his fault. He was trying to be nice. "Sorry, I didn't mean that. I'm upset."

"Has something happened to Ethan?"

"Why do you ask?"

"Well, you're going to marry him. I just thought maybe—"

"Ethan's fine, and I'm not going to marry him. I told him three days ago."

They just stood there, looking at each other.

Now he knows. What difference would it make? she asked herself.

Maybe none. Maybe he was just being polite. Even in Gull's Landing, she doubted a man would walk past a woman bawling her head off and not try to help.

"It's David," she said. "He—"

The back door slammed against the wall, and Ben catapulted into the room, followed by Rebecca. They threw themselves at Liz.

"I won!" Ben shouted.

"You got a head start," Rebecca countered.

"What's all the ruckus about?" Matt asked. He pulled the kids' attention from Liz to himself. "You nearly knocked your mother down."

"I bat first tomorrow," Ben said.

"We had a race to decide," Rebecca explained.

Liz got up, moistened a paper towel at the sink and tried to wash her face. She didn't want the children to know she'd been crying. They'd ask questions. There'd be time for that later when she'd managed to come up with some answers.

"Now that's settled, I think you'd better run and get ready for your baths."

"Mama," Rebecca called.

"She'll be along in a minute," Matt said. "You run along and start getting ready. You, too, sport," he said to Ben. "I'll be up in a minute."

"Thank you," Liz said as she heard the children run down the hall. She turned to face Matt. "You don't have to bathe Ben. You must be tired."

But he didn't turn away. Instead, he crossed the room. He took the paper towel from her hands and threw it into the trash. He took out his handkerchief, wet it and began to moisten her eyes with cold water.

"Why aren't you going to marry Ethan?"

She used his washing her eyes as an excuse to close them so she wouldn't have to look at him.

"I don't love him. I never have. When I came back, I needed a friend very badly. He hoped it was something else."

He placed his hand under her chin and proceeded to wash the tearstains from her cheeks. "You can open your eyes now."

She didn't want to. She was afraid of what she might see. She was even more afraid of what she might not see.

When she opened her eyes, he was looking directly at her. He seemed to look right into her, to see her hidden thoughts. She knew it was foolish, but she still felt naked, exposed.

He tilted her chin back slightly, turned her head from side to side. "Remarkable. You were crying like your heart was broken, and your eyes aren't the least bit red. You're just as beautiful as ever.''

That nearly started her bawling again. She knew she had to look a soggy mess.

''What did David say that upset you so badly?''

''Nothing I can't handle.''

She tried to pull away, but he wouldn't let her. His expression said he wasn't going to let her go until she told him.

''He said if I didn't let the children visit him, he was going to sue for custody.''

''Will he?''

''I'm sure he will. He doesn't really love them. He just wants to…''

She broke down again. It mortified her to cry in front of Matt, but she couldn't stand the thought of losing her children.

He pulled her to him, up against his chest. She knew she shouldn't, that it was dangerous, but she couldn't resist. She didn't want to resist. It felt wonderful to have his arms around her, to be able to lean against him.

For such a long time, she'd had to stand on her own, to hold back her feelings because she couldn't afford to appear vulnerable, couldn't afford to let herself *feel* vulnerable. It was a relief to let go. She hadn't felt so safe since she was a little girl and her daddy held her tight when it thundered.

She was certain she ought to back away, but she couldn't make herself do it. Still, she couldn't stay in his arms forever, no matter how comforting, no matter how enticing. She had children to bathe. She had her face to wash, again. She had her self-esteem to piece back together.

But when she pulled back, Matt's arms didn't let her go. She then made her biggest mistake.

She looked up into his eyes.

The man who looked back at her didn't look like the angry young doctor who wanted to forget he'd ever heard of Iron Springs. He bore no resemblance to the doctor who said he didn't want to become involved with his patients' lives. He didn't make her think of the handsome physician who had every woman in Iron Springs looking for an excuse to feel sickly.

He looked like a man who cared passionately that she was unhappy.

His brown eyes looked luminous with caring, glistened with moisture, as though he were crying with her. She knew he wasn't—men like Matt Dennis didn't cry, they couldn't—but it felt like it, and that melted her heart. When he lowered his head toward her, she didn't turn away.

His lips felt natural on hers, like he had kissed her many times before. Everything else felt just as it should, her palms resting lightly against his chest, his arms around her pressing her against him.

The kiss was very tender at first. His lips seemed to brush hers lightly. Neither tentative nor unsure. Not aggressive or frightening. Just comforting. Reassuring.

She kissed him back. She hadn't meant to, though she knew she'd been wanting to kiss him for quite a long time. She couldn't stop herself. She didn't want to stop. It was too inviting, too wonderful, too perfect.

Then what had begun as a kiss of consolation turned into a greedy kiss of unfulfilled need. Liz felt Matt's lips consume her mouth, the gentle brushing intensified in pressure. His arms closed around her. She felt herself being swallowed up, consumed.

An equally strong desire surged to the surface from somewhere deep inside Liz. Her mouth moved against his with a need deeper and more unrestrained than his own. Her arms slipped around his neck, holding him tightly, pulling him down to her. She ground her body against his. She felt the muscles in his abdomen tense, his thighs become rigid.

"Mama, are you coming?"

Rebecca's words were like an electric shock that drove them apart. For a moment, they stood facing each other. She could see her own reactions in the mirror of his. Their eyes wide, their bodies stiff, their minds in a whirl, their emotions in turmoil.

"Mama!"

"Coming," Liz managed to say. "In a minute."

She tried to look away from Matt, but it was as though their gazes were one.

"I'd better go see that Ben hasn't flooded the bathroom," Matt said. He sounded as shocked as Liz felt.

They stood a moment in silence. She didn't feel like she had the strength to walk down the hall, much less climb the stairs.

"Thanks for listening to me," she finally managed to say. "I'm sorry I cried all over your shirt."

"It was going in the laundry anyway."

They were just saying words, standing there, not moving.

"Mama! Are you coming? The water's getting cold."

"I'd better go. Thanks again."

Liz dropped her gaze and hurried past Matt before he could respond. She didn't know what to say, to him or to herself. She would have to say something, attempt to make some explanation, but not before she'd had time to think. She'd known she was attracted to him, but this was a lot more serious than she'd guessed.

She wanted him to kiss her again. She wanted even more than that.

Matt hesitated before locking his office door. He could go to Charlottesville without going back to the house. He could change his clothes at his friend's apartment. Muttering a curse, he turned the key in the lock and headed down the hall past the reception desk.

"Bye, Beefcake," Salome cooed through red lips. "Don't do anything I wouldn't do."

"If he did half the things you've already done, he'd get arrested," Sadie said.

Matt grinned. He and Salome had come to an understanding. She wouldn't call him Beefcake in public or introduce him to females who purchased their body parts in department stores. In return, he wouldn't duck into his office every time he heard the sound of her voice.

He let himself out the back door and began the short walk

back to the house. He freely admitted to himself he'd been trying to avoid Liz. Six days had passed, and he still hadn't recovered from the shock of finding that he had not only kissed her like he'd never kissed another woman, but also that he was burning to do it again. It didn't matter that he had marshaled every argument he'd ever used against getting involved. It didn't matter that he'd reminded himself almost hourly of his ambitions and what it would take to get there.

Neither did it matter, so it seemed, that he'd been abandoned by everyone who'd ever promised to care for him. He and Liz couldn't agree on the time of day. He couldn't rationally expect this to be anything more than a purely physical attraction. He wanted to take Liz into his arms and kiss her until the ache inside him went away.

For a man who'd prided himself all his life on being rational, on making decisions based on cold, hard facts, this was a terrifying dilemma. He was being controlled by his emotions, and he couldn't do anything about it. To make things worse, he didn't understand what was happening to him. He wasn't in love with Liz. He didn't want to get married. He'd never consider settling down in a place like Iron Springs and having a family, certainly not trying to be a father to another man's children. It would be hard enough with his own children. It would be impossible with someone else's. He of all people ought to know that.

He moved over to the shoulder of the road to let an ancient pickup truck pass. A young woman stuck her head out the window and waved frantically as the truck went past. Matt waved back, hoping she would turn around and watch the road ahead. Iron Springs was a unique community, but trees still didn't get out of the way of pickup trucks.

Matt rounded the corner of Hannah's Drugs. The pickup had come to a stop in front of the ancient gas pump.

"Why don't you come in for a chat?" the driver said. Matt had seen Amy Thurber about a week ago about pains in her back. She might have a crushed disk from years of lifting her bedridden father.

"Can't," Matt said. "I'm on my way out of town."

"Going to kick up your heels in the big city?"

"Something like that."

"Kick 'em up at least once for me," the young woman said with a smile before she disappeared into Hannah's store.

Matt knew she'd probably never kick up her heels in Charlottesville or anywhere else. By the time she was freed from taking care of her parents, she might not be able or interested. She'd spend the rest of her life watching other people go off to have fun.

Matt didn't know why he was letting himself worry about this young woman. People made their choices. Despite their protests, they usually did what they wanted. He was the one in danger of letting himself get caught up in something he didn't want. He'd have to see Dr. Andrews the minute he reached town. He'd take almost any kind of assignment, but he had to get out of Iron Springs.

Away from Liz and her family.

He had hoped to make it back to his room, then to his car, without being seen. Ben spotted him while he was still three houses away. He rode his bicycle to meet Matt. As usual, Matt had to jump out of the way to keep from being run over.

"We're going to have to get you some brakes for that thing," Matt said as he helped Ben turn the bicycle around and point it toward the house. "One of these days you're going to knock me flat."

Ben laughed. "You jump too fast."

"It's a good thing. You don't slow down."

"I like fast."

"So I see. Why don't you see how fast you can ride it back to the house?"

"I want to stay with you," Ben said. He didn't seem to notice that he took up all the sidewalk, forcing Matt to walk in the grass or on the road. "Becca says you got to play ball with us. She says you pitch the best."

"I can't today, sport. I'm going to Charlottesville as soon as I change my clothes."

"No go to 'lottesville," Ben said as his smile crumpled. "Play ball with me and Becca."

Matt wondered why Ben's disappointment upset him so much when his own unhappiness never seemed to bother anybody in Gull's Landing.

"I can't, sport, really I can't. But I'll be back tomorrow. Maybe we can fit in a game then."

He was lying, an awful thing to do to a child. He didn't plan to return until late tomorrow night.

"Now," Ben said, "I want to play now."

"Sorry, but we'll have to wait. Now you'd better go back to your friends. I've got to go."

Ben's bicycle fell over when he jumped off. He ran off around the corner of the house without looking back.

Matt felt like a piece of scum. He was running away from Liz and he'd practically lied to her kid, all because he was too much of a coward to face up to his feelings. He was ashamed of himself. But these feelings were too strong. He'd never felt anything like this before. He didn't know if he could control himself.

He still wanted to kiss her again. He remembered each split second of their kiss. Every emotion, every tactile sensation. He had relived them in his dreams each night. He felt like he was under siege. He had to get away before he lost all will to fight. That's why he was slinking off to Charlottesville like a thief in the night.

Liz turned to exit the pew as the strains of the postlude began its weekly competition with after-church conversation. She wondered if Aunt Marian would mind if she dropped by for lunch. She didn't want to go back to her house. It seemed empty and quiet without Matt. Even the children felt it. Ben had sulked all weekend. No matter what she thought of to do, it wasn't the right thing. She didn't need anyone to tell her that every suggestion she'd made would have been greeted with enthusiasm if Matt had been there.

Rebecca wasn't nearly so obvious, but she wasn't her usual self, either. Ethan had come over Saturday afternoon—he just wouldn't stay away—and offered to play with her. She accepted politely, but she played with a sense of obligation. Even Ethan sensed it.

"Good morning, Liz," The Reverend Pike said. "We missed the doctor this morning."

"He's gone to Charlottesville for the weekend," Liz told him.

"I wonder if it's too much to hope he's attending church there."

"I don't inquire into his business." Liz smiled and moved on so the Reverend Pike could greet his other parishioners.

Several people spoke to her. She nodded and made some response. She was headed toward the nursery to get her children when someone grabbed her by the arm. She couldn't have been more surprised when she found herself face-to-face with Josie Woodhouse.

"Tell Norma that Dr. Dennis is worried about my indigestion. She doesn't believe he wants to give me a thorough physical examination."

"I told her I didn't believe Dr. Dennis would see another doctor's patient," Norma explained. "He's much too nice a man to do anything that unprofessional."

"Josie went to see him without telling him she had a private physician," Liz said. "Her curiosity got the better of her."

"It did not," Josie declared, but Norma winked and grinned at Liz.

"It's true Dr. Dennis thinks she ought to have a thorough physical examination," Liz continued, "but he thinks her own doctor ought to do it."

"He's an old woman," Josie sniffed.

"Then get yourself a new doctor," Liz said.

"It's only indigestion," Josie said.

"Maybe, but—"

"And I wouldn't have that if you would leave Ethan alone."

Liz should have known Josie would get around to her and Ethan sooner or later.

"I'm not going to marry Ethan," she told Josie. "We had a long talk and decided we wouldn't suit."

"Then why did he spend Saturday afternoon playing with your children?"

Liz felt like uttering several curses, even though she was still on church grounds. "Ethan has always played with the children," Liz said. "He's very thoughtful."

"Not nearly as thoughtful as he was before you got your hooks into him," Josie said.

"Well, I've taken them out again. Now make sure you see your doctor about that physical. Bye, Norma."

Liz turned before Josie could say anything else. She was having enough trouble dealing with knowing Matt was avoiding her, that he had gone to Charlottesville to keep from having to be in the same house with her for two days. She didn't want to be blamed for Ethan's refusal to accept that there was no hope of her falling in love with him.

She had tried to keep busy during the weekend. She had worked in the garden, played with the children, started a new dress for Rebecca, visited her aunt, helped her cousin choose wallpaper for her new bathroom.

But none of it had driven thoughts of Matt from her mind any more than it had during the week. Both of them had worked harder than usual, had asked Sadie or Salome to bring things from each other's office they would normally have gotten themselves. It had been so obvious Salome had asked if they'd had a fight.

But meals had been the worst. They couldn't avoid each other then. Neither could they ignore each other. The children wouldn't let them. It was almost as though they had sensed something was wrong and talked louder and longer, hoping it would go away.

Liz had to face it. As long as Matt stayed in her house, they were going to treat him like part of the family. They would want him to play with them, eat with them, watch TV with them, put them to bed. And they wouldn't understand if that suddenly changed.

Poor things! They didn't understand conflicting ambitions

or opposing viewpoints any more than they could understand the need that was tearing her apart.

She knew all the reasons why she should keep her distance from Matt. She knew all the reasons why any relationship between them would end in pain. She understood perfectly why he wouldn't let anything happen even if she were fool enough to want it to. Yet despite knowing all of that, her thoughts of him had grown more frequent, her need to talk to him more urgent, the desire to be with him more intense.

Which was a stupid thing for a woman of her intelligence to let happen. With David and Ethan to deal with, she already had enough problematical men in her life.

Chapter Thirteen

Matt looked at the chart in his hand. It said that Josh Worsley was eight years old and had never seen a doctor for anything more serious than a bad case of poison ivy. The boy sat forward in his chair, his hands folded in his lap, his big gray eyes watching Matt with curiosity rather than fear. His long, straight, dark hair had been ruthlessly combed into place, but Matt guessed that during summer it usually covered about half of his face. His clothes weren't new, but they were clean and neat.

"And what's wrong with you, young man?" Matt asked. "You look far too healthy to be spending a nice summer afternoon in the doctor's office."

"He didn't want to come, but I made him," his mother said. "He's been acting peculiar lately."

"In what way?"

Matt had learned that *peculiar* in Iron Springs didn't always mean the same as it did in other places.

"He's been looking mealy and picking at his dinner for

the last few weeks. This morning he woke up with a head-ache.''

"Has he had a cold, any flulike symptoms? Is anyone else in the house having these symptoms?''

"No. We're a very healthy family,'' Mrs. Worsley said. "Josh has never acted like this before. I don't know what's got into him. I even caught him staring off into space when he was watching ESPN yesterday.''

"How is that significant?'' Matt asked. Mae Worsley looked country, but she didn't look stupid.

"He's crazy about the Washington Redskins. Once the season starts, he near 'bout drives me and his father frantic talking about them, reading about them, quoting numbers till I fair want to scream. They was having a special report on the team before the start of the exhibition season. You know what it's like. They show you all the new players, talk about even more numbers, and make those poor fellas that hardly got out of grade school embarrass their mamas by talking. When I saw Josh wasn't paying attention, I knew something was wrong.''

"Has he been doing this long?''

"This morning was the first time I've noticed it with the television. But he hasn't been rambunctious like usual.''

Matt could see no outward signs that there was anything wrong with the boy, but he was getting an uneasy feeling in his gut.

"Has he been having recurrent or persistent fever?''

"No.''

"Bone pain?''

"He hasn't complained of it.''

"Has he lost any weight?''

"No.''

"How about bruises?''

"Show the doctor your arm, Josh.''

The boy pulled up his sleeve to expose several small bruises on the underside of his arm.

"He got these last week. Shouldn't they be gone by now?''

Matt grew more certain of the probable diagnosis, but he

wouldn't know until he'd completed a physical exam on the boy. He wouldn't even know then until he'd ordered a series of tests. He would never tell a mother that her child had leukemia until he was absolutely certain of his diagnosis.

"Well I think it's best I give him a good going-over. Then maybe I will know what all this means."

"You think there's anything wrong with him, Doctor?"

"I can't say until I've examined him."

"I'm probably being too anxious. Ma says all kids go off color now and again. She says I worry too much, but I can't help it. He's our only young 'un."

"I understand. I'll be very thorough. If I have any questions, I'll order special tests." He ruffled the boy's hair. "I want to make certain he has a clean bill of health."

Mrs. Worsley rose. "You do like the doctor says," she told Josh. "I don't want to hear that you caused a ruckus."

"I'm sure he'll be a little gentleman," Matt said. He just hoped that all the signs meant something else.

"I do need more tests," Matt told Mae Worsley, whom he'd called back in after he'd finished examining Josh.

"Is something wrong?" She looked worried.

"I'm not sure. That's why I need the tests."

"You might as well do them now," she said. "It'll save me coming in again. We only got one car."

"He'll need to go to the hospital in Charlottesville, maybe stay overnight."

Her body stilled, and her entire being seemed to concentrate itself in her eyes, which were focused on him. "Something is wrong. What is it? What can I do to fix it?"

"I can't be sure until I see the test's results."

He couldn't help but admire this small, modest country woman. She didn't fall apart or start crying hysterically. She knew he was talking about the possibility of something life-threatening to her precious child. Her thoughts were centered entirely on what she had to do to help her son. She'd deal with her own feelings later, in private.

"His father and I have never been out of the valley," she said. "You'll have to tell us what to do."

"I'll make all the arrangements. All you have to do is take Josh to the hospital."

"When?"

"I'll call you as soon as I know, probably tomorrow."

That one word *tomorrow,* told her it was serious. She stood, her steady and direct gaze fixed on him. "We'll be ready."

"Come by here before you leave. I'll have maps and directions for you."

She held out her hand. "You've been very nice."

"It's my job."

But after she left, he dropped in his chair. How had he ended up with a job that required him to tell a mother her child might die?

Liz couldn't decide whether she was simply lusting after a handsome man, or if she was falling in love with Matt. Either way, she couldn't continue to avoid him, refusing to speak of what she thought they both knew lay between them. She couldn't expect him to bring it up. He'd told her from the beginning exactly where he stood on marriage, small towns and his career. Falling in love with her would be the antithesis of everything he wanted for himself. But she had to know, had to have it in words.

She waited for him after his last patient. It would be easier to talk while they walked home through the heat of the July afternoon. Too many attentive ears at home or in the office. She might be about to make a fool of herself. She didn't want anybody listening.

"I thought you'd be gone," Matt said when he saw her.

"I had some work to finish up."

He didn't seem nervous. Not even wary. In fact, he seemed pleased to see her. He'd been looking rather down the past few days. It was nice to see him smile.

"You work too hard," he said.

"Not half as hard as you."

"I don't have much choice. There's nobody else to see patients."

"And there's nobody else to run the office."

He smiled at her again, and her heart tried to jump into her throat. "How does it feel to be indispensable?"

"I might be indispensable to my children, but not to anyone else."

"Well I can't do without you. The office wouldn't run half as smoothly."

The afternoon sun shone with waning brightness and warmth. Spencer Mountain rose in the distance, its summit shrouded in mist. A cool breeze, laden with moisture and the scent of humus and wet leaves, flowed down from its tree-shaded slopes to rustle leaves of the ancient oaks that shaded the white clapboard houses of Iron Springs.

The setting was idyllic. The time, the lazy end of the day. And the most romantic thing Matt Dennis could manage to say was that she was indispensable to the running of the clinic.

"Are you going to Charlottesville this weekend? I don't think you should," she continued before he could answer. "The crafts fair starts Friday. It's the biggest weekend of the summer. It would be a crime to miss it."

"Are you going?"

"Of course. I usually take a picnic, even though it's only five minutes from the house. The kids like to eat on the lawn and play down by the lake. Why don't you come with us? The children will be upset if you don't."

Coward! She wasn't asking him for the children. She was asking him for herself. Was she afraid the prospect of spending the afternoon in her company wasn't enough to lure him from Charlottesville?

"What are you fixing to eat?"

"I thought that old saw about getting to a man through his stomach had gone by the boards."

"As one of my foster parents said, it's important to enjoy anything you have to do three times a day."

He was smiling; he seemed perfectly relaxed. Then why had he tried to avoid her for so long?

If he'd been wrestling with his own questions, trying to

make up his mind about her, he'd apparently succeeded. Only she didn't know what he'd decided. Whatever it was, he seemed comfortable with it. That didn't bode well for her. If he was about to violate everything he'd ever thought he believed in life, he'd be upset.

"The children have put in a request for hot dogs. I usually have potato salad and fried chicken for me. Lemonade to drink, chocolate-chip cookies for dessert."

"How do you make your potato salad?"

"With pickles, eggs, and mayonnaise. Is there another way?"

"With mustard, onions, and celery seeds." He made a face. "It's as bad as it sounds."

"Can I bribe you with anything else?"

"No. Just hold out two short thighs for me, and I'll bless your name."

"If I'd known you were that easy, I'd have served fried chicken before."

They turned the corner at Hannah's Drugs only to meet Hannah standing on the steps talking to Solomon Trinket.

"You coming to the fair?" Hannah asked Matt.

"Liz has just talked me into it," he answered.

"I had to bribe him with two chicken legs."

"I'll bet that's not the only legs he's got his eyes on," Solomon said, chuckling wickedly.

Hannah hit him over the head with her baseball cap.

"I declare, Solomon Trinket, you get worse every day. If you don't die soon, we'll have to bury you alive just to keep the town from getting a bad name."

"I'm just telling the truth," he said with another chuckle. "Can't no red-blooded man ignore Liz's legs."

"Speak for yourself, you old coot," Hannah said, giving him another swipe with her hat. "Not that you've got any blood left to speak of."

"I think Liz has great legs," Matt said, winking at Solomon. "I intend to look at them as often as I can."

Matt winked again, and Solomon indulged in a wheezing laugh.

"Ignore them," Liz told Hannah.

"'Shoot 'em' is what I say," Hannah replied.

"I'm leaving," Matt said, starting across the street. "I'm not through looking at legs yet."

"It would serve you right if I wore pants," Liz said when she caught up with him.

"Then you'd pass out from the heat, and I'd get to carry you home."

Liz couldn't understand the change in Matt's attitude. Maybe she'd just imagined he was avoiding her when she was doing all the avoiding herself. She didn't know, but either he'd changed his attitude toward her or she'd misjudged something.

"It'll be more likely that I have to carry you home in a wheelbarrow after Ben and Rebecca keep you playing kick ball all afternoon," she said. "It won't be an easy game like usual. All the kids will be there."

"Good. It'll give me a chance to work off some of the pounds I've gained eating your food."

Liz would have liked to have had Matt to herself a little longer—she hadn't felt so comfortable around him in days—but the children had seen them long before they reached the house. They came running down the sidewalk.

"What are you doing here?" she asked as she caught Ben in one arm, Rebecca in the other. "I thought you were staying with Aunt Marian."

"She said she was tired of campers," Rebecca announced. "She said she could put up with us but not two hundred campers."

"She made Hawaiian punch," Ben announced. A bright red line on his upper lip indicated he'd had more than his share. He took hold of Matt's hand. "You can have some, too."

"Don't I get any?" Liz asked.

"There's lots," Rebecca said. "Aunt Marian said she wasn't moving until supper. She said she was staying and you were fixing."

"She's real tired of campers," Ben announced.

They headed for the backyard and the glasses of punch, Rebecca holding Liz's hand and Ben hanging on to Matt. Liz liked the feeling.

Matt lay in the bed staring at the ceiling, sleep an abandoned hope. It was Saturday, the day of the crafts fair. Everything in Iron Springs was closed. People had come from miles around. Last night a high-school band had played a concert in the shell behind the hotel. Tonight a jazz ensemble would perform. On Sunday there'd be cloggers. It would be a celebration, and he was going to spend it with Liz.

He'd given up trying to pretend he wasn't strongly attracted to her. It was foolish to keep denying the obvious. He'd also given up trying to hide from her. He'd never been a man to run from anything. Yet from the moment he arrived in Iron Springs, he'd been running from just about anyone and everything in sight. He supposed he sensed long before it became conscious thought that something here threatened the plan he'd made for his life.

He now knew that something was Liz…and her children…and people like Salome Halfacre and Aunt Marian. He'd never come across a community like this. He hadn't known they existed. He'd assumed every place was like Gull's Landing.

Despite Dr. Andrews's efforts, he was going to be in Iron Springs for a year. He might as well relax and enjoy himself when he could. That meant being with Liz as often as possible, admitting he liked her, taking a chance things could become even more serious than that.

They'd both tried to keep it from happening. There was nothing but pain and unhappiness ahead if they let their feelings get out of control. He imagined Liz had had enough of that already. He knew he had. He had vowed long ago that he would never again give anyone the power to hurt him.

But the force that was drawing them together was stronger than either one of them. Despite his best efforts, he couldn't control his feelings any longer. There were times when he felt so tense, so rigid, he was certain he'd break. It seemed better to bend just a little.

So he would go to the fair. He would enjoy the picnic and the roughhousing. He would stare at her legs and steal as many kisses as she would allow. He would enjoy not feeling the loneliness that had been his constant companion since his adoptive parents gave him up.

But he wouldn't bend very much. He would remember that letting himself like people meant his getting hurt.

Several hours later, Matt staggered over to Liz's blanket and collapsed. "I don't care what they want to play next, I'm not moving for at least an hour," he said between labored breaths. "I'm too old to keep up with those kids."

"I told you to decide beforehand which games you'd play. That way, they couldn't strong-arm you into everything."

"I didn't know they would come at me in relays. While I'm out there killing myself in every game, they've got reserves resting up in the shade."

Josh Worsley wasn't one of those sitting in the shade. He was home, not feeling well.

"You can't give up now," Ethan said, trotting over to where Liz had spread their blanket in the shade of an oak near the edge of the lake. "We have to defend the honor of the adults in volleyball."

"I'm not moving," Matt insisted.

"I'm still going."

"You spend every day climbing up and down that mountain. I spend it sitting in a chair. I'm out of shape."

"You can't give up. They'll think we're sissies."

"They're welcome to think anything they want as long as I don't have to get up off this blanket."

"We don't have anybody else."

"Ask Amos," Liz suggested.

"He said he can't leave the hotel," Ethan said.

"Set the kids on him," Matt offered. "They'll drag him out of his lair."

"Get Naomi," Liz suggested. "If she plays, Amos will, too."

"What you ought to do is get Salome," Matt said. "She'll kill them."

"She broke three nails last year," Liz told him. "She refuses to come anywhere near a volleyball."

"Forfeit," Matt said as he rolled onto his stomach. "Then we can all get some rest."

Liz giggled inwardly as she stared at Matt spread inelegantly at her feet. If she'd only thought to lay her picnic on a sheet, Salome could have fulfilled her wish to see Matt spread out on a sheet. Liz had to admit he did look delicious. His shirt clung to his back and arms, revealing muscles Matt swore he didn't have. Tight shorts delineated his rounded behind and powerful thighs. Muscled calves tapered down to slim ankles and trim feet. Even out of breath, he looked like a minor god.

"Why don't you take a nap?" she suggested. She was tired of games. She wanted some time alone with Matt. "I'll keep everybody away."

Matt rolled up on his elbow with a sudden display of energy. "I'm not that tired. I just wanted to spend some time with you." He pulled her down next to him.

"Matt, stop it. Everybody will see us."

She sat up, flustered. She wanted to know if he liked her. And if so, how much. But she wasn't prepared to start necking with him in public, especially not rolling around on a blanket in full view of the whole town. She wouldn't put it past Josie Woodhouse to demand she stop making a public spectacle of herself.

Matt started to trace a pattern on the skin of her leg just above her knee. "Nobody will see us."

Liz moved her leg. "Don't let appearances fool you. At least half the gazes in Iron Springs are on us at this moment."

Matt sat up and looked about him. The tents containing the crafts had been set up across from the hotel on the open lawn that ran from the road down to the shore of the lake. Most of the tents were close to the road and the hotel, where guests retreated every hour or so for shade and liquid refreshment. The rest of the lawn had been set off for games. Liz had spread her blanket under trees at an angle from the hotel, but they were still in view of anyone who wished to see them.

Matt came to his knees, held out his hand to her. "Then let's go for a walk in the woods."

"I can't leave the children."

"Of course you can. They're being watched by the other half of the people in Iron Springs."

"We might as well hang a sign around our necks saying Going Necking. Back In An Hour."

"It works for me."

"But not for me. You get to leave Iron Springs. I have to live here."

"We can both run away."

"Don't be silly. I don't want to run away."

Matt looked directly at her, no grinning, no kidding. "I thought you invited me to this fair so we could have a chance to talk. I'm beginning to think you only wanted someone to entertain your kids."

That was coming to the point with a vengeance. She hadn't been nearly so clever as she thought.

"I did. But we can talk without hiding in the woods."

"Then at least let's walk. We won't be such easy targets." They got to their feet. "I don't know how you stand it here. I couldn't, knowing dozens of people were looking over my shoulder, ready to gossip and whisper about every move I made."

"Most of it is friendly, even protective."

"So you told me, but I'd rather take care of myself by myself."

"So you told *me*."

Things weren't getting off to a good start at all. Already they were arguing over one of the fundamental differences between them. It only pointed to the fact they would never want the same thing.

"When you invited me to the fair, did you think one of us

would be so overcome with passion that we'd need the entire town as a chaperon?'' Matt asked.

"I have to admit I wasn't thinking about the town at all,'' she replied. "I just wanted to talk. I couldn't stand us avoiding each other all the time.''

They ambled along side by side, their shoulders occasionally brushing as they tried to stay on the path. The sun had long ago dried the dew. Matt picked stalks of grass and stripped the layers one by one. She fiddled with the collar of her blouse or readjusted her straw hat.

"We could have talked at the house,'' Matt said.

"And have Ben or Rebecca interrupt us every five minutes?''

"We could have talked after they went to bed.''

"Maybe I did want the protection of daylight, open spaces, people watching.''

Matt turned. "Do you distrust me that much?''

"I don't distrust you. But after you spent the whole week hiding in your room, I had to do something to draw you out. Nothing else came to mind.''

"Did you care that much?''

Now he was shifting the burden of confession onto her. Well, she'd already confessed in so many words.

"It made me very uncomfortable to be living in the same house with someone who was avoiding me,'' she said, sidestepping a direct answer to his question. "I'd rather bring the problem out in the open, put a name on it.''

"That's not our problem.''

"What do you mean?''

"We know what the problem is.''

"In a way,'' she temporized. "I mean, I don't know what your feelings are.''

"Do you know what yours are?''

She stopped and turned to face him. She had to shade her eyes from the afternoon sun as she looked up into his face. "Yes. I like you. I tried not to because I knew it was pointless. I tried to use all the things we've argued over to convince myself I couldn't possibly care about you, but it didn't work. Besides, you like my children. What woman could resist that?''

He didn't move for a moment, just looked down at her with his big brown eyes. Why did she find them so fascinating? They were an ordinary brown—not honey or whiskey colored—but they glowed with a warmth that reached out and wrapped itself around her. No wonder his patients wouldn't go to anyone else.

''What if I don't like you?''

''Not even a little bit?''

''Not even that much.''

She turned away. She didn't believe him, but the thought he didn't return as least a small portion of her regard hurt. ''That would simplify things,'' she said, looking out over the small lake.

''Would you prefer it?''

She'd never thought to ask herself that question. Would she prefer an impossible love to a comfortable indifference? She'd no sooner framed the question in her mind than she knew the answer. She turned back to Matt.

''It may sound like a terribly overused cliché, but I'd rather have loved and lost than never have been loved at all.''

He took her by the arm, and they resumed their walk around the lake.

''I never wanted anyone to love me,'' he said after they'd gone a short distance, ''not even like me very much.''

''But that's awful.'' She tried to turn and face him, but he forced her to keep walking.

''I didn't believe in love, at least as far as I was concerned. I didn't want it. It would just get in the way.''

''It doesn't have to.''

''It always does. It makes people do things they don't want to do to make other people happy. They end up with something neither of them wanted.''

''You don't have a very high opinion of mankind, do you?''

''No.''

''Then why did you become a doctor?''

"I wanted to become rich."

"I can't believe that's the only reason. Didn't you want to help people?"

"Yes."

"See, you—"

He stopped abruptly, swung her around to face him. "Don't try to make me out to be better than I am."

"What are you trying to tell me, Matt?"

"I'm not the kind of man you want. I want to be a good doctor—no, I want to be the best—but I have laid out very specific goals for my career. I don't mean to let anything get in the way of my reaching them."

She turned and started walking again. It was a moment before Matt followed. They had reached the far side of the lake and began to circle behind it. The path wound under trees and among small boulders that had tumbled down the mountain eons ago.

"Okay, so you're a clear-eyed pragmatist with no intention of letting your career plans be altered by so much as a single degree," she said. "You still haven't told me whether your heart—and you do have a heart despite your efforts to deny it—has slipped the leash long enough to feel something for once."

He turned her around and pulled her to him. A patch of bull rushes shielded them from view.

"Are you asking me if I like you?"

"I know it's a shocking thing for a bare-legged girl from a small Southern town to ask a sophisticated career man like you, but yes, that's exactly what I'm asking."

His answer wasn't at all what she expected.

Chapter Fourteen

Liz suddenly found herself in Matt's arms being kissed in the most satisfyingly ruthless manner. There was nothing gentle or loverlike about it. His arms had closed around her like steel bands, and his mouth roughly took hers.

He suddenly let her go and stepped back. He looked like a wild man, confused, angry, maybe even frightened by the things that were happening inside him. "Does that answer your question?"

Liz knew it wasn't nice to feel triumphant, but she couldn't help it. It thrilled her to know she had managed to shake this stubborn man so profoundly.

"I think it raises more questions than it answers," she finally managed to say. She touched her lips with the back of her hand. It was a reflex action. She had to touch them to make certain what she thought happened was real.

"I'm leaving—you're staying," Matt said. "We've always known there couldn't be anything permanent between us. That leaves only one question that needs answering."

A choking sensation made it difficult for her to speak.

Maybe he was good at letting himself be whiplashed by conflicting emotions. She wasn't. Her marriage to David had scarred every part of her psyche. She could feel the pain of every tiny rebuff.

"What?" she finally managed to ask.

"Can we live and work together and keep it from growing any stronger?"

"Can you?"

"Yes."

He said it so quickly, so decisively, she wondered if he was trying to convince himself, as well as her. He had always controlled his emotions, had never let them control him. But he'd let go just a moment ago. Would he let go again?

Despite his appearance of control, she felt certain he was as unsure as she. She wasn't a woman of the world, but no one in firm control of his feelings kissed like Matt had just kissed her. That was the kiss of a man who'd been shaken to his foundations, who felt an incredible passion he was fighting with an equally fierce passion. He was on the edge. How long could he hang on?

But if he didn't manage to hang on, could she control her feeling for him? If not, could she let him go?

Liz didn't know the answer to that. She hadn't yet fully come to terms with her feelings for Matt. They were too new. She'd had even less time to figure out how they might affect her life. Her children's lives.

"I don't know if I can do that. I'm not even sure I want to try," she said.

"Where does that leave us?"

"At opposite poles, where we've always been."

He reached out and took her hand. "But you like me."

"Yes."

"And I like you."

"So it seems."

"That doesn't sound too opposite to me." He took hold of her other hand and pulled her toward him until she leaned against him. "Let's not think beyond that."

"I don't understand."

"We can go on liking each other. No more than that."

He was asking her to enjoy the moment, take what they could and not regret the rest. It sounded like something David would say but with one crucial difference. Matt wasn't making any promises. He wasn't expecting any. "I'll have to think it over."

"Is it okay to lobby for my point of view?"

"It depends on what you had in mind."

"I promise it won't hurt."

He kissed her gently this time. He teased her lips, brushing them with his own, tickling them with the tip of his tongue, nibbling, taking her lower lip between his teeth and pulling gently. A wildly irreverent thought crossed her mind. She wanted to ask him if medical schools had special classes to teach doctors the most sensitive and erogenous parts of the body. He certainly had found her combination in one try.

Though his hands barely touched her shoulders, her entire body responded to his touch. She reached out, settled her hands on his waist. She resisted the urge to pull him close, to press her body against his. She was hanging on to her self-control by a thread. She was certain that would break it.

Despite his promises, she wasn't sure this might not hurt more than outright rejection. Yet she couldn't summon up the will to push him away. She was enjoying it too much.

"Mama! Mama!"

Rebecca's frightened voice cut through the fog that clogged Liz's thoughts. She wrenched herself out of the nearly hypnotic trance to see her daughter running toward them.

"Come quick!" Rebecca called. "It's Ben. He's been sick all over everywhere."

Maybe it was the heightened emotion; maybe it was that her nerves were on edge. Liz panicked. She started running as fast as she could. As she rounded the far edge of the lake, the playing field came into view. A knot of people had gathered around someone she couldn't see. She couldn't think of anything but getting to Ben. He had to be all right.

Matt reached Ben before she did.

"Move back," he ordered. "Give me some room."

Ben lay on his side, his knees pulled up, his hands on his stomach, tears in his eyes. He had ruined his clothes.

"Mama," he cried when he saw her. He reached out to her, but Matt motioned her back. It nearly killed her not to grab him up in her arms, but she knew it was more important that Matt examine him.

"I think he just played too hard on a full stomach," Matt said as he straightened up. "We'll take him home and put him to bed."

Ben grabbed hold of his mother and held on tight, but when it came time to pick him up and carry him back to the house, Liz found she was still weak from shock.

"I'll carry him," Matt said.

Before Liz could object, Matt had scooped up the boy and started from the field. She had all she could do to gather up Ben's discarded hat and shirt and hurry after him.

"Are you sure he's all right?" she asked at least half a dozen times before they reached the house.

"I'm certain," Matt reassured her. "But I'll sit with him awhile just to make sure."

It didn't take long to get Ben cleaned up, in his pajamas and in bed. He wasn't satisfied until he had Matt on one side and his mother on the other. Rebecca nestled close to her mother, uneasy as long as there was something wrong in her family.

"Tummy hurts," he said.

"It usually does when you make a pig of yourself over hot dogs." Matt talked and teased until Ben was grinning.

Liz couldn't help but think Matt was a great fool for cutting himself off from people. He'd make a great father. If he'd just open his eyes, he'd see that. Ben and Rebecca adored him. He could already do more with Ben than she could. Most important, he didn't do any of it out of duty. He was genuinely concerned about them.

The thought occurred to her that this was the kind of family relationship she'd hoped to have with David. She'd dreamed of the two of them watching over their children, tending to their cuts and bruises, consoling them when the hurts were deeper and harder to reach. She'd pictured him sitting across the bed where Matt sat, comforting Ben, making him forget that he hurt.

But that dream was dead, and Matt would have her believe her dreams about him would one day be just as dead. Yet Liz couldn't believe he was the kind of person he said he wanted to be. She didn't know what forces had shaped him, what had made him resist all the best parts of life, but she was certain he would realize his mistake if she just gave him time.

For a man like Matt Dennis, she had all the time in the world.

"There can't be any doubt," Matt said to Mr. and Mrs. Worsley. "I had them run all the tests twice. Josh has leukemia."

He could tell from the blank looks on their faces they hadn't understood the full impact of what he'd just said. Maybe they didn't know much about the disease, but apparently Josh did.

"Am I going to die?"

Leave it to a child to go straight to the heart of the matter. There would be no beating around the bush, no avoiding the question. Josh had already asked it.

"I hope not, but it's a very serious disease. It wouldn't be fair to tell you anything else."

"But there is a cure?" his mother asked.

"There is a treatment," Matt said. "We don't have anything that's a one hundred percent effective cure for cancer."

That struck her like a blow. Now both parents understood that their precious son could very well be taken from them before he reached his tenth birthday.

"What is it? We'll do anything you say."

"He must go to Charlottesville every two weeks for treatment."

"Why can't you do them here?"

"The treatments are too specialized, the equipment too expensive, the procedures too complicated and dangerous. There are specialists in Charlottesville, men who do this all the time, who know exactly what to do for Josh.''

''You're a doctor. You ought to know that.''

How could he explain to parents—especially when they'd just been told their only child had a potentially fatal disease—that doctors were not miracle workers. Or that in this day of specialization, no doctor could know all there was to know about every disease and its treatment.

''I do. But as I just said, we don't have the equipment.''

''Can't you go with us?'' Mrs. Worsley asked.

Refusal was on the tip of his tongue. There was nothing he could do. He'd probably be in the way. Some of the doctors might think his presence indicated a lack of confidence in them. He would have to cancel a full day's appointments. That would throw him behind, irritate other patients.

They didn't really need him. He could give them more maps, building diagrams, everything they needed to get in and out of the hospital complex with a minimum of fuss. But that wasn't the reason she asked. She asked because she and her husband needed someone they could trust, a friendly face who understood what was happening and could answer their questions, allay their fears.

''Do you want me to go with you?'' Matt asked Josh.

The boy nodded. He was trying to be brave, but Matt could see the fear in his eyes. He couldn't imagine what it was like to be told you might die. Growing up, he'd been certain nobody's life could be as bad as his own, that he was the most cursed kid in the whole world. He hadn't had any sympathy to waste on anyone else.

But he'd never faced death. Next to that, everything else was easy.

''I'll be happy to go,'' Matt said, giving Josh's knee a squeeze. ''After all the tests are done, I'll show you where the Virginia Cavaliers play football. They're not quite the Redskins, but they're not too shabby.''

That was a fortunate idea. It started Josh on an exhaustive recap of the Cavaliers' past season and their prospects for the coming year. Matt decided he'd have to see if he could talk one of the coaching staff into giving Josh the tour. This child knew a hundred times more about Virginia football than Matt ever had.

There was no time lapse between the knock and Salome's sticking her head inside Liz's office. Her chosen color for today was fuchsia. It looked particularly terrible, but no one could persuade her not to wear it.

"Somebody to see Beefcake," Salome said, arching an eyebrow to expose eye shadow so vivid it made Liz think of vampires and other bloodsucking creatures.

"Why tell me? Tell Matt."

"He's out on a call."

"Then let them wait."

"It's a she."

"Okay, then let *her* wait."

"She wants to wait in here with you."

"Salome, I've got a stack of work that—"

Liz's protest was wasted. Salome had disappeared. Liz didn't know whether to get up and lock her door or try to run interference in the waiting room. Or come back later. She couldn't imagine who it might be. Matt didn't know any woman in Iron Springs but his patients. From what he'd told her, none of his friends from Charlottesville would dare venture this far into the wilderness. She wouldn't be surprised to find they thought panthers still lurked behind trees.

A knock sounded at the door. Before Liz could say "Come in," an expensively dressed woman entered the office.

"Hello, I'm Georgia Allen," she announced with a distinctly Midwestern accent. "I hope you don't mind if I wait in your office, but I couldn't possibly wait in the same room with a woman who makes me look pale by comparison." She smiled in a friendly manner. "Besides, we clash."

Georgia Allen was striking rather than beautiful. Her figure wasn't out of the ordinary. Her clothes were understated and severely tailored. But every inch of her had been styled, airbrushed, toned and dressed to make a statement that here was

a successful female executive. All this was underpinned by
an easy confidence and an appealing femininity that made
Liz feel quite insignificant by comparison.

Georgia held out her hand. Her handshake was businesslike
but friendly. Liz felt immediately at ease.

"I know you must have work to do," Georgia said. "I'll
sit quietly."

"That's okay," Liz said. "I'm glad to finally meet one of
Matthew's friends."

Georgia laughed. "Do you call him that?"

"What?"

"Matthew."

"Why?"

"It's not his name. His mother christened him Matt."

Liz didn't know why Matt hadn't corrected her. She'd just
assumed Matthew was his Christian name.

"But I guess this is a Matthew kind of town."

Liz knew what Georgia meant. She wasn't sure it was a
compliment.

"I could let you wait in Matt's office if you'd rather."

"I'd rather stay here if you don't mind. All that stuff in a
doctor's office make me nervous."

Liz could hardly imagine anyone this relaxed and confident
ever being nervous.

Georgia sat down and crossed her slim legs. "I couldn't
believe it when I heard that that committee had sent Matt
here. He must hate it."

Clearly Georgia wasn't impressed with Iron Springs. But
then neither was Matt.

"Sorry," Georgia said without appearing embarrassed. "I
shouldn't talk about your town like that, but I know Matt."

"He makes no secret that he had hoped to be reassigned,
but it seems he's going to be with us for a year. We're delighted. He's an excellent doctor."

"He's brilliant," Georgia said. "He's practically a genius.
He should be working with a specialist right now. He's going
to be a great doctor."

She talked directly at Liz, her gaze focused and direct. Yet there was nothing aggressive about her. You might hate what she was saying, but you liked her. She reminded Liz of Matt in that regard. Maybe that's why they were such good friends.

Liz could hardly believe the feeling of jealousy that suddenly flooded through her. This was ridiculous. Matt had hardly mentioned this woman. She couldn't be important in his life. Liz might have believed that before she saw Georgia. It wasn't so easy now.

"He did tell me he wanted to become a surgeon."

"I've known Matt since we were undergraduates," Georgia said. "We've spent hours talking about our plans. He had everything mapped out, doctors he wanted to study with, hospitals he wanted to work in. Then Reichenbach decided he needed to learn how to deal with people."

"I think that's important."

"It would be for most people, but not necessarily for a man of Matt's gifts. He should be spending his time improving his skills, gaining experience, building a reputation. He'll have a clinic of his own someday. People will come to him. He'll see them for five minutes—he'll have staff to do the in-depth interviews—then he'll do the surgery. They'll get well and think he's a genius. There's no need for anybody to know what he looks like."

As if any woman could forget Matt!

"I'm afraid I don't agree with you or Matt on that score," Liz said. "What brings you to this part of the world?" If Georgia was so infatuated with Matt, she wondered why she hadn't written, called or visited him before now.

"I help executives deal with stress. I have several unwinding at a retreat between here and Charlottesville. I couldn't be this close without getting Matt to check them out." Her smile was genuine.

She didn't sound very loverlike to Liz, but then neither did Matt. Maybe career people were all different from her.

"Matt never mentions his friends. He hasn't told me anything about you."

"There's no reason. We probably don't see each other more than twice a year. Building my career takes all my time.

By the time I'm established enough to have a little free time, who knows where we'll be.''

"You'll probably be worried about picking out colleges for your children.''

Georgia directed a look at Liz that she found rather daunting, like she'd inadvertently strayed onto forbidden ground.

"My work doesn't leave me time for a husband or children. Matt and I feel exactly the same about that.''

Despite what Matt and Georgia may have decided all those years ago, Liz knew Matt didn't feel that way anymore. He couldn't treat Ben and Rebecca the way he did. He might not know it yet, but Liz did.

She wouldn't let him be lured back into that cold, cynical attitude. She had nothing against Georgia Allen—she seemed like a nice person—but she was nothing like Matt. Liz wouldn't allow either of them to make the mistake of thinking he was.

Liz's thoughts skidded to an abrupt stop. She guessed she now had the answer to at least one question. There was no doubt that she'd fallen in love with Matt. Otherwise, she wouldn't be intending to fight Georgia Allen for his soul. It sounded rather melodramatic when stated that way, but that's what it was.

Matt had a sweet, warm, giving soul. Terrible things must have happened to make him withdraw into himself, to think that people were cruel and unfeeling, to want to be so successful he could strike back at them. He thought he was beyond emotion, beyond feeling. He had just built a shell around himself. Iron Springs had begun to dissolve that shell. Liz had every intention of seeing that it was completely gone by Christmas.

Matt hadn't been out of Iron Springs an hour before he knew leaving with Georgia was a mistake. It wasn't that he didn't like her or find her attractive anymore. It wasn't that they couldn't have fun together. But Georgia thought Matt was the same person she'd known in college. So had he. Now he realized he had changed.

"You should see this one guy," Georgia was saying as they drove up the valley toward Middleburg. "He has an anxiety attack every time I take away his portable phone. He's certain his company is going to fire him and he won't know about it."

"He's probably got two kids in college, a huge mortgage and a credit-card balance the size of the national debt," Matt said.

"Not to mention a wife with a penchant for emeralds and winters in the Caribbean."

Matt couldn't imagine Liz in emeralds. But Liz spread out on a hot Caribbean beach was an image he found hard to forget.

He looked out the window at the Shenandoah River threading its lazy way through the valley. Huge green fields populated by grazing cows bordered the highway. Large white houses or brick mansions nestled placidly in groves of hundred-year-old trees. Like protective barriers, the mountains rose in the distance on both sides of the valley.

It was serene and beautiful despite the cars bulleting down I-81. He actually liked it now, thought fondly of the ambling flow of life. Nobody in Iron Springs ever got stressed out.

"That's all the more reason to stay single," Georgia said, interrupting his thoughts. "When I get home, I can put my feet up—or run out and howl if I like. There's nobody to tell me I've got to cut an important meeting short because of a soccer game or to get angry because I forgot an anniversary dinner."

"Don't you get lonely sometimes?"

"No. I have all the dates I want."

"I don't mean dates," Matt said. "I mean family."

"No. I told you about my family."

He'd forgotten. "What about friends?"

"I have more than I have time for."

"You can't have more than two. You've had a different job practically every year. You've had more addresses than an army brat."

"And it's gotten me right where I want to be. I've paid all

my college debts and I'm making more than two hundred thousand dollars a year. I thought you wanted to make even more than that.''

"I do. Watch the road.'' Georgia was as bad as Salome about looking at her passenger when she was talking.

"I know being here is a great disappointment, but don't let it get you down. You've got a great future. Nothing can hold you back.''

But that wasn't what he was talking about. He hadn't changed his mind about what he wanted to do. But living in Iron Springs these past months had changed something in him, something more than falling halfway in love with Liz.

Just admitting that to himself was a shock. He didn't want to fall in love with anyone, not even halfway. It always meant complications.

But he *did* want to like people, and he wanted them to like him.

He'd never cared before. He didn't know why he should have started to care now. He just knew he had. He would miss Ben and Rebecca when he left next year. Hell, he'd miss them if he left now. It would be a hundred times worse by next summer. He'd miss a lot of other people, too. He'd never find another receptionist who had the nerve to wear fluorescent lipstick and call him Beefcake.

And of course he'd miss Liz. She had gotten firmly under his skin. Pretending did no good. He would leave something very important behind when he left Iron Springs, and Liz was a great part of it.

"You've got to do spectacular checkups on my stressed-out CEOs,'' Georgia said. "I want to know if the slightest thing is wrong with them. I've never had one go bad on me yet. It would ruin my reputation if one did now.''

"I'll do the best I can,'' Matt said. "What happened to your regular physician?''

"He had a heart attack. His partner was all set to take over, but I knew you were in the area so I insisted we bring you in.''

"But I'm only a consultant.''

"That's what it says on the paper, but you'll be doing the real work."

"Does he know?"

"Sure. He doesn't care."

"But he'll get the blame if I do anything wrong."

"Nobody will. And after you're done, we can go someplace nice for dinner. I know just the spot. And after that…well, tomorrow's Sunday. I have this great view of the mountain and a waterfall from my window. I can't wait for you to see it."

Matt should have known Georgia would expect him to spend the night. He always had when their schedules allowed. He'd even anticipated it when he found her in Liz's office. After several weeks of enforced celibacy, his body was screaming for physical release. But he also knew that he wasn't going to find that release with Georgia.

Sexual release in itself was no longer enough. He wanted something more. He wasn't sure what that was. Nothing had been what he'd wanted or expected since he arrived in Iron Springs. Someone had changed the rules without warning. He was growing more and more certain that someone was Liz Rawlins.

Chapter Fifteen

"He's sick all the time," Mae Worsley was saying. "He doesn't complain much, but I can tell. He hurts, too, in his joints. He says they near 'bout kill him sometimes."

Josh lay in a big four-poster bed, his normally bright eyes dulled with pain. Despite the heat, he lay under a handmade quilt. The air-conditioning unit in the window kept the temperature in the upstairs room relatively cool, but it was under the eaves. Matt doubted even the branches of a huge black walnut tree could keep out the heat of the summer sun.

Josh had covered the walls with pictures of his favorite Redskin players. Matt figured he must have cut up every issue of *Sports Illustrated* for the past ten years.

"Have you taken the painkillers I prescribed?" Matt asked Josh.

The boy nodded his head.

"He don't complain no matter what I give him," his mother said. "There's times I give him more than it says, but it don't do no good. Now he's started spitting up his dinner. How's he going to get well if he don't keep nothing down?"

"I can give him something to settle his stomach," Matt said.

"It's not just his stomach, Doctor," Mae said. "It's everything. Seems like every day he wakes up there's something else wrong with him. Do you think the treatments are working?"

"It's too soon to tell."

"How long before we'll know something?"

"I can't say. Each case is different." Mae was no more anxious than Matt to see signs the chemotherapy was working. If it didn't, the only other choice was a bone-marrow transplant.

Matt examined Josh carefully but found nothing he could do. Everything that was wrong stemmed directly from the leukemia or the chemotherapy. All Matt could do was try to make the boy more comfortable.

He wrote out a couple of prescriptions. "Have these filled and follow the instructions carefully. Don't overdose him."

"But he moans so pitifully."

"Still, don't do it."

"I can't help myself," Mae said. "I can't just sit here listening to him cry and do nothing. I'm his mother. I'm supposed to be able to make him feel better. Could you sit here and listen to your child crying from pain and not do something for him?"

Matt thought of Ben the night he threw up. It had been hard to sit by his side, doing nothing even though he knew the discomfort would soon go away. How much worse must the Worsleys feel having to watch their son suffer terrible pain, knowing he might not get better?

"I don't know," Matt answered truthfully. "I wish there was something more I could do."

"You've done all you know how to do," Mr. Worsley said. "Nobody's expecting you to work miracles."

But Matt could see that's exactly what they were hoping for. "I'll call the hospital first thing tomorrow," Matt said.

He knew his call wouldn't make any difference, but it would make Josh's parents feel better.

Matt wondered who took care of the farm. With chemotherapy treatments, they were away for days at a time. Maybe
weeks if Josh reacted badly. He didn't know much about
farms, but he did know you couldn't just walk off and expect
it to take care of itself.

"Who takes care of things while you're away?"

Mr. Worsley's face relaxed for the first time since Matt
had met him. "We got kin, Doctor. They'll see to everything
as long as need be."

"They've been here ever since Josh took sick," Mae said,
"cooking, cleaning and doing all the outside work so me and
Addison could sit with Josh. They know he's all we got."

But they had so much more. Strange how everybody in
Iron Springs took it for granted. They shouldn't.

Liz smelled beer on his breath, smoke in his clothes.
"You've been drinking."

She shouldn't have said anything. He wasn't drunk. Besides, it wasn't her business. It was just the surprise. Matt
had never drunk anything before, at least not to her knowledge.

He gave her a look she hadn't seen in a long time, the one
that said she was sticking her nose into things that didn't
concern her.

"Sorry, I shouldn't have said anything. It's just so unexpected. Did you have an emergency? The children waited up
for you."

He'd left the house after dinner to see Josh Worsley. She'd
expected him back hours ago. He had become part of Ben's
and Rebecca's bedtime rituals. She'd only gotten Ben to sleep
by promising Matt would come tell him good-night the minute he got back.

"No. I drove around for a while after I left the Worsleys.
I wanted to think. I stopped in Newmarket and had a couple
of beers while I was there."

He wasn't acting like himself. He didn't look like himself,
either. He looked mussed up. She couldn't ever remember
him looking the slightest bit rumpled.

"How is Josh doing? You were gone so long I worried he was worse."

"He's okay. There won't be any change for a while yet."

He obviously didn't want to talk about it. Probably more of his professional reticence. He still couldn't understand there was a difference between wanting to know confidential medical information and being worried about a neighbor.

"You're looking mighty pretty tonight," Matt said.

He had changed the subject, so she gave up. She didn't mind receiving compliments, and this was the first compliment she'd had since he'd gone off with Georgia Allen. He hadn't come back until the next day. She'd expected that. She hadn't expected to dislike it so much.

But almost immediately she got the feeling she might have misjudged the situation. Matt seemed almost relieved to be back. He told the kids funny stories about the people he'd met. He told her about the views of the mountain and the waterfall. He spoke of Georgia like he would a sister. Liz was an only child, so she wasn't certain how brothers and sisters past the ages of three and four acted toward one another, but her jealousy told her there was nothing loverlike in Matt's attitude toward Georgia.

She hated to admit how pleased that made her.

But something was wrong with Matt now. He wasn't acting like himself. Not even like he had at the lake.

"It's cooler on the porch. Why don't we sit out there."

This was a side of Matt she hadn't seen. She wondered if two beers were enough to cause him to let down his barriers far enough for her to get a look at the real Matt Dennis.

Prudence told her she ought to decline his invitation. Desire to be near him made her accept.

She followed him onto the porch. He removed his coat and tie, carefully folded them and laid them over the back of a chair. That was one thing the beer hadn't changed. Then he sat down in the swing and patted the place beside him.

She cocked her head, looked at him quizzically.

"I am human. I even show it on occasion."

The temptation to throw herself at him was enormous. But

she couldn't do that without letting down her protective barriers. She wasn't sure enough of her own feelings to risk that.

"That's some confession."

"You've been telling me for weeks I ought to be more human, to try to get to know people. Now when I make an attempt, you stand there looking like my third-grade teacher."

"Why start with me?"

"Why not? I like you more than anybody else in Iron Springs."

"More than Ben and Rebecca?"

She hated herself for saying that. It sounded small, but she couldn't help it. It hurt that he liked her children better than her.

"There's nothing complicated about liking children. You play with them, read them a story and that's all there is to it. It's different with adults. Even more so with women."

"We're too big to believe in fairy tales, and our games have very different rules."

"Why are you snapping at me tonight?"

"Last week you were as cold to me as a winter storm. Now you want to get cozy and you ask why I don't jump at the chance. In between, you went howling at the moon with Georgia Allen."

"Georgia has nothing to do with this. I had some thinking to do. I was still fighting getting involved, but it didn't do any good. I am involved."

"Are you sure you can tell the difference between me and Georgia? It is dark out here."

"Don't be ridiculous. You're nothing alike."

"So now I'm ridiculous. I'll bet you didn't say that to Georgia."

"You're jealous." He sounded surprised.

"No, I'm not."

"Yes, you are. You think I slept with Georgia."

"I wouldn't be out here if I did." She hadn't meant to expose herself that far, but it was too late now. "Actually I haven't thought about it at all. What you do is none of my business."

"It is when I can't think of anything I'd rather do than kiss you." He got up from the swing and started toward her. Liz felt like she was being stalked. "I bored Georgia silly. I talked about you and the kids all night. I would have come back early if I'd had enough sense to drive."

"You could have called."

"I almost did. I thought about you."

She'd missed him, too, but he didn't need to know that. "I was very busy."

"I kept thinking of what I'd like to do to you."

"Matthew Dennis! If you dared—"

"I wanted to kiss you. I wanted to hold you tight."

"I don't believe you."

"I want to do it this very minute."

She backed away. She wasn't going to be ignored for days on end, then be his plaything the minute he felt in the mood. "What makes you think I feel the same way?"

"You came out on the porch with me."

"As you correctly pointed out, it's cooler out here."

He came closer, and she backed farther away.

"You were worried about me."

"Worried about Josh. Curious as to why you were gone so long."

He kept advancing. She kept backing—around a chair, around the corner to the side porch.

"You let me kiss you at the lake."

"You're much stronger than I am."

"You kissed me back."

Matt had her backed up at the end of the porch. She had nowhere to go. He closed in on her. She felt his fingertips brush her cheek. She shivered despite the heat.

"Liz."

His voice was a hoarse whisper, heavy with desire. Liz felt an answering response surge up from somewhere deep inside her. In an instant, her whole body felt taut with the sweet ache she had denied for so long.

He brushed his fingertip across her lips. He took her face in his hands and caressed her lips with his thumbs.

"They're made for kissing and loving."

She wished she could see his eyes more clearly. The huge oaks surrounding the house blocked out the moonlight. The light from inside the house came from behind him, turning him into a dark shadow looming above her.

His voice sounded soft and sensual; his touch felt gentle and caressing. But she needed to see his eyes. Only then could she tell whether he spoke from his heart or from somewhere a bit farther south.

"I kiss and love my children every day," she replied.

His hands moved to the back of her neck, the top of her shoulders, rubbed away the tension. The feel of his fingers on her bare skin turned up the heat in a way his words couldn't. Liz felt as though she would melt, sag against him, abandon herself to him, but she fought off the desire to toss away all restraint and let herself be washed about on this sensual tide. She had given herself over to a man once before, and he had rejected her. She wasn't sure she could endure that a second time.

But Matt wasn't just any man, and his effect on her was mesmerizing.

"I wasn't talking about children," he purred. "Only a man can kiss you the way you ought to be kissed, can love you the way a woman ought to be loved."

She wasn't thinking clearly. The most irrational thoughts kept floating to the surface of her mind. The feel of his lips on her mouth sent her thoughts scattering like dry leaves before an October wind.

It was a greedy, hungry, sloppy kiss, like the kiss down by the lake. Liz abandoned any sense of restraint, any intention of merely testing the waters. She dived straight into the center of the pool and let the heat of passion wash over her.

Liz felt particularly vulnerable. Only a halter top and a thin pair of shorts kept her body from being completely open to Matt's exploring hands. The rapidity with which they roamed over every part of her made her feel no clothing would have given her enough protection tonight.

The fact that he was fully dressed didn't reduce the feeling of intimacy. Feelings, emotions, needs that had been carefully locked away tumbled forth in one wild jumble. She didn't know what she felt, what she wanted, not even what she feared. She only knew Matt had something she needed desperately, something she could not do without any longer.

She pressed herself against him. She couldn't hold back. The pressure on her breasts caused her nipples to grow hard and sensitive. She felt his erection through his clothes. She had fought with herself over this man, agonized over him. It was a relief to finally know, to admit what she wanted to do.

She felt his hands on her breasts. She knew she ought to back away, but it felt too good to stop. No one had touched her in years. Her body ached for it, longed for it. He kissed her neck, her shoulders, her ears.

Liz felt completely at the mercy of her body, her senses, the need that had gone ignored and unfulfilled for so long. Matt's mouth and hands had stoked into flame the simmering heat that had been burning deep inside her since the day he walked up on her porch.

Matt's hands slipped inside her top, and her breath caught in her throat. She had to stop him now. No matter what she felt, no matter how shrilly her body cried out for the release only Matt could provide, she couldn't let herself be seduced on her own porch.

"Matt—"

She couldn't talk when his lips covered her mouth. She tried to push his hands away, but he was so much stronger. He didn't seem to notice her feeble resistance. She had to try harder. She must.

Summoning up all her willpower, she slipped out of his arms.

"What the hell?" he muttered. He looked stunned, like he didn't understand what had just happened.

Liz felt almost too weak to stand. For a moment, she couldn't move. She just stood there, leaning against the wall, waiting for some strength to return to her muscles. She was breathing like she'd been running. "We got a little carried away," she said when she finally managed to catch her breath.

Apparently still under the sway of his passion, Matt reached out for her. "We were only kissing," he said.

She sidestepped his grasp. With the first of her returning strength, she adjusted her top to cover her breasts. "We were about to do a whole lot more than that."

The sight of her bra askew seemed to bring him back to reality. She could see a stiffening of his expression, the slow spread of chagrin as he realized what had almost happened.

"I didn't mean... I don't want you to think I always... It must have been the beer," he said in the end.

"I'd like to think a little bit of it was me."

"It was all you," he said, gradually regaining control of himself, "it always has been. It's just that I knew it couldn't work and I managed to keep my distance. The beer just loosened enough restraints so I could do what I'd been wanting to do for a long time."

"I don't have beer as an excuse. I should have known what I was doing."

"It's all right, Liz. Don't beat yourself up over it. Nothing happened."

"But I wanted it to. I know all your reasons and mine about why I shouldn't—why it can't work—but I wanted it anyway.

"It doesn't change anything, though. I want a husband, a father for my children, a man who loves me and will come home to me at night, who thinks of me before his career. I don't want an affair."

"I didn't mean to—"

"I'm not blaming you. I'm just as much at fault. I'd like for you to go up and say good-night to Ben. I'm sure he's lying awake waiting for you."

He stood there a moment, silent, immobile. He looked so unhappy she wanted to reach out and hold him in her arms.

But she didn't dare. If she so much as touched him, her will-power would vanish completely.

"I've never loved anybody in my life," he said when he finally spoke. "Nobody ever loved me. I didn't know what it feels like. I always thought I didn't want it, but we have something I don't want to lose. Yet I'm afraid of what it'll make me do. I feel like I want to run away and hide. Is that what love feels like?"

"What you're feeling is fear, panic. Something has come along that upset your carefully organized world, made you question your preconceived notions, made you start to reevaluate your goals. You can't possibly know what you feel until you stop being scared. Love will make you do things you don't want to do, but it will give you something more precious than all the careers you could ever have."

"How do you know?"

"Because I was in love once."

"But that marriage went sour."

"Not because I didn't love David enough. I just didn't pick a worthy man to love."

"How do you know it won't happen again?"

"I don't. I have to be willing to take a chance and follow my heart."

"I couldn't do that."

Liz lifted her shoulders to rid herself of the last of the tension. "Then you'll never know the greatest joy a person can experience. Now, please go tell Ben good-night before he gets out of his bed."

"We're not through with this yet," Matt said.

"Yes, we are. We never got started."

She waited without moving until he rounded the corner of the porch. She still didn't move until she heard him open the front door. She fell into a rocking chair and burst into tears.

Matt's steps as he climbed the stairs were slow and deliberate. The whole evening had been a surprise to him. He almost didn't know himself anymore. What was he doing?

What was he becoming? He wasn't sure he disapproved so much as he simply didn't understand.

That frightened him. He'd never been happy with his life, but he'd understood what he was doing and why. He'd always felt in control of his own feelings. But that wasn't true any longer, and today had shown that very clearly.

He'd always maintained that a doctor should keep an emotional distance between himself and his patients, but he'd failed entirely with Josh Worsley. It upset him that he couldn't relieve the boy's pain. He felt guilty for calling himself a doctor and being so helpless.

Then he'd had a few beers and virtually attacked Liz. Putting aside the fact she didn't deserve such treatment and he didn't want to do anything like that to someone he liked so much, he couldn't imagine what had caused him to come undone. He knew Liz didn't want casual sex. She was a one-man woman. She wanted a home, a full-time husband, all the things he either didn't want, didn't trust or didn't have time for.

What in the hell was wrong with him? He didn't want to change. Was this transformation some genetic time bomb his unknown parents had planted inside of him, or was it caused by Iron Springs and the people who lived here? Hell if he knew. He supposed it was that alien at work again.

He tiptoed into Rebecca's room without cutting on the light. She was sound asleep, a stuffed rabbit clutched to her chest. He bent over and gave her a kiss on the cheek.

It was warm and soft. She didn't move, but she smiled and something inside him went a little funny. He tiptoed out of the room. He was coming apart at the seams. He had to get to Charlottesville soon. Maybe away from Iron Springs, he could figure out what was happening to him.

Ben's room was as messy as Rebecca's was neat. Shoes, books, a train and a set of wooden blocks testified to what he'd been doing when he should have been sleeping. He was curled up on the floor, his favorite book, *The Three Billy Goats Gruff,* under his cheek. He'd gone to sleep waiting for Matt to read to him.

Matt picked Ben up as gently as he could and put him in his bed. His chubby little legs stuck out of shorty pajamas. Matt pulled a sheet over him.

"Matt?" Ben mumbled as he turned over, his eyes still closed.

"Yes, sport. It's me."

"I wanted you to read me a story." He opened one eye a tiny bit, but Matt was certain he couldn't see.

"Sorry. I got home late. We'll read it tomorrow night."

"Becca says it's her turn."

"Then we'll read two stories."

Ben smiled, closed his eye and snuggled into his pillow. "Night, Matt."

"Night, sport," Matt said. The peculiar feeling grew more intense.

"I love you," Ben murmured as he drifted off to sleep.

That did it. A man could only take so much.

Matt sat down on the bed and brushed away the first tear to roll down his cheek since he was four years old. What the hell was he supposed to do now?

Chapter Sixteen

"She says it's just indigestion," Ethan told Matt, two nights later, "but it seems a lot worse this time."

Josie Woodhouse lay in her bed, her body so twisted by pain Matt could hardly examine her.

"Have you called her doctor?" he asked Ethan.

"Yes, but Mama insisted I call you first."

"We ought to wait for Dr. Kennedy."

"He's not coming. He said to give her a double dose of her usual medicine and call him in the morning."

Matt hadn't formed a positive impression of Dr. Isaac Kennedy, but this destroyed any willingness to give him the benefit of the doubt.

"Has your mother had the physical examination I recommended?"

"No. Dr. Kennedy didn't think it was necessary."

"If she had, this could have been prevented," Matt said.

"What could have been prevented?"

"I think your mother has an ovarian cyst. We're going to have to take her to the hospital immediately. We can get an

X ray there. If it is a cyst, we'll have to operate as soon as possible.''

''Are you sure?''

''No. That's why I recommended a complete examination. That's why we're going to take an X ray. You get your car ready. I'll telephone Dr. Kennedy to meet us at the hospital.''

Several hours later, after admitting Josie to the hospital in Woodstock, Matt explained the X ray.

''There's no question,'' he told Ethan. ''It's a cyst. I'll have them set up the operation as soon as possible.''

''How soon will that be?''

''I can't say. We have to find a surgeon first.''

''Why can't you operate?''

''I'm not her doctor.''

''Dr. Kennedy isn't here. Mama wants you to do the operation.''

''You don't know a thing about me.''

''Liz told me you plan to be a surgeon, that you've been studying for years. Everybody knows you were on your way to a big hospital when you got sent here by mistake.''

''Yes, but—''

''Please do the operation. Mother's an old crab, even mean at times, but she's all I've got. I can't lose her.''

''It's not a dangerous operation. Any staff surgeon can do it.''

''So you won't do it?''

''It's not that.''

''Then what is it?''

He didn't know himself. Operating on people he didn't know was easy. It was nothing more than solving a problem. But it never occurred to him that anybody he knew would trust him with their life. That seemed downright dumb now that he thought about it, but that's what it was.

''Nothing. Tell your mother I'll be honored to do the operation.''

Matt drove the last miles between Woodstock and Iron Springs. The sun had been up for hours, the day was well under way and he hadn't had a minute's sleep. He was too tired to appreciate the clarity of the morning, the coolness of the air. He had no time to waste enjoying the panorama of mountainsides covered in a mantle of rich green or the pristine water that tumbled over rocks in the stream that ran alongside the road.

He was too busy cursing himself for breaking one of his most basic rules and becoming involved with his patients. If he'd done what he'd always done, he wouldn't have been spending several hours each evening with Josh and his family. He wouldn't have spent the whole night with Josie Woodhouse. Nor would he be driving back to his office, facing a full day of work, so tired he couldn't see straight.

He slammed on the brakes and cursed again. A buck stood in the middle of the road, imperiously staring at Matt, daring him not to slow down.

"Move, you great big lice motel!" he shouted out the window when he came to a stop. "I don't have time to admire your great rack of horns."

The buck ignored Matt. Just as Matt was about to honk his horn, a doe slipped out of the brush next to the road. Two fawns tumbled down the bank behind her. She walked across the road without looking at Matt, confident the buck would protect her. She bounded up the far bank, and the fawns scrambled up behind her. The buck gave Matt one more look, almost as if to say, "There, you stupid human, you didn't think I was standing in the middle of the road for nothing, did you?" then sprang up the bank after his family.

Matt started his car forward, but not nearly so fast this time. The oddest thing had happened. For some reason, he suddenly felt good. Almost wonderful. And it had taken a deer to make him see it.

He felt good about helping Josh and Josie. It had been emotionally draining, it had been physically exhausting, it had taken up all his spare time, but he felt good about doing it. There *was* more to being a doctor than just making people well.

People trusted him because he was a doctor. Not because

he was personally worthy of it, not even because he had done anything to deserve it. They trusted him because he'd promised to do the most important thing one human being can do for others, help preserve their lives and the lives of the people they loved.

The magnitude of that trust, the responsibility, nearly overwhelmed him. It made his goal of becoming rich and famous seem cheap and tawdry. It put him in the same category as everybody in Gull's Landing. They wanted only to put him somewhere and forget about him. He'd wanted to treat his patients like that, to use them to achieve his own ends without any concern for theirs.

The problem was he'd never learned to care about people. It didn't matter that the people of Gull's Landing didn't care about him. The problem was with him. If he didn't fix it, what the rest of the world did wouldn't matter.

But he hadn't failed. Not completely. Not yet. He did care about Josh and Josie and all the other people of Iron Springs. He really didn't mind all the work he'd done studying charts. He really didn't mind being dragged to picnics, church, even chicken dinners.

The car suddenly lurched as the left front wheel hit the narrow shoulder. Jerking his attention back to his driving, Matt pulled the car back on the road. He shivered as he looked at the yawning abyss beyond. He was exhausted. He should have rented a motel room in Woodstock and gotten some sleep. But it would throw the office into chaos if he missed a whole day. He had a full schedule of patients.

Besides, he didn't want to skip the office. These people needed him, and that was important. It was something of a surprise to realize that. He'd always thought doctors were interchangeable, that patients wouldn't care as long as they got proper care.

Josh Worsley and Josie Woodhouse had dispelled that theory. Matt still couldn't get over the fact they had turned to him. How could they trust him after only a few weeks? He'd spent his whole life distrusting people, suspecting their motives, avoiding any emotional involvement with them. Yet this little community hidden away in the mountains had turned to him, accepted him with trust from the start.

He pulled into his parking space behind the clinic, rubbed his eyes. No use trying to puzzle through it. He had work to do.

"How's Josie?" Salome asked the minute he walked in the door. She was wearing fluorescent turquoise today. It hurt Matt's tired eyes just to look at her.

"She'll have to stay at the hospital a few days," Matt said, "but she'll be as good as new in a couple of months."

"Good. She can be a pain in the behind, but I'd miss her."

"That's no way to refer to Mrs. Woodhouse," Sadie said.

"Woodhouse, Smoodhouse. She's a pretentious old bat, and you know it." Salome directed a critical gaze at Matt. "I never thought I'd say this, Beefcake, but you look like hell."

"He's worn-out," Sadie said, "what with spending a couple of hours every night with Josh and now staying up all night operating on Josie. You want me to cancel your morning appointments?"

"No. Just keep bringing me cups of black coffee."

Matt headed back to his office. He stopped at the coffee machine.

"He looks dead on his feet," he heard Sadie say.

"He's got no business seeing all these people," Salome replied. He heard the rustling of pages as she thumbed through a book, probably the appointment book. "Half these people could just as easily wait until tomorrow."

"I'll call some and see if they're willing to postpone," Sadie volunteered.

"I'll do it," Salome said. "You're such a pushover you'll end up with more appointments instead of less. They won't give me any backchat."

"You can't bully them," Sadie said.

"They bully Beefcake, wanting to see him for everything from a hangnail to a runny nose. They can damned well wait for a change. Tell him his patients from eleven to twelve-thirty canceled. That'll give him time for a nap. It kills me to see him so tired he looks almost ordinary. Hell, how am I going to get hot flashes if we work him so hard he turns ugly?"

Matt carried his coffee into his office and closed the door, a smile on his lips. He didn't know how it had happened, but the sense of community that had closed around Liz when she came back, that had closed around Josh's family when he fell ill, had now closed around him. He was no longer an outsider. He was in.

He belonged.

"Nothing's wrong, David."

"Then why did you call? You never call."

She'd waited until Matt and the kids were outside. If things went wrong, she didn't want anybody to know she'd had this conversation. "I've been thinking about what you said about letting the kids visit, but I think it would be better if you and your wife came here. The kids need time to get to know you and your wife. I know you're their father, but you have to realize you're a stranger to them. This will give them a chance to get used to you in a comfortable environment. That may not seem important to you, but they're little children. They get frightened when they're in a strange place."

Silence.

"Are you listening?"

"Yes."

"Will you do it?"

"It won't be easy to get away."

Good. She wouldn't mind if he put this off for years.

"I'll have to call you."

"Good."

"Thanks, Liz. I appreciate it."

She decided not to tell him she was following Matt's advice, that if she had her way, he'd never see his children. But Matt had said the kids needed their father, that she'd scar them emotionally if she kept them apart. If anybody would know about that, it would be Matt. She wouldn't do any favors for David. She'd do anything for her children.

* * *

The tension inside Liz had been building for the past three days ever since that evening on the porch when she'd nearly let Matt seduce her. He'd apologized, said he'd do it all over again if he got the chance, kissed her in front of the kids to prove it and headed off to work. Since then, she'd been the one to hide from him, to be relieved he spent so many nights with Josh Worsley.

But the crisis over Josie Woodhouse had turned everything around. Between visiting Josh, checking on Josie, coping with Dr. Kennedy's anger at being at fault over a missed diagnosis, and trying to catch up on his office visits, she had hardly set eyes on Matt for three days. When she did see him, he was too exhausted or preoccupied to do much more than eat and collapse into bed.

She couldn't help but wonder if he'd ceased to be interested in her, if his desire for her had burned only briefly, if her refusal to let him go any further had caused him to strike her off his list. She didn't believe he was that coldhearted, but she had to know. So she had waited up for him tonight.

He was frowning when he entered the house, but he smiled when he saw her.

"Is Josh any better?" she asked.

"I can't tell," he replied. "Everything depends on the chemotherapy. If it doesn't work, they will try a bone-marrow. But he doesn't have any brothers and sisters, so the chance of finding a match isn't good."

"What are his chances of being cured?"

"That's impossible to say." He came over to her, lifted her chin with his hand so he could see her face better. "What's worrying you?" he asked.

She didn't know how she could have thought he was insensitive or had forgotten her. Only a person who cared could have looked into her eyes and known she was worried.

"I'm worried about us."

"I thought you said there couldn't be any *us*."

"Okay, I'm worried about you and me."

"Don't. I care for you very much, but we've each set our hearts on mutually exclusive goals."

That was the confirmation Liz had wanted. Matt did care for her, but he recognized they could never have a future together. Yet the very minute she got confirmation, Liz couldn't accept it. It was impossible for her to think of living without Matt.

"I care for you very much," she said. "I really do, but I can't sleep with you just for sex. It would hurt too much."

"I understand, Liz. I don't like it, but I understand. But if you keep telling me how much you care, I'm liable to drag you up those stairs and make love to you all night long."

Liz found it difficult to believe how powerfully his words affected her. It was all she could do to keep from throwing herself into his arms.

"I think it's important to say how we feel, to get it out in the open."

"Why?"

"I need to hear you say you care for me. Even if words are all you can give me—all I can accept from you—I need that."

"I don't understand. If you don't tell me you love me, then I can pretend *you* don't. But if I know you love me, how am I supposed to stand here and keep my hands to myself?"

"Because you love me," she answered.

"That would be the very reason I couldn't do it."

"A woman would—"

"Don't tell me what a woman would do. I'm not a woman. My inclination when I see something I want is to take it. It may not be right, it may not be fair, but that's what instinct tells me to do. Do you think I could declare my undying love, then walk away to separate bedrooms? How can you do that? What are you women made of?"

His intensity frightened her a little. The only time David had ever been this wrought up, he'd hit her. But Matt was on the edge of losing control because he cared for her, because he wanted her so much he could hardly stand it. Maybe she wasn't built as much like other women as she thought. She'd like nothing better than to go upstairs with him this very minute.

But she couldn't. If a single breath of scandal reached David, he'd be down on her in a second with a court order for the children. She kept telling herself to think of the children. No matter what she wanted, no matter what her body screamed for, think of the children. And think of what it would mean to her afterward. How much greater the pain would be when he left. She wouldn't, couldn't, do that to herself.

Gradually she felt herself grow more calm, under control.

"I guess what I wanted to say was that my feelings for you are more than just sexual attraction. You are a very attractive man. I'm sure I'm not the only woman whose dreams you invade each night. But as important as that is, it's the rest of you I find so appealing. Your kindness, your thoughtfulness and your genuine caring. You're better with my children than their own father ever was. You were from that very first day. It's because you care. That's a very attractive quality, even more attractive than your beefcake backside."

"Are you trying to turn me off with flattery?"

Liz laughed even though she didn't feel much like it. "I'm saying there's something worthwhile about you that still will be worth loving when you start to look old and ugly like everyone else. Isn't there something about me that appeals to you besides my legs?"

The surprised look on his face caused her heart to plummet.

"Forget I asked that question. I was married long enough to know when a man looks at a woman, he doesn't see beyond her face and the shape of her body."

"You're wrong," Matt said. "I never thought about it before because that's all I wanted to see. But you're different."

"How?" She didn't need much. Just a crumb would do.

"You've got spunk. I don't always agree with what you do, but when you believe in something, you go after it full tilt. You've got courage, too. It wasn't easy to tackle that heart-attack case alone, but you didn't hesitate. It couldn't have been easy to leave a comfortable existence and come back here without an education or a job, especially with people like Josie hounding your every step. You haven't gone around feeling sorry for yourself. You turned down Ethan, the answer to all your problems, because you didn't love him. Not everyone can do that. It's pretty special."

It was all Liz could do to keep from crying. This was a man she could love with all her heart, and she couldn't have him. It wasn't fair of God to tease her.

"But what I admire most is the way that, in the midst of all the upheaval in your life, you've created an island of calm and security for your children. I don't say they don't miss having a father, but they are remarkably happy in spite of it."

She was crying.

"But I've got a very personal reason to think you're pretty special. I came to Iron Springs a bitter and angry man. I'd closed myself up into a tight little ball, where no one could ever get to me. You cared enough to keep prodding me until I came to my senses.

"But something more than that happened. Maybe more than you planned. Certainly more than I'd expected."

"What?" She didn't bother to brush the tears away. She didn't care. She wasn't wearing makeup anyway.

"I started to care, *really* care, for the first time in my life. I was so stupid I didn't even realize it at first. But when those tears started running down your cheeks, I knew I wanted to hold you in my arms and kiss away the sadness, protect you from anything that would cause that smile to disappear from your lips." He held his arms out to her.

Liz had made many mistakes in her life she wasn't aware of until later. This time she knew she was making a mistake but she did it anyway. She didn't care. She couldn't help herself. She walked into Matt's embrace.

Nothing in her whole life had ever felt so good as his arms around her, holding her tight, cradling her against his chest. She felt like she'd come home after a long and turbulent journey, that she could rest secure in the knowledge the man she loved so much loved her, too.

She held him tight. She wanted to absorb the feeling of her arms around him. She wanted to give herself up to being protected, shielded, cherished. She wasn't an impulsive girl this time, falling in love with a pretty face, flattered by the attention of a man who could have had any woman he wanted.

She was a woman, tried by misfortune, who could tell this time it would last.

"I didn't want to care for you," Matt said. "I didn't want to care for anybody."

"I know. I wore down your defenses with my children."

"You wore down my defenses by your stubborn refusal to let me hide behind my excuses. And your children. And your wonderfully long legs. And your cooking."

"Chauvinist!"

"Not guilty. I'll be happy to share the cooking, but I'm only good with sandwiches and the microwave. I dread to think what Rebecca would say about my fried chicken. And I'm perfectly willing to let you admire *my* wonderfully long legs. We can begin right now if you like."

Laughter bubbled up inside Liz. "You are a brazen man, and you know it wouldn't take much to make me just as bad as you."

"Let's play dare."

"How do you do that?"

"I make a dare, and you've got to top it."

"Absolutely not! You have no shame."

"Not anymore. I'll do anything it takes to keep that smile on your face."

She was certain he hadn't meant to introduce a sobering thought, but he had. He couldn't keep the smile on her face because they couldn't share a life together.

"What did I say?" he asked when her smile vanished.

"Nothing. It was a lovely thought."

"Then why are you looking like you want to cry again?"

"How can you expect me to keep smiling when you know you'll leave in less than a year and I'll stay here?"

"It doesn't have to be that way."

"Yes, it does. Everything you want is in places like New York. Going back there would make you the person you were when you came here. It would make me the woman David rejected."

"No, it wouldn't."

"You'd have to be like that to survive. And I'll never fit. I know. I tried."

"This is no way to figure out what to do," Matt said. "Both of us are too emotional. We need to wait until we have time to think about it logically."

"Nothing's going to change. You still want—"

The shrill ring of the telephone cut her off. Liz turned to answer it.

"Ignore it," Matt said.

"I can't. Somebody might be hurt."

The phone sounded shrill and insistent.

"They can call 911."

"Matt, you know you'd never forgive yourself if someone was hurt and you didn't go."

The ringing was getting on her nerves. She jerked up the receiver. "Hello." She listened a moment, then turned to Matt. "It's Josh's mother. He's screaming in pain, and she doesn't know what's wrong."

Matt didn't hesitate. "Wait up for me. We have to talk," he said as he turned and started for the door. "Tell Mae I'm on my way," he called back over his shoulder.

"He'll be there in five minutes," she told Mae Worsley. "Don't worry. Matt will fix Josh up in no time."

Liz hung up the phone. Any woman who married Matt Dennis would have to share him with his patients. Any time of the day or night. But his job wouldn't close her out as David's did. It would bring all his patients together into one tight-knit group around him. She and the children would be in the center with him. She could stand that.

She walked to the front door. She reached it in time to see

Matt turn the corner at Hannah's Drugs. The Worsleys lived about five miles out of town on the road that passed by the clinic. She felt certain no matter what troubled Josh, Matt would be able to fix it. But would he be able to fix what troubled her? What troubled them?

Could anybody fix two lives so badly broken?

Chapter Seventeen

It was past 4:00 a.m. when Liz heard Matt's car pull into the driveway. She sat up in the bed and cut on the light. She waited. She expected his knock.

"Come in."

She knew the moment he stepped through the door they weren't going to continue their conversation. He stood in the doorway, tie gone, shoes in his hand, looking straight at her. He looked so down, so defeated, she immediately feared the worst.

"Is Josh all right? He isn't dead, is he?"

It didn't seem possible, but she didn't know what else could have affected Matt so profoundly.

"He's okay now," Matt said.

"What happened?" It made her frantic to see him standing there like he didn't know where he was and didn't care.

"He was bleeding internally. We had to take him to the hospital at Woodstock. I stayed until he was feeling better. They'll send him to Charlottesville first thing this morning."

"Are you going with him?" She moved over and patted

the bed. He sat down, dropped his shoes and gripped her hands.

"No. There's nothing else I can do. Hell, I never could do anything."

"You've just spent hours taking him to the hospital, making sure he was as comfortable as possible."

Matt broke away. "I didn't become a doctor to make appointments and pass out aspirin. I did it to make people well."

Liz had never seen him with his confidence shaken. She'd never seen him vulnerable in any way.

"Here's a great kid, his parents' only child. It'll kill them to lose him, and I can't do a damned thing but take him to the hospital and hold his hand. Hell, a drunk off the street could do that much."

"That's not true," she said. "You do a great deal."

"What? Tell me one way that Josh Worsley is better off than he was the day he came to my office."

"You've identified his disease and set up treatment. You've counseled his parents, explained everything—"

"And he's not one bit better for it," Matt said, his voice rising in frustration. "He was screaming when I reached his house. Screaming! Do you know what it's like to watch an eight-year-old boy scream with pain and know there's not a damned thing you can do about it?"

This was just the kind of thing Matt had tried to protect himself against by keeping his distance. She'd talked him into letting down his barriers, into caring for his patients. He cared now, far more than she ever thought possible, and it was hurting him as badly as anything that had happened to him in Gull's Landing.

It was all her fault. "It must be very difficult," she said. "I can't imagine—"

"It makes me feel like a fraud who gives people hope, then ducks out before they realize he hasn't really given them anything."

"But you haven't ducked out. You've been to see him nearly every night."

"I spent four years in college, three years in medical school, two as an intern, three specializing. Twelve years! That ought to be enough to educate even the dumbest college freshman, but not me. I can't even fix up a kid whose greatest wish is to see a Redskins football game."

"Matt, you can't beat yourself up over this. Nobody could have done more for Josh than you did, regardless of how many years they spent in school. You have to accept the fact that you can't do everything."

"But that's just it. They expect us to do everything."

"No, they don't. Mae and Addison know there's nothing you can do."

"There ought to be. A kid like that shouldn't have to die."

Liz shivered. Matt had turned away. She touched his arm and he looked up at her. "Is he going to die?"

"I don't know."

"Is this the first time you've actually known a patient who might die?"

"Yes."

She put her arms around him, and he pulled her to him. They sat without moving for several minutes. She didn't know what to do except hold him. She couldn't imagine what it must feel like to know people put their lives in your hands and then not be able to save them. It must be a terrible feeling of helplessness, of failure. Georgia had told her about his many successes when he was a resident, but she was certain it would be the failures that stood out in his memory.

Who would be with him in the future to comfort him when one of his patients didn't make it, when a little part of him died because he felt he'd failed? Not a wife too busy with her own career to see his suffering. Not an office staff anxious to scrub up and get home when their shift ended. No, he'd be left to go through it on his own.

And it was her fault. She'd forced him to tear down his barriers, all because she thought *she* knew what was best for him. It might make him more human, but just how much could one human stand?

Matt seemed to stiffen slightly. He released her and stood. "Sorry. I guess I kind of lost it."

He had collected himself. His moment of weakness was gone. But she couldn't let him retreat into his shell blaming himself either for Josh or for reacting like a human being.

"No, you were grieving. All people have to do that, and doctors are people, no matter how much they try to deny it."

He kissed her on the mouth. "I do love you," he said. "You never fail to keep me straight."

She scrutinized his face. He didn't look devastated anymore. A moment of weakness. But he was all right now. "You don't need me or anybody else to tell you what to do. But it's nice for a woman to know her man needs her, that he has to lean on her for a change."

"I need you. Especially tonight."

Liz didn't know when she said yes. She supposed she'd said it days, even weeks before, but she couldn't force him to go back to his room tonight. He would go through this again and again, but tonight was the hardest. It was the first time.

Besides, she loved him. It would be impossible to send him away.

"Come sit next to me," she said. She put the extra pillow behind his back, and he enfolded her in his arms. She rested her head against his chest. She could hear the sound of his heart beating. She pulled his shirttail out of his pants and slid her hand inside, against his warm skin.

His heart beat a little faster.

He held her closer and kissed the top of her head. "I was afraid you'd be asleep," he said softly.

She looked up at him. "You said you wanted to talk."

He smiled. "I've changed my mind." She sat up and he kissed her, gently, lingeringly. "I decided we've been talking too much."

She rested her head on his shoulder. She could feel his hands playing over her back, the thin fabric of her pajamas a fragile barrier between them. "Take off your shirt," she said. "I want to touch you."

"Only if you let me take off your top."

"You first."

Matt pulled his shirt over his head and dropped it on the floor. Liz couldn't wait for him to remove her top before she started running her hands over his chest. She'd wanted this for so long, dreamed of it, told herself it would never happen. She couldn't get enough of touching him. She put her arms around him and absorbed his warmth. She kissed his abdomen, his chest, his nipples; she smiled to herself when she felt his heart skip a beat then race forward.

"You're so warm and soft," she murmured.

"A man's supposed to be strong and rough."

Liz tilted her face so she could look up at him. "Not my man."

"At least strong and virile."

Liz placed her hand over his groin. "I think that question's been answered."

With a growl Liz swore came all the way from his toes, Matt pushed Liz down on the bed and dived beneath her pajama top. Even before she could pull it over her head, he buried his face between her breasts. The effect on her body was so overwhelming she could barely summon the strength to take off her top and toss it aside.

Her muscles ached, became heavy with tension, which caused her to shiver despite the heat rushing through her veins. The touch of his hands on her skin—the feel of his lips on her breasts—caused her nerve ends to become so acutely sensitive her skin hurt. Need flowed through her body with the speed of a brushfire.

Matt was kissing the tops of her breasts, tracing her collarbone with the tip of his tongue, kissing her breasts again. All the while, he gently massaged her nipples. Shafts of desire shot through Liz like a wildly disorganized display of fireworks. When he touched her with his tongue, then his lips, she gasped for breath.

"You're...having...all the...fun," she managed to say.

"I'll try to do better."

"I didn't...mean that. I...want...to touch...you."

She ran her hands along his neck, his shoulders, his back. She felt the corded muscle, skin that burned to her touch. But the roughness of his jeans against her bare legs reminded her he was still wearing enough clothes to appear in public.

"You're still wearing your jeans."

He must not have heard her. He kissed the underside of her breasts, meandered down her side, began to trace designs on her stomach with his tongue. Liz decided that when it came to being a lover, an M.D. beat an M.B.A. any day. David had never done anything like this.

Matt distracted her so completely she hardly noticed when he eased her out of her pajama bottoms.

"You, too," she said. "I want to touch you."

"Not yet." He moved up to take her mouth in a deep kiss. His tongue forced its way between her teeth. She gasped. His hands began to knead her breasts. She couldn't get enough of him. Forcing her hands between their bodies, she struggled with his pants. No one but Matt would wear a belt with jeans.

He broke their kiss long enough to say, "I'll do that."

A few moments of scrambling movements, and she had the sheer pleasure of feeling his hot, bare skin next to her own. She reached for him, but he slid down her body, kissing chest, breast and belly.

"Not fair," she murmured.

"I'll explode if you touch me."

"I'm exploding already."

"It's not the same."

She sat up in the bed and turned her body completely around. He was ahead of her. They ended up nose to nose, their heads at the foot of the bed, their feet on the pillows.

"You're not going to let me touch you?"

"Not yet."

"When?"

"When you're ready."

He touched her, entered her with one finger, and heat pooled in her loins. Gently moving within her, he touched a spot that acted on her like an electric shock. Her body arched off the bed.

"What are you doing?" she gasped. Nothing like that had ever happened with David.

"Trying to give you pleasure. Did you like that?" He touched her again.

"Yes," she said when she could manage to speak.

Liz didn't know if she could wait much longer. Matt touched that spot again, and she moaned.

"Now?"

"Yes."

"Can I touch you?"

"Gently."

Liz reached out and closed her fingers around him. He felt so soft and hot. And so hard. She wondered if it was uncomfortable. He touched her on that spot again, and she squeezed him. It was pure reflex, but it forced an anguished moan from him. He pushed her hands away.

"Open for me."

She relaxed. His body became one with her own.

He kissed her long and languidly. But as the tempo of their lovemaking increased, as their bodies became slick with the heat of their passion, their kisses turned into a battle. Each one seemed driven to consume the other. Mouths, tongues, hands searched for ways to deepen and intensify the melding until Liz had no thought of anything but the waves of pure pleasure that washed over her with increasing intensity.

Finally their kisses became noisy gasps. Their bodies reached that fulfillment they'd been striving for ever since that first kiss. Liz reached the peak, let go and floated down the other side.

When her breath returned to normal, she lay nestled in the embrace of the man she loved.

Matt woke to find himself in an unfamiliar bed. It took a moment before he remembered what happened the night before. He and Liz had made love. He turned over, but the space next to him was empty. He lay back.

For a moment, he didn't know what he actually felt about that. He loved Liz, but he wasn't ready to face the consequences of what loving her meant.

He had to now. He couldn't make love to a woman, then act like nothing had happened, not with the woman he loved.

Much to his surprise, a knot somewhere inside of him seemed to loosen. He had already begun to face the consequences of loving Liz. Making love to her was just one step. Next he had to convince her that they could have a future together. Her marriage to David would have failed no matter where they lived. People could hate in small towns. They could love in big towns. Sure, things would be different, but everything in his life was different now.

He'd find a place in the suburbs where Rebecca and Ben could have a big yard. They couldn't be expected to give up kick ball. Besides, there had to be room for brothers and sisters. Matt had never wanted children before, but now he wanted them with Liz.

It hit him like a thunderclap. He hadn't used any protection last night! He'd been so caught up in his own problems, he hadn't even thought about it.

He sat up in bed and banged his head with his open palm. He was a doctor. If he couldn't remember, how could he expect anyone else to? Judas! Liz must be thinking he was the prize chump. Let his hormones get a little wrought up, and he wasn't any different from any other man hungry for a woman.

He had to talk to her.

He looked at the clock—11:18 a.m. Hell, he was hours late! He leaped out of bed but came to a halt before he opened the door. He was naked. His clothes were on the floor. He quickly put them on and eased the door open. He didn't hear any sounds. Liz must have gone to work as usual. He grabbed up the rest of his clothes and dashed upstairs.

He'd showered and shaved when he came down twenty minutes later. He found Liz's note in the middle of the kitchen table.

You were so tired I decided to let you sleep. I'll ask Salome to reschedule your morning appointments. If you're not there by noon, I'll come wake you up.
We have to talk.

Liz

They certainly did. He had a lot he wanted to tell her.

"You sure you don't want to come?" Aunt Marian asked. "You've always enjoyed the skits the drama camp puts on."

"Matt and I have some things to talk over. It'll be easier if we don't have the kids interrupting us every five minutes."

"Well, if you finish up early, come on down. I understand the last skit will make you laugh till your sides hurt."

"I'll try, but don't wait for us. And don't put up with any nonsense from Ben or Rebecca."

"They're wonderfully behaved. Considering how so many children behave, I'm proud to claim them."

Liz watched her children dance around their great-uncle as they waited for her aunt to catch up with them. It seemed incredible that everybody else was involved in such humdrum activities when she was about to face the dissolution of a dream. She wanted to shout at everybody, to tell them they couldn't carry on as usual when her world was falling apart.

But she couldn't share this with anyone. It was her own private tragedy, and it would have to stay that way.

Dinner had been the most difficult meal of her life. She'd been able to avoid Matt during the day. But she'd not only had to spend thirty consecutive minutes in the same room with him, she'd also spent half of it sitting directly across the table from him. For the children's benefit, she'd had to act like nothing had changed.

But everything had changed.

She had made love to Matt. It didn't matter why it happened or who had been most responsible. She had said she loved him and yielded up herself. Such an action implied different things to different people, but Liz had no doubt what it meant for her. Love, marriage, family, fidelity. It meant freely offering to each other what could never be demanded or taken, only given.

That meant not trapping a man because you were going to have his baby.

Liz doubted she was pregnant—she couldn't possibly know for several weeks—but she did know neither one of them had stopped to think of protection or of the consequences of not using it. Under no circumstances did she want to bring an unwanted baby into the world. There were many reasons why she and Matt couldn't go on as before. That was one of the most crucial.

She took a deep breath and walked into the house.

He smiled at her when she reentered the kitchen, and her resolve nearly disappeared. How could any woman in her right mind push such a man away? He was sweet, kind, handsome. He had a brilliant future. He loved her and her children. What more could she want?

She sighed inwardly. It was no longer a question of wants. It was a question of need—what she must have to survive, to bring her children up the way she wanted. She'd entered one marriage without knowing that. She'd tried to preserve it by compromising her principles. She wouldn't do that again.

He opened his mouth to speak. "Let me go first," she said. It was almost a plea. "If I don't, I'll forget everything I want to say."

"It sounds ominous." His expression gave the lie to his attempt to sound lighthearted.

"About last night—"

"Look, I didn't mean to take advantage of you. I—"

"I'm not blaming you. I knew what was going on. If I have to be honest—and I suppose this is the best time to be honest—I wanted it as much as you."

His expression softened. Whether from guilt or relief, she didn't try to discover. It would make no difference either way.

"But that has no bearing on the situation."

"Of course it does."

"Look, Matt, we don't want the same things out of this. I can't indulge in an affair. Setting aside what it would do to me and my children if this ever got out, it's not something I want or would ever do. I want marriage, a family, a husband who loves me and will come home every night, who'll have time for me and the children."

"I do love you."

"Are you ready for all the rest?"

"I'd rather take all this one step at a time. I haven't even gotten used to being in love yet."

"I don't see how that's possible. We skipped way ahead last night."

"I know. I—"

"It's possible I'm pregnant."

She could tell he'd already thought of the possibility. He didn't look shocked or stunned. He didn't start blaming her, but all the animation drained out of him. He seemed to turn slowly to stone.

"I'm sure I'm not, but it's possible. We weren't careful."

"That's my fault. A doctor should never do anything so stupid."

"Could you stop thinking like a doctor and for once think like a man?"

"I did last night."

"Good. You know how. Now do it again."

He looked at her with an intensity and longing that was tangible. "If I did, I'd get out of this chair, kiss you until you were breathless, then make love to you again and again."

Liz instinctively backed up behind a chair. "Maybe being a doctor is safer."

She looked at him more closely. He seemed to be having as much difficulty staying away from her as she was having keeping her distance from him. His hands gripped the table. His knuckles were white. His whole body seemed rigid to the point of pain.

"We can't go on like this," Liz said.

"Go on like what?"

"You living here, letting my children treat you like part of the family, encouraging me to feel the same way."

"Why not?"

"We started out disliking each other, but in two months we've made so much progress in the other direction we slept with each other."

"Don't make it sound cheap. I love you."

"I love you, too, far more than I thought I could love any man. Why else do you think I abandoned everything I believe and made love with you?"

"Because you knew I needed you last night more than I've ever needed anybody in my life."

"But you'll need me again, and I'll make love to you again. I'll do it myself—you won't have to talk me into it—but I can't live with that. It has nothing to do with living in Iron Springs. I couldn't do it if I were back in New York."

"I know."

"Then you'll understand when I ask you to move."

Chapter Eighteen

He didn't understand. His expression told her that immediately.

"No, I don't. Besides, there's no place for me to go."

"I talked to Josie Woodhouse. She has plenty of room in that huge house. She said you could stay with her."

"What the hell did you do that for!"

His anger surprised her. He never got angry. He always kept everything inside.

"You can't stay here."

"You could at least have talked to me first."

"What difference would it make?"

"It could make a lot, you stubborn, hardheaded woman. I love you, Liz Rawlins. I've never loved anybody in my whole life. I don't intend to let you slip away like that."

"I'm not a commodity to be captured and held until you decide to let me go. I'm a woman with feelings."

"That's what we've been talking about—feelings, yours and mine. You were the one who said we had to be honest. You can't start by denying what we feel for each other."

"I'm not denying it. I'm afraid of it."

"Hell, that's what I'm supposed to say. When did you start?"

"When I couldn't wait to get you into my bed. When I never stopped to think I could get pregnant. When I realized I wanted to have your baby more than anything in the world."

The last sentence came out as a strangled whisper, but it affected Matt more visibly than anything she'd said.

"Now do you understand?"

He shook his head.

"I'd do anything you want because I want to be with you for the rest of my life. Soon I would begin to compromise. Then I'd lie to myself. It would happen by slow degrees so I wouldn't notice it. But it would happen, and it would destroy everything we feel for each other."

"You have the advantage over me. You've been in love before. I never have, and I'm not willing to give up so easily."

"Matt, we can't agree on anything."

"We've never talked about it seriously, not from the standpoint of being in love, what we're willing to do for each other."

"I did, and it didn't work."

"You haven't done it with me."

"How will it be different with you?"

"I don't know. I haven't had a chance to find out."

"Well, you can think about it from Josie's guest bedroom."

"Can't we wait?"

"No. It won't be long before last night happens again."

"I promise to keep my distance."

"Don't you understand? I *want* to make love to you. I want your baby. But I don't want to use it to trap you into marriage."

Matt's expression told her that was an aspect of the problem he hadn't considered.

"Don't you see it wouldn't work?"

"No, I don't. I admit I don't have any answers. With all my planning, I never thought of this happening, but I'm not willing to give up. I love you. I love Ben and Rebecca. I don't know where it will lead me, but I intend to find out. No matter what, I don't mean to let you go. Some way, we're going to work it out."

It would be so easy to give in, to believe him, to have faith it would work out. Liz could almost feel herself tipping over the edge, feel her tongue forming words of capitulation. At the last minute, she drew back. She couldn't do it. She couldn't chance failure again. She didn't think she'd survive it this time. She wasn't sure her children would, either.

"You'll be here until next summer. We'll have plenty of time to think about it."

"You don't sound very hopeful." He sounded angry.

"Matt, your ambition has always been to work in a famous city hospital. I'm not leaving Iron Springs ever again. I don't see that leaves us anything to talk about."

"You're giving up too soon."

"I've already tried to think of a way out. There isn't one."

Matt rose and walked around the table. "When did you fall in love with me?" he asked. He was standing within reach. His anger had disappeared. His gaze bore into her. She looked away.

"I don't know."

He put his hand under her chin and forced her to look at him. "Are you sure?"

"I wasn't expecting it. I thought you were a coldhearted opportunist who looked at medicine as a way to gain the riches and fame you craved. Then I found you had memorized all those charts."

"Any reputable doctor would do that."

"Then there was Ben and Rebecca. You were so different with them. It was like there were two of you. But liking the one, I started to understand the other one." She grinned. "Somewhere along the way, I guess I caught a glimpse of your beefcake backside or your long legs and fell in love."

"Don't joke with me."

"There's no reason a woman can't be attracted to a man's body."

"I fell in love with your long, slim legs, but they're not the reason I don't mean to let go of you. I'll move to Josie's house, but we're going to talk. And keep on talking. We're going to date like any normal couple. We're going to figure out how we can spend the rest of our lives together. Do you understand?"

"Yes."

"I know you're not convinced, but you always said I was smart. Well if these brains are good for anything, they ought to be capable of finding a way to preserve my own happiness. I will. I promise."

He kissed her then, and her resolve nearly disappeared once again.

"I'm not going anywhere," Liz said. "I'll always be here, but I'll never change my mind."

"Never say never. I did, and look what it almost cost me."

She didn't want to say never, but it didn't do any good to ignore reality. Still, she couldn't give up hope. Matt had changed a lot already. No telling what might happen tomorrow.

"Okay, Beefcake, give me the real scoop before I start spreading malicious rumors all over town."

Salome had greeted him at the door wearing the most bilious shade of vaguely purple lipstick he'd ever seen. She followed him to the coffee machine.

"Where do you get that lipstick?" he asked, unable to contain his curiosity.

"Do you like it?" she asked, preening.

"It's the most horrible color you've ever worn. The manufacturer ought to be arrested for making it."

"It is ugly, isn't it?"

"It's hideous. Why do you wear it?"

"So you'll notice me. Now stop stalling, and tell me why you moved. Nobody's talking about anything else."

In one brief moment of suspended intelligence, Matt had

hoped the people of Iron Springs might not demand to know every detail of his move from Liz's house. He realized now how foolish he'd been.

"If I tell you the truth, will you promise not to embellish it before you repeat it?"

"Cross my heart." She crossed a chest encased in a uniform that seemed to have shrunk another size during the past week. "Now spill it."

"Wait a minute. I want Sadie here, too. I want a witness."

"Sadie!" The name was a screech that scraped its way up and down Matt's spine. "Get your tail in here on the double. Beefcake is about to spill his guts."

"Nothing quite so dramatic," Matt said.

"Considering this is the dullest summer on record, it's going to be a real headliner."

Matt groaned. Maybe he could talk Solomon Trinket into putting the moves on one of those sex-starved artists up at the hotel.

"Okay," Sadie said, coming up with coffee cup in hand. "What's the scandal?"

"No scandal," Matt said. "And I'm only going to tell you if you promise not to put Liz through the third degree when she gets here."

"I wondered why you were here early," Salome said.

"To spike your guns," Matt said. But then he had to smile. He knew Salome wouldn't say anything to hurt either one of them. "I moved out because I've decided I want to court Liz. We decided it wouldn't look very good if I were living in her house at the same time."

"Is that all?" Salome said, disgust written large on her face. "Hell, everybody in town knows you two are sweet on each other. Why do you think she broke up with Ethan?"

Matt couldn't decide whether he felt like cussing or laughing. He should have known everybody would know what was going on between him and Liz. They knew everything else.

"You got me all excited, and that's all there is?" Sadie complained.

"Sorry, but that's it," he said.

"Damn, this is real disappointing," Salome said. "I expected something that would at least last through the week. This won't even make it to lunch."

"You shouldn't be so nosy," Matt said. "Then you wouldn't be disappointed."

"That's the price you pay for living in Iron Springs," Liz said, entering through the back. They all turned. "Have they put you through the inquisition?"

"I told them we'd decided to date and thought it would be better if we weren't living in the same house."

"Which is no news at all," Salome said. "I've got some calls to make." Salome followed Sadie down the hall.

"I told them I moved because we wanted to start dating," Matt said.

"I heard."

"How about Wednesday night?"

"What about it?"

"Can we go to dinner?"

"I have to take care of the kids. I—"

"I've already spoken to your cousin. She has agreed to keep them for the evening."

"Matt, you can't—"

"Yes, I can." Matt pulled her into his office and closed the door. "I knew if I left it to you, you'd use those children as an excuse." He tried to take her in his arms, to kiss her, but she pushed him away.

"I can't take advantage of my cousin."

"You aren't. They're going out to dinner. I'm paying."

"You're paying for eight people to eat out!"

"Can you come up with a better plan?"

"Yes. We can all stay home."

"It won't work. If we don't go out, everybody will know we lied and they'll start pestering us for the real reason I moved out."

"And when we don't tell them, they'll come up with their own ideas, probably embarrassingly close to the truth."

"Your version, not mine."

"This is not a matter of versions, Matt."

"Yes, it is. Just like we don't look at the chances of our working something out for the future the same way."

"I've got a full day's work ahead of me," Liz said. "I'll never get through it if we get into this now."

"We can talk about it Wednesday night. What's your favorite restaurant?"

"We can't do this. I know how much money the county pays you, and you can't afford it."

"I have a private trust fund."

"Right, left to you by the good people of Gull's Landing."

"I hadn't thought of that. They might have paid me to leave town."

"Matt, be serious."

"I am. I want to see you. I want to be with you. I want to touch you, kiss you, hold you in my arms."

"I can't do this," Liz protested. "I'm going to my office."

"You still haven't given me an answer about Wednesday."

She opened the door. "I'll think about it," she said as she left.

He knew she meant she intended to refuse and hadn't figured out how to do it yet. But he wasn't going to give up that easily.

A knock sounded on the door, and it opened at the same time. Salome and her purplish lips appeared in the doorway. "I thought you'd want this. It just came in over the fax."

"What is it?" Matt asked.

"I don't know. I can't understand all this medical gibberish, but it's got Josh Worsley's name on it."

Matt practically snatched the paper from Salome's hand.

"What does it say?" Salome asked impatiently as he quickly read the sheet.

"Translating medical gibberish into the vernacular, it says Josh has finally had a positive result from his chemotherapy."

"Does that mean he's going to get well?"

"I can't guarantee anything, but his chances are now one hundred percent better."

Salome flashed an ear-to-ear purple smile that acted like a

needle shot to Matt's nerves. "One hundred percent sounds like a cure to me. Wait till I tell Sadie."

Matt wanted to call her back, to remind her to be cautious, but he couldn't contain his own elation. After so many problems, Josh seemed to have turned the corner. Matt was so relieved he felt like letting out a whoop.

Yet he felt a tinge of shame. He couldn't be sure whether he was more relieved for Josh or for himself. The specter of failure had hung over him for weeks. It had seeped into his thinking so thoroughly he questioned nearly every diagnosis he made. After an unbroken string of academic successes, he wasn't prepared for failure. He'd always known the possibility was there, but it had been an abstract kind of knowledge.

He would be relieved to get back to a research hospital. There would be inevitable failures—even the most successful doctors had them—but at least it wouldn't be happening to people he knew.

He left his office to tell Liz. He knew she'd be as relieved as he was.

"I want Matt," Ben whined. "I want him to read me a story."

"He can't," Liz said. "He's staying at Ethan's house now."

"Why?" Rebecca asked. "Ethan doesn't like Matt."

"I like Matt better'n Ethan," Ben said.

"That's not a nice thing to say," Liz said as she put Ben into bed and pulled the sheet over him. "Don't say it again."

"But Ethan *doesn't* like Matt, Mama," Rebecca said. "I know he doesn't."

"What makes you say that?"

"He was always trying to get between you and Matt," she said. "He always wanted us to choose him for our side."

"I want Matt," Ben stated.

So do I, Liz thought to herself. But she couldn't allow herself to think of that. She knew what she had to do. It wouldn't help anybody if she started thinking about what might have been. She'd only end up crying and upsetting the children again.

"I'm sure he'll still play kick ball with you," Liz said as she kissed her son good-night. "Maybe he'll even read you a story." He probably would. All Ben had to do was shove a book into his hands. But not a bedtime story. Liz didn't trust herself to let him back into the house. She might decide she really couldn't do without him after all.

"Now go to sleep. If you're good, I'll see if Josie will let you play in her yard." Josie had built an entire playground for the grandchildren she'd expected to have by now. Her yard had become the favorite playground for the children in Iron Springs.

Liz accompanied Rebecca to her room and waited while her daughter climbed into bed. Rebecca always went to bed without the fuss Ben created, but Liz knew her daughter was missing Matt, as well. There was something about his presence that had made their little family seem complete.

She'd been a fool to think love would make a difference. She'd also been unfair. She had expected Matt to do all the changing. She had called him stubborn, selfish and some other things she didn't want to remember. All the while, she had refused to consider changing her plans for herself and her children by even the smallest detail.

She wanted to, but she couldn't.

She couldn't expect Matt to change his plans for her if she wasn't willing to change for him. And the bottom line was that she wouldn't.

If it had to end, it would hurt less if it ended now. And it couldn't end with him in the house.

As long as she saw him across the breakfast and dinner table, as long as he played with her children and put them to bed, as long as he touched and kissed and held her and told her he loved her, she would never stop hoping some miracle would come along to make everything work out.

She'd stopped believing in miracles with David.

"Is our real daddy ever coming back?" Rebecca asked.

The question was unexpected, but Liz decided this was as

good a time as any to tell Rebecca about David's upcoming visit.

"He's coming sometime this summer."

"When?"

"I don't know yet. He said he'd call and let me know."

"Is he going to take us away?"

"No, sugar. Nobody will ever take you away from me." Rebecca hugged her mother tightly. "I want to stay with you always."

Liz hugged her back. "You will, darling. You will. But your father misses you. He wants to see you and Ben."

"Will I like him? What does he look like?"

Liz realized she didn't have a single picture of David in the house. He was nothing but an abstract idea to her children. Suddenly she thought of what Matt had said and felt guilty. She might have been greatly disappointed in David, but she had divorced him. He was out of her life. He would always be Rebecca's father. She deserved—she *needed*—a good image of him. Ben did, too.

"Yes, I think you'll like him," Liz said. David could charm anyone when he tried. "When I first saw him, I thought he was the most handsome man in the whole world."

"Even handsomer than Matt? Salome says Matt's to die for."

Liz would have to have a word with Salome. "I don't think he's as handsome as Matt, but you've got the best-looking daddy of any little girl in Iron Springs."

"Is he going to live here?"

"No. He lives in New York."

"Why?" To her children, there was nowhere else but Iron Springs. They couldn't imagine living anywhere else.

"His job is in New York," Liz explained. "So is his wife. He may soon have a new family."

"Will he bring his new family to see us?"

"I doubt it."

"Won't his new family be our family, too?"

"Yes, in a way."

"Then why can't we see them?"

"We might, but I can't tell you for sure. I don't know."

"Are we going to have any more family?"

Liz's heart slammed into her throat. For a wild moment, she thought Rebecca must somehow know she and Matt had slept together. But a moment's rational thought told her that couldn't be true.

"I'd have to get married first," Liz replied.

But she wouldn't, even though she might already be in the process of giving them a brother or a sister.

"You could marry Matt. Then we could have more family."

Life was full of irony. Everyone said children were helpless. Yet with a single sentence, they could bring a parent to her knees.

"Matt will go away soon, and we'll never see him again."

"Would he stay if you married him?"

"No."

"Why? Doesn't he like us?"

"He likes you very much, but he has something he wants to do very much. He's been training for it all his life. He wouldn't be able to do it if he stays here."

"Where's he going?"

"I don't know."

"Can't we go with him?"

Liz didn't think she could stand much more. Rebecca was asking all the questions she'd already asked and answered. Hearing them all over again only made it more painful.

"This is our home," Liz said, "where Aunt Marian and all the rest of our family live. We belong here. Matt doesn't. He has to go away."

"I don't understand."

"I'm not sure I do, either, but that's the way things are. We just have to accept it."

But could she? What a mess! All because she'd let her emotions get away from her one time too many. Well, she'd learned her lesson. She wouldn't do it again. She would keep her emotions under control if it killed her. Because if she didn't, it probably would.

Chapter Nineteen

Matt glanced over at Liz sitting stiffly in the front seat of the station wagon next to him. They were going to dinner, but it had taken him two weeks to talk her into it.

"You sure you don't have a favorite restaurant?" he asked. She'd been sulky from the moment he picked her up. You'd think she was being punished.

"I never eat out. I can't afford it."

"There's a nice buffet just off the interstate at Newmarket."

"That sounds fine."

"We could catch a movie in Harrisonburg afterward."

"I can't be out that late."

"Why? The children are staying overnight with your cousin."

"I just won't feel comfortable."

She hadn't been communicative since telling him he had to move. She told him she didn't see any point in teasing herself with impossible dreams, but he knew she wasn't dreaming at all. She'd given up.

"I have some good news I've been saving until tonight."

"Has Dr. Andrews finally managed to get you recalled to the hospital?"

"I wouldn't consider that good news. Well, yes, I would, but not the way I would have months ago."

"It would get you out of Iron Springs. What could be better news than that?"

"Your leaving with me."

"Matt, I've told you a hundred—"

"I know. You had a terrible time in New York and you won't trust anybody outside of Iron Springs ever again. That sounds as much like a crybaby as my whining about being born a bastard. And for a whole lot less reason, as I see it."

"Maybe, but that's how I feel."

Great! She wasn't going to try to defend her position. She was going to stick to it and to hell with what he said or thought or felt. It was impossible to reason with her.

"Do you want to hear my news?"

"If you want to tell me."

He'd need radar to detect any enthusiasm in her voice.

"Georgia Allen called me earlier this week."

"Correction. She has called you every day this week."

Matt smiled to himself, relieved to know the source of her pique wasn't entirely something he'd done. He suspected Salome had let Liz know every time Georgia called.

"It's good news. One of the CEOs I checked out for Georgia was so impressed I discovered a bleeding ulcer his regular physician had missed that he offered me a job."

"How wonderful for you."

"No, for us." He wished he weren't driving. He'd love to take Liz by the shoulders and shake her until she stopped acting like they were strangers going out on a blind date.

"Okay, how is Georgia's job going to affect me?"

He gripped the steering wheel to keep from saying something that would only make things worse.

"The man wants his company to have their own physician. They've got a lot of highly stressed executives who want someone to hold their hands."

"How is that going to advance your career as a surgeon?"

"It won't take all my time. I'll be on call, do routine physicals, monitor any problem cases. The rest of the time will be mine. There are several hospitals in New York I could work with."

"What about your job here?"

"They're willing to buy up my scholarship obligation. I wouldn't ever have to work in a place like Iron Springs again." He hadn't meant the words to come out exactly like that. "I mean, nobody will be able to make me go anywhere that wouldn't help my career. The company would pay me a salary, and after five years I'd be free of any obligation."

"It sounds like a great opportunity for you."

"It is. I'll miss working with Dr. Andrews, but there are lots of opportunities in New York. The company also has offices in Chicago, Houston and Seattle. I don't have to stay in one place."

"What does Georgia think about this?"

"She's the one who pushed me as a candidate for the job. They originally wanted someone older. She convinced them I was good enough to handle the job now."

"You must be very grateful to her."

"I am. Georgia's the greatest."

"I'm sure you'll be very happy together."

"I doubt I'll see her. She's a stress-management consultant. She moves all over the country with each new job."

He thought Liz turned to stare at him, but he only caught the movement out of the corner of his eye so he couldn't be sure. He didn't dare look away from the road, especially at dusk. He still hadn't gotten used to driving through these mountains.

Her stiff, stubborn silence frustrated him. "Well, say something."

"What do you want me to say?"

"That you'll love me forever, that you'll follow me anywhere, that we'll be so insanely happy we'll both forget we've been through some rough patches."

The silence didn't auger well for the kind of response he

wanted, but then he hadn't expected it. Still, he didn't know how she could complain about his being cold when she was giving a very convincing imitation of an iceberg.

He thought heat was supposed to melt ice. God only knew he'd been as hot as a Bunsen burner for the past two weeks.

"This is the perfect opportunity for us," Matt said. "I get to pursue my career. I'll be making enough money for us to put the kids in day care so you can go back and finish your degree."

"Haven't you forgotten something?" she said.

"What?"

"You haven't asked me to marry you?"

"I thought you understood...I assumed—"

"Any woman who assumes a man wants to marry her before he actually says the words is a fool."

"I want you to marry me. Will you?"

"Haven't you listened to anything I've said?"

"Of course I have."

"Then you know the answer."

"No, I don't. As you just pointed out, I've never asked the question."

"Matt, you know I can't marry you. It hurts when you won't recognize that and let me alone."

"Why?"

"I've already told you. I won't leave Iron Springs. You won't stay."

"There's nothing for me here."

"I know that, but it doesn't change the fact that everything I want is here. Besides, I won't marry a man who wants to be one of the most famous or successful men in his field. Men like that don't have time for wives and families. I've been there. I know."

"Anything else?" Much to his surprise, he was no longer nervous or frustrated. He was mad through and through.

"I won't like the wives of the men you'll be working with, women only interested in the size of their houses, the number of servants they can afford, the cost of their jewels. They

ave their husbands to eat in restaurants, or with their mis-
esses, and their children to nannies and boarding schools.''

"Anything else?"

"I think that ought to do it."

"It sure as hell does." He jammed his foot on the brake
edal. The tires squealed as the car skidded off the road and
nto the shoulder of a curve that would have scared him to
eath if he hadn't been too angry to pay attention. The car
ame to a stop that would probably give them both a serious
ase of whiplash. He slammed the gearshift into park and
rned to Liz. He grabbed her roughly by the shoulder.

"Now you listen to me, Liz Rawlins. I've never heard so
any foolish words come out of the mouth of an intelligent
oman in so little time in my whole life. When did you get
be such a mass of ignorant prejudices? To characterize all
eople who live in cities as lacking soul and conscience is
st as bigoted as my thinking everybody in Iron Springs had
red neck and descended from the same branch of the family
ee. That's just plain stupid, and I won't accept it from you."

"You don't have any choice. I—"

"You're a coward. Did you know that? I used to think you
ere courageous, but I was dead wrong. You're a certified,
rade-A,   quivering-like-jelly,   stick-your-head-in-the-sand
oward. Josh Worsley has more courage in his little finger
an you have in your whole body. Ben and Rebecca, too.
ou should be ashamed to call yourself their mother. No
onder David wants them back. You'll have them growing
p afraid to take a deep breath."

It was a dangerous gamble. He had hit her where she was
ost vulnerable, but she wasn't an iceberg ignoring him any
nger. She was giving a riveting imitation of a snarling wild-
at.

"Don't you ever accuse me of not being a good mother to
y children," she cried, trying to break free from his hold.
There's nothing I wouldn't do for them."

"Then let them see their father."

She tried to hit him, but he grabbed her wrist.

"Don't you tell me what to do with my children."

"Let them have a normal life, with all its risks and plea sures. Let yourself have the same thing."

"I suppose you mean by that I ought to marry you, tha being your wife would be such a pleasure I could forget ev erything terrible that might happen."

"Dammit, Liz, I'm talking about two people who lov each other wanting to be together for the rest of their lives.

"That sounds strange coming from a man who wanted t be a good doctor but wanted nothing to do with his patients.

"Who was convinced I was wrong, that I ought to giv people a chance?"

"Getting to know your patients isn't the same as gettin married."

"It's more of a risk than you're willing to take."

"I divorced David. I came back here without a job."

"You came here because you were afraid to go anywhei else. Admit it, Liz, you've been running scared since you le New York."

"I am not. I turned my back on something I didn't want.

"And you turned your back on finishing your degree an building a career that would give you and your children better life. Admit it! You were running then, and you're rui ning now."

"Damn you, let me go."

"I love you. I want to marry you."

"Well, I don't love you."

"Liar!"

He took her in his arms and kissed her. It was like the mood—hard and brutal. She fought him just as hard.

"Let me go," she demanded.

"Not until you admit you love me."

The steering wheel had caught him painfully on the hi but he refused to let her go. She turned her head when tried to kiss her, so he kissed her neck. When she twiste away from him, he kissed her ear. Then suddenly she wa kissing him back with all the fervor of their night of lov They didn't stop until both of them were out of breath.

"I love you," she said, sounding as if the words wei

ulled from her unwillingly. "I can't stop myself from making that mistake, but I can stop myself from making the big-
er mistake of marrying you."

"It won't be a mistake."

"Yes, it will. We'd always be pulling against each other.
: wouldn't be long before it would destroy our love. We'd
row to hate each other."

"You aren't going to give us a chance, are you?"

"Don't you see we don't have a chance?"

"What you mean is you're too afraid to try."

She pulled back from him. She might as well have pulled
piece of plate glass between them. The barrier she threw
p was that hard. "Go to New York, Matt. Take that job and
nake lots of money. I'll be very proud of you when you
ecome one of the most famous surgeons in the whole coun-
y. All of us will be proud. Forget you ever heard of a place
alled Iron Springs. Forget us. We're not part of your world.
Ve never were."

She was closing him out, putting so much distance between
nem he couldn't even talk to her. He was on the outside
nocking as hard as he could, but he couldn't get in. Every-
ody else had let him in, made him feel a part of the com-
nunity, but none of it mattered as long as Liz refused to even
sten to him.

It was just like Gull's Landing all over again. It didn't
natter that he'd been rejected for different reasons. He'd been
ejected. It hurt just the same.

He moved back to his part of the seat. "Maybe you're
ght," he said, letting the anger run freely through his voice.
'Not about Iron Springs, but about marrying you." He
rned on the ignition. The engine sputtered. He turned the
ey again, ramming his foot down on the accelerator repeat-
dly. "I don't want to marry a woman who's afraid of life.
don't know who my parents were, what they were doing,
hat they dreamed about, but somehow I know they were
earching for something they were willing to risk everything
r. I don't know what it was, but I can feel it. That's what
want in my wife, in the children we'll have together."

The engine caught. He threw the car in reverse and backe across the road in the beginning of a three-point turn.

"I want someone solid and dependable, too. Doctors ar called away at all hours. I won't always be around for im portant events. I want someone reliable enough to stand i for me when I can't be there."

He put the gearshift in drive, and the car jumped acros the road. Liz shrieked when it came to a halt with the tire on the edge of the shoulder. There was nothing beyond, bu Matt was too angry to be scared.

"There'll be more Joshes in my life," Matt continuec "kids I'll get to know and care about. Not all of them ar going to get well. I'll need a wife strong enough to suppo me while I get over the emotional devastation."

He backed up and pointed the station wagon toward Irc Springs.

"But just as important, I want a wife who'll have the cou age to love me and to have faith I'll love her, that I'll nev shortchange our love no matter where my career takes me. want someone who can enjoy life, endure the rough, deligh in the good. We only go around one time, and now that I'v finally understood what it means, I don't want to waste i The irony is that you pulled me into life and now want back out."

He took a curve dangerously fast. He didn't care. If Salom could drive through these mountains like a maniac, so coul he.

"I want a woman willing to look life in the teeth and da it to do its worst. I thought I wanted the woman who taugh me that lesson, but I guess she's a whole lot better at talkin than she is at doing."

He pushed the accelerator to the floor, but not even th roar of the engine or the screeching of tires as he skidde through a curve could cool the anger that boiled in him.

"Aren't you going to say anything?" he asked.

"Everything's been said."

He skidded through another curve. He didn't know why h

hould have been so afraid of this mountain before. All it
ok was a little guts.

"Not everything. First thing when you get to the office
omorrow, notify the medical board in Richmond that I'm
lying to New York to look at a job. If I take it, I could be
one in a matter of days. They'd better see about getting
omeone to replace me."

As he hurtled down the mountain, he realized he was prac-
ically holding his breath. He still hoped Liz would say some-
hing so he could change his mind. He didn't want to go to
New York. His ambition to become a surgeon was un-
hanged, but it wouldn't mean anything without Liz, or the
ids. Even though they weren't his biological children, he
elt like they belonged together. All four of them.

But they couldn't do it without Liz. She was the glue that
vould hold everything together. Or keep it apart.

She didn't say a word.

Liz paused, her hand on the knob. Matt had been gone for
ve days, but it felt like a lifetime. She didn't know if she
ould stand to enter the clinic one more day. The days before
e left had been difficult, but the ones since he'd been gone
ad been agony. She hadn't thought it was possible to miss
nyone so much. Her children only made it worse. If they
ad known she was the reason Matt had moved out of the
ouse, the reason he was in New York, they'd never forgive
er.

She wasn't sure she could forgive herself.

She wasn't pregnant, but despite the difficulties it would
ave caused, she couldn't help regretting she wouldn't have
Matt's baby. It was stupid, but she couldn't change the way
he felt. Rebecca's sudden interest in having a bigger family
nly made things worse.

She entered the office in time to hear Salome's pungent
eply before slamming down the phone.

"I ought to make you answer this damned phone," Salome
aid accusingly the moment she spied Liz. "It's your fault
veryone's as cranky as a bear in heat."

Liz didn't have to ask what Salome was talking about. Since the clinic patients learned Matt had left town, that he was likely to take a job in New York, they'd been mad as plucked hens. They'd also been trying their best to get in one last appointment with him. When they couldn't, they took out their frustrations on Salome. Naturally that didn't improve her temper.

"It's not my fault," Liz said, collecting her paperwork and hoping to hide in her office for the rest of the day.

The phone rang, and Salome picked it up. "All of our representatives are busy serving other customers," she growled. "Call back later." She slammed down the phone.

"Salome, you can't cut people off like that. That could have been an emergency."

Salome slid the phone in Liz's direction. "You want somebody to talk to them, you do it."

"It's not my job."

"It's not going to be mine if things don't get better around here pretty damned fast." She compressed her electric blue lips into a tight, dark line. "Why the hell didn't you marry Beefcake and keep him in Iron Springs?"

"I'm not responsible for providing the town with medical care."

"Come off it. We both know what we're talking about. He wanted to marry you, and you were too afraid to take the chance."

"What…how…?"

"How did I know?" Salome asked. "Hell, everybody knows you two are nuts about each other. Everybody also knows he talked himself blue in the face trying to get you to go out with him. When he finally did, he comes roaring back into town hardly fifteen minutes later looking madder than a stomped-on snake. You looked like you'd swallowed a mouthful of alum. Next day he's making plane reservations for New York. What none of us can figure out is why you'd do anything so stupid. Folks always thought you were a smart woman. Hell, I even used to look up to you."

"You don't know what you're talking about."

"No, I don't know why you got cold feet. I do know you let the best man you're ever going to find get away. No, you ran him off. That's so dumb it makes me want to hit you."

The phone rang. She snatched it up and shouted, "Not now!" in the receiver and hung up again. "Now get out of here before I do."

Sadie entered the office. "Salome, what on earth have you been doing? I've got people on the other phone threatening to come out here and—"

"I know, I know," Salome said. "I'll call 'em back. Just do something about Liz. Just looking at her makes me so mad I could start spitting all over again."

Liz snatched up the rest of her paperwork and headed toward her office.

"Don't pay any attention to Salome," Sadie said. "She—"

Liz spun back around. "She didn't say anything other people aren't thinking and feeling," Liz said. "There's no use pretending otherwise."

"Well, it is true people are wondering why you drove the doctor off. He was mighty well liked."

"I didn't drive him off," Liz nearly screamed. "He wouldn't have stayed."

"He was thinking about it. I bet you could have talked him into it, at least for a while."

Liz started to repeat herself then stopped, her mouth still open. "What do you mean he was thinking about it?"

"It was the day you were supposed to have dinner. He heard the county was considering closing this clinic. That was just after we'd heard Dr. Kennedy was going to retire after the mess he made over Josie's cyst. Anyway, he said if they moved the clinic to Woodstock, he'd have to stay until they decided to move it back. He said people around here couldn't do without a doctor. He said what would have happened to Josie if he hadn't been here? Then there's Dr. Kennedy's patients to consider. Maybe they do think they're too good to come to the clinic, but they've got to have a doctor. Who's going to take care of them if Matt leaves?"

"How do you know all this?" Liz asked.

"I listened in on the phone," Sadie said, "the way I always do."

Ethan Woodhouse had been instrumental in convincing Dr. Kennedy to retire, but Josie had been the one who convinced him to recommend Matt to his patients. In her usual subtle way, Josie had said she'd sue him for malpractice if he didn't.

"Why don't you try to talk him into staying?" Sadie asked. "With all Dr. Kennedy's patients, it won't be like he has to start a practice from scratch."

Liz mumbled an excuse and stumbled away to her office. She couldn't believe Matt had actually considered staying in Iron Springs. She, on the other hand, hadn't been willing to consider anything *but* staying in Iron Springs.

What had happened to her? Why had she lost the courage she had as a teenager, the desire to see more of the world, experience more of life than Iron Springs could offer her? When had she lost her desire to live rather than hide?

It didn't matter so much when or why it happened, just that she realized it and was willing to do something about it.

She couldn't live without Matt. She'd already proved that to herself. Her children couldn't live without him, either. The fact that everybody in town apparently knew it proved she was trying to ignore a truth that was too big to hide. No matter what she had to face, even if it was discrimination or snobbery, nothing could be worse than facing the rest of her life without Matt.

She also had to admit a truth she had denied up until now. Everything she was looking for in life depended on people and relationships, not location. She could have been content in White Plains if David had loved her the way Matt did.

She had to call him. She couldn't wait. Matt said he wanted a wife who was willing to go after the things she wanted in life. Well, she finally knew what she wanted, and she meant to go after it. She just hoped she hadn't waited too late.

Thirty minutes later, she still didn't know the answer.

"Dr. Dennis has checked out of the hotel," the desk clerk

told Liz. ''He left for the airport to catch a flight to Richmond, Virginia.''

Richmond! Why hadn't he gone to Charlottesville? That's where he'd left his car.

Chapter Twenty

Liz was anxious to get home. She'd been called in to help the doctor covering for Matt deal with a small emergency. That wouldn't normally have been a problem, but it was Saturday, and none of her usual baby-sitters were available. She'd had to leave Ben and Rebecca with a neighbor. It wasn't that she didn't trust Marjorie. She hated to impose.

She didn't want to admit it, but she had spent more of the morning thinking about Matt than about her children or helping the doctor. She'd heard from Matt only once since he left, a short note saying he'd be later getting back than he'd planned. Actually the note hadn't come to her. It had come to the doctor in charge during Matt's absence. Though she'd tried several times, Liz hadn't been able to reach Matt.

She kept going over in her mind what she intended to say to him when he returned, but none of that would matter if he no longer wanted to marry her. She wouldn't give up yet. Matt loved her. She was sure of that. She'd disappointed him, but she'd been running scared. She wasn't now.

She had returned to Iron Springs because it represented so

much of what she valued in life. But she'd also come back with her tail between her legs. She was ashamed to admit it, but she'd accepted Ethan's attention because she needed to feel attractive again. Rather than borrowing the money to go back to school, she had taken a job in the clinic because it represented security. She held off from dealing with David's desire to see his children because everything about him reminded her of her failure.

She hadn't even noticed it, but over and over again she'd acted like the coward Matt had accused her of being.

She wouldn't do that again. She didn't know what it would take to get Matt back, but if it meant moving to New York, she'd start packing this afternoon. All she wanted was to see him again, talk to him, convince him that she loved him as much as he loved her, that she would never again be afraid to follow him wherever he wanted to go. If she'd known where to find him, she'd have driven to Charlottesville or Richmond to see him.

But she didn't know anything about his life in Charlottesville, not his friends or their telephone numbers. That was another mistake she wouldn't make again.

The thread of her thoughts snapped when she saw Marjorie and Marjorie's children in their front yard. She didn't see Ben or Rebecca. She had told the children to stay outside. She didn't want them tracking mud or leaves through Marjorie's house. She hoped the children hadn't had a falling-out.

"Where have you got them locked up?" Liz asked when she entered Marjorie's yard.

Marjorie looked confused. "They've gone with their father."

Liz's whole universe came to a screeching halt. "What are you talking about?"

"They went with Mr. Rawlins. He came by about an hour ago. He said you knew he was coming."

David hadn't called, written or anything. Why? Maybe he didn't want her to know when he was coming. Maybe he wanted to swoop down and spirit her children away.

"I wouldn't have let them go," Marjorie said, "but Rebecca said you'd told her he was coming. She said she and Ben were supposed to go with him."

Paralyzing fear rose in Liz's throat. David had kidnapped her children, and she'd made it easy for him. She'd heard of numerous cases where fathers had kidnapped their own children and disappeared.

"He said he was taking them on a picnic," Marjorie continued. "He said he'd be back in a few hours."

Liz didn't believe a word of it. He was just trying to keep her from looking for him so he'd have more time to get away.

"His wife was with him."

Any woman who helped kidnap another woman's children was lower than dirt.

Liz started toward her house. She was determined not to run, but she could feel her feet moving faster and faster. Wild thoughts whipped through her mind—thoughts of her children whisked away to a foreign country, held prisoners on a mountain estate patrolled by armed guards. She told herself not to be foolish. David was selfish and thoughtless, not crazy. But the nightmarish images wouldn't leave her mind. Then, when she was halfway there, she saw Matt's station wagon turn the corner at Hannah's Drugs.

Liz started running.

All remembrance of their differences went out of her mind. Now everything would be all right. "David has kidnapped the children," she cried. She threw herself into his arms and kissed him with all the hunger of seven lonely, desperate days.

She'd never thought anything could feel so wonderful, so right as Matt's arms around her. The feel of his body pressed tightly against hers, of his lips kissing her hungrily, were like a safe haven. She didn't have to stand alone anymore, didn't have to be afraid. He still loved her.

"He didn't kidnap them. He took them on a picnic."

The jolting sound of Marjorie's voice reminded Liz that David had her children.

"Where did he take them?" Matt said. He turned to face Marjorie, but he kept a satisfyingly firm hold on Liz.

"I didn't ask, but he said Liz knew he was coming."

"He lied," Liz said to Matt. "I mean I invited him to come see the kids, but he said he'd have to let me know. I'd never let him take my kids without me being with them. We've got to find him."

"I'm sorry," Marjorie said, "but Rebecca was so set on going I figured it was all right. She said he looked just like the picture you gave her."

Realizing her children wouldn't recognize their own father, Liz had given them a picture of David. Rebecca had taken it to her room, had started asking questions about her father several times a day. She asked most often about the new family he might have with his new wife. Rebecca had decided she, too, wanted more family. Liz wouldn't put it past her daughter to have asked David and his wife what they were going to do about it within thirty minutes of meeting them.

"There are dozens of places where they could go for a picnic," Marjorie said. "It would take you the whole weekend to check them all."

"Where's he staying?" Liz asked. "He probably asked directions from somebody at the motel."

"He didn't say," Marjorie said.

"We can call all the motels in the area," Matt said. "There aren't that many."

"I'll help," Marjorie said.

They called all the motels within fifty miles, but none of them had a David Rawlins registered.

"I told you he took my children," Liz said. Her fear had grown as motel after motel proved to be a dead end. "He just drove in, picked them up and drove away again."

"Did they take any clothes?" Matt asked.

"Why should he? He can buy them anything they need."

"Why don't you look?"

Liz didn't know why she hadn't thought of that herself. Only one drawer in each room had been disturbed. Each child had taken a bathing suit.

"It looks like they really did go on a picnic," Matt said. "They'll probably come rolling up about dinnertime."

Liz was feeling a little less frantic, even a little embarrassed, but she had to know her children were all right.

"He said something about taking them out to dinner," Marjorie said.

"Then why can't we find him at a motel?" Liz demanded. "If he weren't such a snob, he'd have stayed at the hotel."

Their gazes locked. None of them had thought to check with the old Civil War hotel down the street.

"He sure is staying here," the clerk said. "Booked the Robert E. Lee suite for three nights."

"Did he say anything about going on a picnic?"

"Yeah. He asked directions to the Blue Ridge Parkway. I told him it was too far away. I talked him into going to the battlefield outside of Newmarket."

Liz turned to Matt. "That's only fifteen miles from here."

"You want to go?"

"I have to."

As soon as they were in the car, Matt turned to Liz. "I'll help you find David on one condition."

"What?"

"You've got to stop fighting him and work out some terms. The kids are obviously not afraid of him, or they wouldn't have left Marjorie's. He has a right, legal and moral."

"I know. That's why I called him, why I gave Rebecca his picture. I'm just afraid he doesn't really care about them. He never did before."

"People change. I did. Give him the benefit of the doubt."

"Okay." It wasn't much of a concession. She didn't really have a choice. But as her fear for her children subsided, her worry over what Matt had done resurfaced. Why hadn't he come back to Iron Springs sooner? Why had he gone to Richmond?

"I missed you," Matt said as he started the station wagon and backed out of the driveway.

Liz's head snapped around until she was facing him. He

was looking both ways before he backed out into Iron Springs's nearly always empty street. For the first time, she wasn't overwhelmed with how handsome he was or his great body. The only really important fact at this moment was that he was there, next to her, that they were looking for her children together.

"I missed you, too."

"They offered me the job," Matt said as he pulled out onto the road. "It's even better than I thought. In addition to everything Georgia told me, they'll help me set up my own practice. With their connections, I can go almost anywhere in the country I want. It's a dream job."

Liz held her breath. He hadn't said anything about her or the kids going with him. Surely he hadn't changed his mind. She didn't care if she had to join two country clubs and learn to make polite conversation with all the mothers at the most exclusive school in town, please, God, don't let him have changed his mind.

"I turned it down."

"Why?" The word came out almost like a squeak. She couldn't believe what she was hearing. That job was everything he'd ever wanted, virtually handed to him, and he had turned it down.

"Like I said, I missed you. And the kids. And Iron Springs. No job is worth it if I have to do without all of you."

She wanted to speak, to say something to express even a fraction of the emotion that was choking her, but she couldn't. Her willingness to compromise, to follow him, seemed insignificant by comparison.

"But that wasn't the only reason I turned it down," Matt said as they headed out of town and up the grade over the mountain. "I've been wanting to become rich and famous for all the wrong reasons. You were right. I should have gotten over what happened in Gull's Landing long ago. Maybe I did. It just took you and the kids to show me. I've been depending on money to give me a sense of security. I've also been depending on keeping my distance to keep me from being hurt.

"I was just as big a coward as I accused you of being. I can't cure everybody. It's going to hurt when I fail, but getting close to people like Josh gives meaning to my work. I changed my mind about what I want to do."

"You can't give up your dream because of me," Liz said. "I won't let you. I know I've been selfish and stubborn and cowardly, but I'd never make you give up something that means so much to you. You can't stay in Iron Springs just because of me."

"What are you talking about?"

"Sadie told me about the clinic being moved."

"I talked them out of it. In fact, with Dr. Kennedy's retirement, they're going to expand it, send us another doctor."

"Is that what you were doing in Richmond?"

"Part of it."

"And the rest?"

"I've decided I want to become a pediatric surgeon. I was seeing what I can arrange. They're thinking about letting me set up a unit at the hospital in Harrisonburg. I'll stay in Iron Springs until they decide."

"Matt, why are you doing this? You could start a unit nearly anywhere in the country. Why should you choose Harrisonburg?"

"I realized I've been trying to belong my whole life. I never did until I was sent to a place I hated before I ever set eyes on it. I don't pretend to understand it, but I belong here. Maybe my mother came from a place like this. Or my father. I don't know. I just know I discovered security isn't about money or fame. It's being connected to people, putting down roots, belonging somewhere."

They reached the top of the grade and started down the other side. Liz realized she didn't remember a single curve on the way up. Matt hadn't been tense. He'd finally gotten used to the roads. Maybe he really did belong. He reached over and gave her hand a squeeze.

"I want to marry you, Elizabeth Rawlins. I want to be your husband, your lover and your friend. I know I have to share

Ben and Rebecca with their real father, but I feel like we're a family already.''

Liz wanted to throw her arms around him and kiss him senseless. Instead, she had to watch through her tears as he negotiated one hairpin curve after another. But she could wait. There would be ten miles of easy driving to hang on to his arm while she told him how wrong she'd been, that she would follow him anywhere, convince him she would never again put any conditions on her love.

But after all that, if he still wanted to stay in the valley...well, she supposed she'd just have to put up with a cup of life that insisted upon running over.

By the time they reached the battlefield park, Liz was so happy she would have given David anything he wanted. Except her children. They both came running the minute they spotted Matt. Liz was certain they loved her best of all, but today she had to take second place to Matt. Today she didn't mind.

They both jumped on him, calling his name, wanting to know where he'd been. It made Liz tear up to see how much they'd missed him. They didn't stop until he'd picked them both up.

"I thought you were never coming back." Rebecca said when she was securely settled in his left arm.

"Come play with us," Ben said. "Daddy can't play kick ball as good as you."

"That's because you haven't dragged him outside every night for the past two months," Matt said. "Give him time. He'll learn."

"Who is that man?"

Liz turned as David spoke. Her breath caught in her throat as, for the first time in three years, she faced the man who'd been her husband. Her first reaction was to wonder how she could have been married to a man who seemed like such a stranger to her now. Her second impression was that he seemed even more handsome than she remembered.

"Hello, David."

"I want to know who that man is."

He was jealous. If he hadn't been such a louse, she could have almost felt sorry for him. "This is Matt Dennis," she said, "the doctor at our clinic."

Matt let the kids slide out of his arms. "They're a great pair," Matt said as he shook hands with David. "I'm going to marry their mother, so I imagine I'll be seeing a lot of them."

"Ben hasn't stopped talking about you since he got in the car," the woman said.

"I'd like you to meet my wife, Phyllis," David said belatedly, still looking stunned.

Everyone shook hands.

"I've heard so much about you," Phyllis said.

Liz didn't know how to respond in the awkward silence that followed. She could tell from Phyllis's tone that none of it had been complimentary.

"Can we have a bigger family now?" Rebecca asked.

Matt picked Rebecca up and tossed her in the air. "If I find any babies lying around the hospital, I'll be sure to bring one home for you."

"I want one, too," Ben said.

"Babies can't play kick ball," Matt warned.

"Then I don't want one," Ben replied.

Matt took the kids by their hands. "Why don't you two come with me and Phyllis, and I'll tell you what I've been doing while I've been gone?"

"What about Mama and Daddy?" Rebecca asked.

"They'll be along in a minute."

Liz watched them walk away, each child holding one of Matt's hands, both talking at once, neither listening to what the other was saying. Phyllis followed behind, throwing irritated glances over her shoulder at her husband.

"Are you really going to marry him?" David asked.

"Yes."

"He can't have any ambition if he means to stay in a place like this. He'll never make any money. Don't think I'm going to support you as well as the kids."

Liz bit her tongue. "I don't want your money, David. I never did."

"Well, I'm going to send it. And I want an accounting every month."

Liz vowed to herself that she'd never touch David's money. Every penny would go into a college fund.

"Now let's talk about some regular visits."

Liz knew David hadn't changed, that he would never be able to give his children the love and understanding they needed. But that wasn't such a problem anymore. They had Matt.

And so did she.

"I'm glad you let the children stay with David," Matt said to Liz as he brought the station wagon to a halt in the driveway. He was relieved she had made her peace with David. He was also looking forward to a little time alone with her.

"There wouldn't have been any point in bringing them all back here," Liz answered. "Both of them ignore David when you're around."

"I know you're still unsure about him. But for their sakes, you've got to do everything you can to help them build a good relationship with their father."

"You're very strong on this father relationship, aren't you?"

"I intend to be the best stepfather possible. But no matter how much they love me, I'll never be their real father. There's something only he can give them. I can't explain it, but I know it's true."

"Your love may not be enough for them, but it's more than enough for me," Liz said as she leaned over and kissed him. "I'm very glad you came back. It saved me having to find a baby-sitter while I went looking for you."

A thrill of satisfaction raced through Matt. "You'd have come after me?"

"I spent days phoning half the medical establishments in Richmond and Charlottesville. I don't know your friends, Matt. I have no idea where you go when you leave Iron

Springs. You might as well have disappeared off the face of the earth. Don't ever do that again.''

She came into his arms. They didn't have a lot of room in the front seat of the station wagon, but he couldn't wait long enough for them to go inside the house.

"I had a terrible time while you were gone," Liz said once she was comfortably settled in his arms. "I was miserable, cranky, no good for anybody. Even Salome missed you."

"I'm not marrying Salome."

"I'm glad. She's discovered a new brand of lipstick that actually glows in the dark. I don't think you'll like it."

Matt laughed. It felt good to be home. Incredibly, Salome and her lipstick were part of it. But the best part was right here in his arms, and that's where he meant for Liz to stay.

A knocking on the window disturbed them in the beginning of a very satisfactory kiss. He looked up to see Marjorie peering in at them. It was obvious she wasn't going to go away. Liz sat up and rolled down the window.

"Did you find the kids okay?"

"David had taken them to the Newmarket battlefield. They'll be back for supper."

"Why don't you bring them over to my house?"

"I couldn't do that. There's six of us."

"That's no problem. After all, it'll be sort of an engagement dinner, won't it?"

Matt and Liz both stared at Marjorie.

"You two are engaged, aren't you?"

"Yes, but—"

"Good. Everybody's been wondering when you'd get around to it. Now we can start planning the wedding."

Liz turned to Matt. "I'm sorry."

Matt laughed. "Don't be. I've always wanted to feel like I belonged. Now I do."

Liz ended up with a much bigger wedding than she had wanted. David and his wife flew back for the wedding. Georgia arrived looking resplendent in a red suit that for once outshone Salome's lipstick. A small contingent of doctors from Richmond and Charlottesville showed up.

Everybody in Iron Springs turned out, from Solomon Trinket to Ben and Rebecca's playmates. Everyone considered it a community affair.

Matt wore a navy suit. Liz wore a blue dress. Aunt Marian was the matron of honor, Dr. Andrews the best man. Rebecca was the flower girl, Ben the ring bearer. He dropped one of the rings halfway down the aisle, but he promptly retrieved it by crawling between the legs of several laughing guests.

Afterward they ate fried chicken and drank lemonade on the lawn down by the lake. Matt had just bitten into his third drumstick when Ben started begging him to play kick ball.

"Not today," Matt said. "I've eaten too much. Besides, I'm all dressed up."

"I'm all dressed up, too," Ben said, "but Mama doesn't care."

"Oh, yes, she does," Liz said. "That's a brand-new suit. You'll have to wear it to church for at least a year. Now go visit with your father. He has to go back to New York tomorrow afternoon."

Ben went off, but Rebecca didn't. "Why aren't you playing?" Liz asked.

"Can we have a bigger family now?" Rebecca asked.

Matt laughed. Liz blushed.

"We can talk about that later."

"Salome said you could start working on one as soon as you married Matt. I waited a long time to ask. Can't you start working on one now? Please."

Matt choked on his chicken.

"Stop it," Liz hissed under her breath, on the verge of laughter.

"I'm willing to start immediately," Matt managed to say between coughing and laughing, "but your mother is dragging her feet."

"Mama, couldn't you—?"

Liz punched Matt, but he only laughed harder. Liz looked around. There was no hope of avoiding the circle of curious gazes or listening ears. She had wanted an attentive com munity. Well, she had one.

"I promise I'll think about it real soon. But if there's an justice in this world, Matt will be the one to get pregnant.'

Matt laughed harder.

"With triplets," Liz added.

"How do you get a pregnant?" Rebecca asked Matt.

Attracted by the laughter, Ben had come running back. "I Matt gets one, can I have one, too?" he asked.

Matt collapsed on the ground. Liz snatched up his plate t keep him from rolling over on it.

She looked at her husband, helpless with laughter, at th grinning faces all around her and at her two wonderful chil dren. Life had a lot to make up to both her and Matt, but i had made an awfully good start.

Silhouette

SPECIAL EDITION®

TM

**In March 1999 watch for a brand-new
book in the beloved MacGregor series:**

THE PERFECT NEIGHBOR
(SSE#1232)

by

 # 1 *New York Times* bestselling author

NORA ROBERTS

Brooding loner Preston McQuinn wants nothing more
to do with love, until his vivacious neighbor, Cybil
Campbell, barges into his secluded life—and his heart.

**Also, watch for the MacGregor stories
where it all began in the exciting 2-in-1 edition!**

Coming in April 1999:

THE MacGREGORS: Daniel—Ian

Available at your favorite retail outlet,
only from

Silhouette®

TM

Silhouette

SPECIAL EDITION®

That's My Baby!

Don't miss these poignant stories coming to
THAT'S MY BABY!—only from
Silhouette Special Edition!

December 1998 THEIR CHILD
by Penny Richards (SE# 1213)
Drew McShane married Kim Campion to give her baby a name. Could their daughter unite them in love?

February 1999 BABY, OUR BABY!
by Patricia Thayer (SE# 1225)
Her baby girl would always remind Ali Pierce of her night of love with Jake Hawkins. Now he was back—and proposing marriage!

April 1999 A FATHER FOR HER BABY
by Celeste Hamilton (SE #1237)
When Jarrett McMullen located his long-lost runaway bride, could he convince the amnesiac, expectant mother-to-be he wanted her for always?

THAT'S MY BABY!
Sometimes bringing up baby can bring surprises...
and showers of love.

Available at your favorite retail outlet.

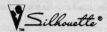

Silhouette®

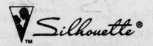

Bestselling author

LINDSAY McKENNA

continues the drama and adventure of her
popular series with an all-new, longer-length
single-title romance:

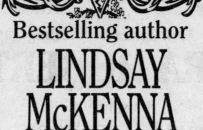

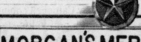

HEART OF THE JAGUAR

Major Mike Houston and Dr. Ann Parsons were in the heat
of the jungle, deep in enemy territory. She knew Mike's
warrior blood kept him from the life—and the love—he
silently craved. And now she had so much more at stake.
For the beautiful doctor carried a child. His child...

Available in January 1999, at your favorite retail outlet!

Look for more **MORGAN'S MERCENARIES** in 1999,
as the excitement continues in the Special Edition line!

Silhouette®

PSMORGMERC

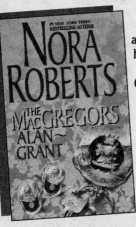
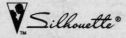

Silhouette®

SPECIAL EDITION®

COMING NEXT MONTH

#1225 BABY, OUR BABY!—Patricia Thayer
That's My Baby!
When Jake Hawkins returned to town, he discovered that one unforgettable night of passion with Ali Pierce had made him a daddy. He'd never forgotten about shy, sweetly insecure Ali—or how she touched his heart. Now that they shared a child, he vowed to be there for his family—forever!

#1226 THE PRESIDENT'S DAUGHTER—Annette Broadrick
Formidable Special Agent Nick Logan was bound to protect the president's daughter, but he was on the verge of losing his steely self-control when Ashley Sullivan drove him to distraction with her feisty spirit and beguiling innocence. Dare he risk getting close to the one woman he couldn't have?

#1227 ANYTHING, ANY TIME, ANY PLACE—Lucy Gordon
Just as Kaye Devenham was about to wed another, Jack Masefield whisked her off to marry him instead, insisting he had a prior claim on her! A love-smitten Kaye dreamt that one day this mesmerizing man would ask her to be more than his strictly *convenient* bride....

#1228 THE MAJOR AND THE LIBRARIAN—Nikki Benjamin
When dashing pilot Sam Griffin came face-to-face with Emma Dalton again, he realized his aching, impossible desire for the lovely librarian was more powerful than ever. He couldn't resist her before—and he certainly couldn't deny her now. Were they destined to be together after all this time?

#1229 HOMETOWN GIRL—Robin Lee Hatcher
Way back when, Monica Fletcher thought it was right to let her baby's father go. But now she knew better. Her daughter deserved to know her daddy—and Monica longed for a second chance with her true love. Finally the time had come for this man, woman and child to build a home together!

#1230 UNEXPECTED FAMILY—Laurie Campbell
Meg McConnell's world changed forever when her husband, Joe, introduced her...to his nine-year-old son! Meg never imagined she'd be asked to mother another woman's child. But she loved Joe, and his little boy was slowly capturing her heart. Could this unexpected family live happily ever after?